Cover Design and Interior format by The Killion Group
http://thekilliongroupinc.com

Thank you.

THE BEST OF ALEXANDER GRANT

KEIRA MONTCLAIR

Foreword

WELCOME TO THE Highlights Series! Yes, you have read most of these scenes! Most books will have new, exclusive scenes that have only been seen by a few but please know you, my faithful fans, have ALREADY READ most of these scenes in my previous books. You don't want to pay for them again? Then please don't. Wait until they are all out and sign up for Kindle Unlimited. Then you can read them for free.

Now a little bit about this series.

The inspiration for the series came from the fact that I have fifty-five books in the combined Grant/Ramsay series, and even I can no longer remember everything. I have so many different notebooks, software notes, journals, and story bibles that tracking down any one bit of information had become a true labor.

The first issue? I couldn't recall the ages and hair colors of all the bairns. There are simply too many of them. I often wished I had a book with just the bairns listed so I could easily retrieve their ages and characteristics.

Then along came the faeries, the swords, the angels, and seers. Who had what power? I lost track.

So I decided to go through all fifty-five books

and copy and paste the relevant scenes into a reference file. My next thought? Wouldn't my readers love it if I did the same thing with Alex Grant and Logan Ramsay? Would they buy a book like that?

I'm hoping you'll say yes!

The project grew from there. As of this writing, I have plans for the following highlight books, to be titled *The Best of*:

Alexander Grant
Madeline Grant
Logan Ramsay
Gwyneth Ramsay
Loki Grant
Brenna Ramsay
Torrian Ramsay
Connor Grant
Maitland Menzie
Dyna Grant
The Bairns, Part 1 and 2
The Pets, Ghosts, and Spirits
My Favorite Scenes

That's right. It quickly went from four books to thirteen, and a few of them have too many favorite scenes to fit in one volume. Logan wins for the longest, but he would tell you that it was only right.

I may not have chosen your favorite, but each collection had to be long enough to reach novella size. You loved Drew, Quade, or Aedan more? Not enough for a book. There are other possibilities, if you my beloved readers ask for them. The best of the weddings, the Camerons, the villains? Maybe someday in the future, but it will be a while before I add any because this was a long, tedious project. Long. Did I say long? It took me forever!

I tried to stick to a few rules:

There is no set order to read the series. You can read in any order. I also will have a random release schedule, not necessarily in the order listed.

I tried to take only three or four scenes from the character's main book. I took the scenes that most represented his or her personality or an important stage in their life.

Excerpts are listed *exactly* as they appeared in each book. All those comma errors? I didn't change them. Other than a few glaring typos, nothing was changed.

I did my best to orient the reader to each scene by adding a line or two in the beginning of each scene. Chapters are listed with the title of each book so you can reference them if you like.

The series and books are ordered by timeline. In other words, Highland Healers comes before Highland Swords, which is *not* how I released them.

Did I miss your favorite scene? Probably. Understand that I had thirteen tabs open on my laptop as I slowly perused each book.

I will also add a trigger warning here as a reminder that Medieval times were brutal.

Are you ready for the Best of Alexander Grant?

Then read on. The first scene is not in any book but is a gift sent to anyone who signed up for my newsletter.

My thoughts will be written in italics before the beginning of each scene.

Let me know what you think!

Keira Montclair

CONTENT WARNING: The world in which my beloved Grants and Ramsays live is violent in many ways. You will read about the horrors of war, sexual assault, traumatic births, child abuse and other events we find shocking today. Please be aware of your reactions as you read and step away if you need to.

NOVELS BY
KEIRA MONTCLAIR

Clan Grant/Clan Ramsay World

THE CLAN GRANT SERIES
#1- RESCUED BY A HIGHLANDER-
Alex and Maddie
#2- HEALING A HIGHLANDER'S HEART-
Brenna and Quade
#3- LOVE LETTERS FROM LARGS-
Brodie and Celestina
#4-JOURNEY TO THE HIGHLANDS-
Robbie and Caralyn
#5-HIGHLAND SPARKS-
Logan and Gwyneth
#6-MY DESPERATE HIGHLANDER-
Micheil and Diana
#7-THE BRIGHTEST STAR IN THE
HIGHLANDS-
Jennie and Aedan
#8- HIGHLAND HARMONY-
Avelina and Drew
#9-YULETIDE ANGELS

THE HIGHLAND CLAN
LOKI-Book One
TORRIAN-Book Two
LILY-Book Three

THE SCOT'S DECEPTION
THE SCOT'S ANGEL

HIGHLAND HUNTERS
THE SCOT'S CONFLICT
THE SCOT'S TRAITOR
THE SCOT'S PROTECTOR
THE SCOT'S VOW
THE SCOT'S DESTINY
THE SCOT'S WARNING
THE SCOT'S RECKONING
THE SCOT'S LEGACY

CLANS OF MULL
THE PLIGHT OF A SCOTTISH LASS
THE BURDEN OF A SCOTTISH
CHIEFTAIN
THE ANGUISH OF THE SCOTTISH
LAIRDS
THE TORMENT OF A SCOTTISH
WARRIOR
THE DEFIANCE OF A SCOTTISH HEART
THE WRATH OF A SCOTTISH BLADE

YOUNG ALEX GRANT

*Stand-alone short story sent
to new newsletter subscribers*

*A*LEX IS DEFINITELY *the favorite of more than
half my readers. Readers tell me it's because of
his patience, his love for his wife, his strength, the way
he carries his bairns on his chest, how he sits behind
Maddie when she delivers their bairns, and the way
he leads.*

*So I thought to share a wee insight into what made
Alex, well, Alex…*

*This story is sent to anyone who signs up for my
newsletter. It was written to stand alone, so I won't say
anything more about it..*

CHAPTER ONE

ALEX GRANT SPUN around with his sword
in hand, close enough to his brother Robbie
that he nicked the skin on his wrist.

"Ow," Robbie howled.

Alex paused to check his brother's injury. "'Tis just a nick. Stop hollering so." He practiced his sword skills with his younger brothers because his sire wouldn't yet allow him to train in the lists with the Grant warriors.

Even though Alex had told his father multiple times that he was ready.

"Alex!" a booming voice called to him. Their father, John Alexander Grant, was headed straight for them, his long strides telling them he was conducting important business. Whenever he spoke to them in that tone and walked so his boots clicked on the stones, they knew better than to disobey. "You will apologize to your brother and meet me in the stables."

Which meant he'd witnessed everything.

Alex, wide-eyed, didn't hesitate but turned to Robbie and said, "My apologies."

Their father had already whirled around and was headed for the stables, his dark locks waving in the wind, his right hand resting on his sheathed sword. His coloring was nearly the same as Brodie's. Robbie's fair looks came from their mother, Elizabeth. Alex had always looked up to him because he was such a tall man, broad-shouldered and powerful. Lately, he could nearly look him in the eye, though his sire had made no mention of it.

Brodie gave his official opinion. "Oooh, Alex. You're in trouble. Papa will be whipping you for sure."

Alex just rolled his eyes and said, "Brodie, go to the keep with Robbie. Mama will take care of his wound." Then he took off after his sire, sheathing his weapon first.

While none of them had ever been whipped by the laird of Clan Grant, Alex didn't think it was outside the realm of possibility that it could happen someday. He was a loving father, but also strict when it came to his lads. He doubted it would happen this day, but that didn't stop his heart from pounding out of his chest on the way to the stables.

He'd never been summoned to the stables before.

Nearly there, he noticed a number of steeds had been gathered outside the gates. His father barked orders at his second, telling him to ready one hundred guards for travel.

Alex's heart pounded even faster, if that were possible. Where were they headed with so many guards? He'd never seen his father's men in such a flurry of activity.

"Alex, inside," his father said, pointing to the stables.

"Papa, what is it?"

"One of our allies has been attacked by a neighboring clan. We go to defend them, and I wish for you to join us."

Excitement coursed through Alex. A mission at last! His sire had finally decided he was ready to ride with the other men. Mayhap he would fight in his first battle. How he wished he could brag to his brothers.

Once they were inside the stables, his sire turned to face him, and his voice pulled him away from the fantasy taking place in his mind. "You must promise me before we leave."

"Anything, Da. Whatever you wish." He stood stock still, not wanting to give his father any reason to change his mind.

"You will stay behind me at all times. You will not speak if we are greeted by anyone. You will follow my instructions without question or hesitation. Can you do that, son?"

"Aye, I promise."

His father sighed and moved closer to grasp his shoulder. "Lad, this could be difficult for you, but I feel 'tis time for you to travel with us."

"Why would it be difficult?" Everyone had always told him the Grant warriors were the strongest, the best in battle. Surely, they could handle whatever they faced.

"Because we may be too late." His father turned to address a stable lad. "Saddle Midnight for my son."

Alex's pride soared. He didn't have to saddle his own horse. That made him feel quite important. In fact, he puffed his chest out a bit just to see what it felt like.

He'd always looked up to his sire, wanted to be like him. Part of it was the knowledge that he would one day follow him as laird.

Chieftain Alexander Grant. That would be his title someday.

Would he be worthy of it?

He prayed he would.

CHAPTER TWO

Where did Alex learn to lead so well?
Judge for yourself…

THEY'D BEEN TRAVELING for half a day and only stopped once. Alex had paid close attention to everything his sire did and said, knowing he might one day be asked to lead these same men or their sons. They were on the last leg of the journey. With his sire's permission, Alex was riding beside him—the better to observe the warriors—but his father made a sudden motion for him to move behind him again. He had already ordered his men to surround and protect his first-born son if they were attacked, something that shamed Alex, although he intended to do as he'd promised and listen to his sire's orders.

"Alex, you will draw your sword to protect yourself from marauders," his sire ordered.

"Aye, Sir."

He'd always been instructed never to let their enemies know they were related, lest they attempt to use him against his father. And he was also told not to call him chief or laird.

Sir seemed appropriate.

A hush settled over the group, his father leading the way with two men on either side of him, all ready to draw their weapons if necessary.

It was quiet—oddly quiet.

As they drew closer to the small village outside the castle, the smell of burned thatched roofs reached them.

Alex hadn't thought anything could be worse than the eerie quiet, but he soon revised his opinion. A horrible moaning met their ears, many voices keening as one.

His father's fists clenched and rage lit his eyes. He cursed and sent the majority of his men around the village to clear the area. The rest rode with him to the gates.

Once they reached the open gates, Alex's sire called out to anyone on the curtain wall, but there was no answer. They led their horses through the courtyard.

There were as many dead bodies here as they'd seen on arrival.

The courtyard was littered with men who'd lost their life fighting. A few still lived, and it was their agonized moans that had carried on the wind. Although Alex had seen bodies before, he'd never seen anything so gruesome. The gore and the flies made him want to retch, but he would not.

Not in front of his father.

His father barked orders to their men, who rushed to do his bidding without question. He told some men to take a crew to dig a large grave behind the curtain wall, instructed others to pile the dead onto carts. Others were tasked with gathering the wounded so they might be brought back to Grant land for treatment.

Every once in a while, his father would turn sideways and give his son an explanation for his instructions. "As every Highlander would do for his brethren," was his explanation for burying the dead.

"Alex," his sire said, jumping down from his horse, "we will check inside for the laird's family. He had two daughters and I fear what could have happened to them."

He dismounted and hurried to catch up to his father, doing his best to match his strides as they headed toward the keep. As they walked, three men accompanying them, his sire tipped his head toward him with an approving look. "I see you've finally surpassed your sire's height, son. Will you never stop growing?"

Alex didn't know how to reply to that remark, but there was no need. His father began giving orders to the three men entering the keep with him.

"Always allow your second to lead you, Alex. We know not if the marauders are still inside. Draw your weapon before you enter. Never forget that."

He nodded to his men, instructing them to go ahead of him, then he followed. Alex came last, although he was determined to protect his sire if they were attacked. Blood roared through his vessels with each step, his senses heightened.

They stepped inside, weapons drawn, then fanned out inside the great hall. Dead bodies were everywhere, and everything inside had been destroyed.

"Bastards. Watch your back, men. The English committed this heinous crime."

The English? How could he know that?

Four men came barreling out of a chamber close to the tower room, their weapons drawn. They attacked silently, unlike most Highlanders in battle.

Alex let out his Grant war cry and went after the man headed toward his sire, cutting the fool down with one swing. Although he'd never been in battle before, he didn't hesitate. Protecting his sire came as naturally as breathing.

"Back!" his sire bellowed in a tone he'd not heard before.

Alex stepped back, allowing his father the opportunity to take the next man down, but another came at them from the side. Alex turned and cut him down with one swing. The four men were dead.

His father said, "Jeffrey, check the tower chambers and the kitchens."

Panting from exertion, Alex stared down at the blood on his sword and the man splayed beneath him. The man's eyes were still open, staring at naught. And Alex couldn't stop staring at the blood spilling from his body. His dead body.

His father moved closer and set his hand on Alex's wrists. "Lower your weapon, son. You killed because you had to. You saved yourself and your sire. The Lord will forgive you. Clean your blade on the enemy, then sheathe your weapon."

He did his best to do as his father told him, but his hands shook too much. He hadn't killed one man but two. His father steadied his hands and helped him to clean his blade. "I'll forgive your defiance this once because 'twas your first experience in battle."

Defiance? He stared in confusion. He hadn't defied his sire, had he?

"You stepped in front of me. I gave you a clear instruction to stand behind me at all times. Howbeit, since you killed a man who was about to cut me down, I'll say naught this time. But you must listen to your chief's orders. Had I not guessed you might step in front of me, I may have driven my blade into your back."

Alex didn't know what to say. He finished cleaning his blade and held it at his side, the tip striking the floor. "Forgive me, Da."

His father clasped his shoulder and said, "Go upstairs and check the bedchambers. Keep your weapon at the ready."

Alex crept up the staircase, gripping his weapon so tightly his fingers were going numb. Sweat dotted his brow, enough that he wished to swipe at it but he didn't dare lose focus. He checked the first two chambers and they were empty.

The last chamber was not.

Two people were sprawled across the bed, both dead. Blood soaked their clothing and the linens. It appeared the husband had been reaching for his weapon when he'd been stabbed in the belly. The wife had her throat cut.

The stench in the chamber was unbearable. He

did his best not to heave in the corner, leaving quickly. He yelled over the balustrade to his sire. "I believe the castle's chieftain and his wife are in their bedchamber, both dead."

His father took the stairs two at a time and bolted into the chamber, only to curse vehemently.

"Bastards!" He stormed back out and stood next to Alex.

"Da, how do you know the English did this?" Alex said softly. "You knew before we saw them."

"Because they have no code of honor. They rape and kill women and bairns. You may not have seen it, but I saw the mountain of bairns dead at the edge of the clearing outside the castle walls. They must have been trying to escape." He ran a hand through his dark hair peppered with gray strands, tugging on the ends, a movement Alex knew was often used to express his frustration.

"Where are the women?" Alex asked.

"I heard some female cries upon our arrival, yet we found none inside other than the chief's wife. Clan Gordon is no more. But where are the women?"

"Would they have taken them captive?"

"Lord help them if they did. The English are brutal. Come, we'll check outside the walls. We'll speak with the men whom I sent to search the village."

Alex followed his sire down the stairs and through the hall, keeping his gaze averted from the death and blood everywhere. Once in the courtyard, the buzz of the flies overtook all other sounds.

Blood and gore were everywhere.

Several of their warriors were busy burying the dead, while others were loading injured Gordon warriors into a cart to be taken to a healer. Alex's sire headed out the castle wall, consulting with men along the way.

"Women? Have you seen any women, young lasses?"

"Aye," one guard said. "There are many dead inside a few cottages. Most are in their night rails. This must have happened at night."

"Did you see any lasses you would suspect to be the laird's daughters?"

"One, aye. She was protected by five others. She wore a noblewoman's slippers, Chief."

"Bury the others, but I'll check the noblewoman," he said, heading toward the indicated cottage. "Alex, wait here."

He did as he was told, although he couldn't stand to be in this courtyard full of death. Thankfully, his father returned quickly. "'Tis one of his daughters, I'm sure of it. Now we must locate the other so we can bury them together. There is one more daughter somewhere." His gaze scanned the area. "You search that area behind the keep while I check with the others."

Alex headed across the sea of bodies and around the keep, looking for any sign of a lass, but they were all men. His father called to him a few minutes later.

"Inside the keep, Alex."

CHAPTER THREE

Why did he hate the English so?

ALEX RUSHED TO his sire's side. "I was told by a dying man that there is a hidden chamber near the tower room," his da explained. Once inside, he pointed down a passageway, indicating that Alex should go first. "You did a fine job during your first battle, so you may lead here, though I don't expect many to be down this way. They would have joined the four men who attacked us before. I suspect they came from the hidden chamber and I fear what we'll find."

As they moved closer, the voice of a sobbing lass reached them. Alex stopped at the door, drew his weapon, then glanced at his sire. The Grant chieftain nodded for him to open the door.

A beautiful red-haired lass lay in the middle of a bed, sobbing and covered in blood. The bedcovers were pulled up to her chin, but blood soaked through the coverlet, making it a dark red color.

Alex couldn't believe the lass could still be alive after bleeding so heavily.

"Go to her, Alex. 'Tis the laird's daughter."

Her sobbing stopped, though her breathing

hitched as she stared at him, her gaze unwavering, much like a deer who'd been shot by an arrow but wasn't yet dead. He strode toward her and asked, "Where are you hurt?"

She squealed and pulled away from him, clearly afraid.

He set his weapon on the floor and said, "I'll not hurt you. I'll put my weapon down."

Somehow he knew she would die soon. There was too much blood, her coloring was eerily pale and dusky, her skin dry. But he would not look away from her. He would not let her die alone.

"I'll fix the pillows behind you to make you more comfortable." He made a move toward her, but she screamed and pulled back.

Alex didn't understand her fear. Couldn't she see he wanted to help her? He stood back, glancing at his father for guidance.

The look on his father's face was a sadness he didn't often see. "She's afraid of you, Alex."

"But why? I'm trying to be helpful."

"She's afraid of *all* men, not just you."

She made an attempt to push herself out of the other side of the bed, nearly tumbling off the side. Alex rushed over to catch her, but she screamed, an odd sound because her voice was so weak. Her body trembled with fear.

"Your name?" Alex asked, desperate to comfort her. "What's your name?"

"Sarah," she whispered.

"Your sire is laird of Clan Gordon?" Alex's sire whispered from the door.

She nodded, still looking at Alex in fear, her

knuckles gripping the coverlet so hard that her skin was white.

"He'll not rape you, lass. 'Twas the English who mistreated you. We're from Clan Grant."

"Rape? I'd never..." The meaning of his sire's comment finally dawned on him, clarifying the poor girl's actions.

The poor lass expected to be beaten and brutalized again.

He peered at his sire, who said nothing, but Alex did not require further instruction. He would do whatever he could to ease her suffering. Perhaps she sensed it in his touch because her grip on him relaxed and her head fell back, her eyelids closing.

The Grant chieftain came closer to the bed and quietly said, "She'll not last more than a few hours. She's lost too much blood. There's naught we can do for her. Those men brutalized her."

"I'm not leaving," Alex said, his tone definite. He knew from his sire's arched brow that he'd surprised him. "I mean, if I have your approval, I'd like to stay with her. No one should die..."

Her eyes flew open again, but only for a moment.

"Alone."

"As you wish. 'Tis a kind thought to stay with her. I will be down below with our men. We have much to do before we leave."

His father nodded to him and left.

Alex pulled a large chair closer and sat in it, lifting Sarah and settling her onto his lap. He tossed the bloody coverlet off to the side and found two furs in a basket and covered her with them.

She shivered against him so he tucked her close. Blood still seeped from below her waist, but he refused to acknowledge it. The fact that she still lived was a testament to her strength and will. The least he could do was hold her. Listen to her story if she chose to tell it.

Tucking her close, he said, "My apologies we did not arrive sooner. My sire thinks your attackers were English. Do you agree?"

She opened her eyes, gazed at him, and nodded. "Aye," she choked out. "Who are you?"

"Alex Grant. We came because my father heard you were to be attacked, but we came too late." Tears blurred his vision just from watching the poor girl. Did she know she was about to die?

"My thanks for coming. You have kind eyes, unlike the others." Her fingers reached up to touch his jawline, but she quickly lost strength and they tumbled into her lap. "Are they still here?" She stiffened at the thought. "Can they return?"

"Nay, I'll protect you, lass. I promise. They're all dead."

Her eyes closed again, and she attempted to take a deep breath but failed. Her eyes opened and locked on his. "Why did they…Why would anyone…Why?" Fresh tears dotted her lashes. "Cruel monsters."

"I'm sorry. I don't understand how anyone could treat another so poorly." The words seemed paltry given the horrors he'd seen in this place, the horrors that had been visited upon Sarah and her loved ones, but he had no idea what to say.

She rested her head on his shoulder and closed her eyes, sighing twice, her hands gripping his tunic. "Don't leave me. Please?"

"Nay, I'll not leave. I promise." He smoothed loose strands away from her face, but she closed her eyes again. "If you like, Sarah, I can try to get you to my mother. She is a healer, and mayhap she can help you."

The trembling in her body started again. "Nay, please nay." She gulped, apparently from expending the effort to speak.

"I'll carry you on my lap. There may yet be time." He prayed that he could still save her. That this whole mission would not be for naught.

"Nay!" Tears fell down her cheeks and she shook her head.

"But why not?"

"I'd rather die."

CHAPTER FOUR

*The beginning of the draw of the parapets…
and why he respected women…*

ALEX DIDN'T KNOW what to say. Why would someone choose death? Sarah stared at him, her gaze locked on his, her hands still gripping his tunic.

"Please."

"I'll honor your wishes. I don't understand them, but I'll honor them."

He tucked her head back under his chin, doing his best to give her his warmth because she shivered so.

"The memories…" she whispered. She took several quick breaths, then said, "Too painful. I'd rather die."

Her words bit into him, more painful than a physical wound. He held her, talking softly to her about his family, naming everyone in their clan, saying aught he could to distract her.

Every once in a while, she would take quick breaths then sigh. He knew she'd not last much longer because she was so cold. Everything about her was cold. If he could ease her passing, he would.

How could men be so brutal? They'd taken her by force, which was horrifying enough, but that alone wouldn't have killed her. They'd beaten her bloody.

Why?

Because she'd fought so hard? He doubted that. She wasn't any bigger than Brodie had been at ten summers.

To entertain each other? What fun could that be? Beating someone smaller than you...nay. There had to be another reason.

She sighed again and then nothing. Her grip eased on his tunic. He watched the rise and fall of her chest to see if she still breathed, but he saw nothing.

She was dead. He knew it without checking for the beating of her heart. They sat like that for several moments more, Alex not daring to move. Then he got up, settled her on the bed and sat next to her, staring at her. Time passed, but he had no idea how much because he was still trying to process what had happened. The lass couldn't be more than twenty summers.

Dead.

Eventually, the door opened and his sire came inside. He moved closer and all Alex could say was one thing. "Why, Da? Why would four men treat a lass so?"

"Some men are fools, son. Lasses carry their babes inside them for nine moons, then they feed them from their breast. Without our mothers to protect and care for us, we'd cease to exist. Someday, mayhap they'll tire of our cruel treatment and choose to let us die. But they have a powerful instinct to feed and protect us. Small men with minds full of ignorance repay their mothers' nurturing by treating lasses cruelly. They're stronger and they use it to their advantage.

"I'll tell you to never raise a hand to a lass. 'Tis dishonorable." His father strode toward the door, grabbed the handle, then spun around and said, "I'll haunt you and your brothers if you don't respect lasses and bairns. Remember that. Come with me. We're searching for a spot to bury the laird's family together. There's naught more you can do for her."

Alex looked at the dead woman on the bed—so young, so sweet—and started to gag. Repulsed by what had happened, he stood up whirled around to face the door, still gagging. He looked to his sire for help but knew there was naught he could do to change what had happened. Naught he could do to bring Sarah back.

John Alexander Grant held the door open and said, "Go to the parapets, Alex. The fresh air will clear your mind of all you've seen."

He raced through the door and headed toward the end of the passageway, throwing the door open with a bang. Taking the steps two at a time, he hurried to the top. He hung over the side of the parapets for a moment before tipping his head up to the gray sky, breathing in great gulps of fresh air. A sudden calmness traveled through him, the heaving deep in his belly finally settling. He took several more deep breaths.

The door opened and his sire stepped out. "You are better?"

"Aye, my thanks. 'Tis much better up here." His hands still gripped the cold stone as if to anchor him to something he understood.

"Use it, my son. Whenever you need a reminder of the good in the land of the Scots, climb to the parapets."

Alex nodded, taking in the beauty of the mountains in the distance, the meadows, the rocky glens. The view was indescribable.

"Promise me you'll never abuse a lass, never take her without her consent, and never raise a hand to her in anger. The fairer sex deserves our respect, and I'm asking you, as the future laird of Clan Grant, to see to it that every man in our clan knows it. Vow to me now that you'll never accept brutality to the women of our land."

He glanced at his sire and whispered, "I promise. As God as my witness, I pledge to you that I will respect women and expect the same from all in our clan."

His sire clasped his shoulder and they stood together, looking over the land, the mounds of dead beneath them, and all the implications of battle.

Battle was not a lark. It was not something to be entered into lightly. The stakes were life and death.

He knew this moment would be locked in his memory forever.

When Alex arrived home the next day, he had the compulsion to do only one thing. After jumping off his horse and handing the reins to a stable lad, he asked his father if he could take his leave. His wish was granted.

Fortunately.

He hurried across the courtyard, followed by Robbie and Brodie and their many probing questions.

"What happened, Alex?"

"Was there a battle?"

"Did you use your sword?"

"Did you kill someone?"

"Did you see a dead body?"

He didn't know how to answer, nor did he wish to, so he just continued jogging toward the keep. He had a sore need to do something, and he wouldn't stop until he did.

His brothers continued to pester him, so he finally stopped inside the great hall. Turning to them, he said, "Aye. Aye to everything. I saw everything, I killed a couple of bastards who deserved it, and wish I'd killed more. Now leave me be for a bit."

He spun on his heel and headed toward the staircase, ignoring his brothers' persistent quest for more information. But he did smile at one thing he heard.

Robbie said to Brodie, "'Tis just as the stablemaster said. He left a lad and came back a man, I think."

He paused to look back at them just before he turned the corner at the top of the staircase. Brodie pushed Robbie out of the way and said, "Nay, he's still Alex."

Alex smirked at that, but then he continued in his quest—charging down the passageway and opening the door at the end.

He had to see if it was the same here at Grant Castle.

Taking a deep breath, he opened the door at the end and made his way up to the parapets. Smiling, he lifted his face to the sun as he stepped out into the fresh air. The view was even more spectacular here on Grant land. There were more mountains, more birds, more everything. This was his land, and someday he would be the chieftain of it.

Then the green eyes of a lass popped into his head. Sarah Gordon.

Mayhap he had come back a man.

CLAN GRANT
1260

RESCUED
BY A
HIGHLANDER

BOOK 1

I never thought I would sell more than ten books, so when I sold sixty the first day, I was shocked. I found out many of you loved Alex Grant.

CHAPTER ONE

*After this one moment, Alex Grant
will never be the same…*

BRODIE FOLLOWED ALEX through the corridor to the two chambers they had been given for the night.

"Alex, you must be out of your head. Why stay in this filthy place? I would rather sleep under the stars with our men."

"I don't know why, but something is no' right. We stay. Get some sleep." Alex nodded toward Brodie's door down the corridor before stepping into his own chamber.

After spying the thin straw mattress on the pallet, he sighed. Why was he here? He peered around the chamber. Dust covered almost every surface. Though he removed his sword, he set it next to his bed in case of an attack in the night. He wrinkled his nose at the smell of the stale rushes on the floor. A small knock on the door interrupted his thoughts, and a dark-haired woman crept into the room when he bade her to enter.

She curtsied to Alex. "My laird sent me to be at your service this night." She leaned toward him, offering him a view of her ample bosom.

Alex stared at the woman. She had soft curves,

and he hadn't been with a woman in a sennight. He should probably accept the gift.

But he could not. The fear in her eyes was too much for him. What a cruel man her laird must be.

"Lass, I will tell your laird that you served me well, but I find I am too tired to see to it."

"Please, I will do anything you ask, but do no' send me back now."

Alex searched her face and found it to be truthful. The lass had chewed her lip hard enough to draw blood.

"See to my brother, lass. I will not send you back to your laird."

"Thank you, thank you." She spun on her heel and rushed out the door.

Alex sat on the pallet, stirring up a cloud of dust. What was wrong with him lately? He used to pay frequent visits to certain women in his village, but he had yet to meet any woman who sparked anything beyond lust. And lust was easily sated. In truth, he wanted a relationship like his parents had enjoyed. They had adored each other. Of late, he was less interested in the meaningless dalliances he used to seek out.

Now that he had lost his father not long ago and officially became laird of his clan, he was too busy to think about finding a partner. He had been betrothed once, but it had left him cold. The woman had not been one of his choosing, so the breakup certainly had not upset him. Maybe he was not meant to be a husband or a father. His father had told him he was born to lead. Would that be enough?

Alex found himself walking toward the door. He entered the corridor and looked in both directions. The parapet, he needed to find the parapet. That was what he needed this night. He knew the cool night air would help clear his head. If he opened enough doors, he was certain he would find the right one.

He headed down the corridor, shaking his head at the giggling sounds he heard from within his brother's chamber. The next chamber was empty. He moved on to the door after that and opened it quietly.

Just as he was about to close it, he froze. The room was dark, but the candle from the corridor lit the side of a woman's face asleep on the bed. Following his instincts once more, he took two more steps into the room, found a nearby candle, and closed the door behind him.

She was asleep on her side. Her gentle curves were visible through the thin blanket that covered her to her chin. He wanted to step closer, but did not dare, lest he wake her. As he inhaled her lavender scent, a strange sense of peace entered him. Her hair fell in soft golden waves over her shoulders. Who was she? Was this the laird's sister?

His eyes fell on her full pink lips and he was hard instantly. He ran his eyes down her body again. She had to be the most beautiful woman he had ever seen. He returned his gaze to her face and took note of her porcelain skin and her small pert nose. Her long lashes rested on high cheekbones. But what he noticed next caused his erection to leave him in an instant.

She had been beaten. He stepped closer and brought the candle close enough for him to see the dried blood and swollen bruises on the other side of her face. She was the vision of an angel, and someone had beaten her. Anger raced through his veins, followed fast by protectiveness. He could see some discolorations on the soft, exposed skin of her neck. He reached down, wanting to touch her and comfort her. Wanting to protect her from whoever had done this.

Her eyes flew open, and he was instantly lost in an ocean of blue. Realizing how she would probably interpret his sudden presence in her room, he expected a scream. Instead, she pulled away from him, groaned in pain and whispered, "Nay."

Not wanting to confuse or frighten her, he turned and fled. He found the door to the parapet at the end of the corridor and raced up the stairs.

But neither the view nor the night air brought him any peace. Who was the beautiful woman? And who had hurt her?

He would find out.

CHAPTER EIGHTEEN

When Alex learns that Maddie's betrothed raped her, he brings him to Grant Castle and challenges him to a duel. Alex's reputation as the finest swordsman in the land is born.

ALEX PATIENTLY WAITED for Niles to make the first move. He preferred to get a careful measure of his opponent's strengths and weaknesses. The crowd grew impatient and broke into a chant waiting for their laird to make his move. Niles raised his sword and came at Alex from above. He drove his sword over and over at him. The clash of steel on steel rang out as Alex easily blocked all of Niles's parries.

Niles took a step back. "You will not get her, Grant. She is mine, and she was good, too!"

Alex turned and swung his claymore in a sideways arc at Niles. Niles blocked the blow, just missing having his belly sliced open. Alex parried at him again and again, swinging his powerful arms repeatedly at his adversary. The crowd's chants grew louder. Sparks flew as the sounds of crashing metal continued. The ruthless drive continued, spurred by a power even Alex didn't fully comprehend. Then a shout wrenched from the crowd as Alex slipped on the gravel and took the edge of Niles's sword in his right thigh. The crowd booed at the injury to their laird. First blood had been drawn.

Alex stepped back to reassess. The wound was a small one, but he smiled. It was a reminder to him that he needed to stay in control. Niles would try to anger him with his taunts and lies about Madeline. He had to shut his mind to them if he was to win. He expected the Comming to be a dirty fighter. The man knew nothing of the word "honor" as he expected.

The crowd cheered Alex on. He couldn't see Madeline but preferred it that way. He wanted no distractions. His brothers would take care of her and his sister. He would not have to see the fear in Madeline's eyes anymore because of Niles Comming.

Alex lunged at Niles. Niles anticipated the move and rolled out of the way, but not before Alex sliced into his shoulder. The crowd roared. Niles still got up and was able to block two more blows.

Both men stepped to the outside of their circle. Niles paced as Alex held firm, both changing their strategies. The crowd quieted as they noted the blood dripping on the ground. Alex's thigh was still trickling red, and Niles's shoulder bled profusely. Alex knew he now had a weak spot on Niles. His shoulder had to be paining him and would weaken quickly. He glanced at his thigh. The pain was minimal and the bleeding was already slowing. But not on Niles. His shoulder continued to bleed heavily. He had to force him to swing overhead.

Alex glowered at his enemy. Slowly, Niles smiled. He walked a little closer to Alex and said quietly, "Did your lassie tell you how much I made her bleed? She was such a screamer." Alex's eyes turned dark as coal, but he refused to be baited.

At that, Niles swung his claymore over his head and brought it straight down on Alex, trying to slice him in two. Alex blocked the swing, but stumbled and fell to his left. Niles saw his opening and quickly brought his sword over his head again for the killing blow. Just as he swung in a downward arc, Alex turned back to his right in a flash and forced his blade into Niles's belly and pulled up. Niles looked at him briefly, stunned, before crumpling to the ground, dropping his sword.

A cheer erupted from the crowd as the Comming went down. Alex's men pounded his back as he lowered his sword. He turned to search for Madeline but couldn't find her in the throng of people. Sweat dripped down his face. He shook his head because his vision blurred, but he couldn't stop. He frantically scanned the area for her. Kenneth was still out there and she was no longer with his brothers.

CHAPTER TWENTY-ONE

Maddie learns how patient and loving Alex Grant is.

MADDIE FORCED HERSELF to meet the gaze of the man she loved. How could she explain? She was so humiliated. Her arms wrapped tight around her middle. She hated Kenneth for what he had done to her. She knew God did not want her to hate anyone, but she could not help it.

And what would Alex say about this? She was aware there was a possibility he would be so disgusted he would walk out of the water and never return. Then what would she do? Her humiliation would be complete. Maddie buried her face into her arms and reached back with her hands to fist her hair. Everyone would hate her, just like Kenneth had always wanted. He had always been jealous of the affection and respect people gave her, and he had tried to ruin her in every way possible. Mayhap he would have the last laugh.

But if she gave up now, when she was this close to happiness, she would be *letting* him win. Alice had advised her to always be honest with Alex, and this was the time for honesty, even if it hurt.

"I need to tell you something," she said, her arms still crossed in front of her.

Alex's head dropped momentarily, but then rose to look at her. "I am listening."

Madeline fought to keep herself from crying. "My stepbrother was very angry that I refused to marry the Comming."

"I know that, Maddie," he whispered. "I bore witness to his brutality."

"I had refused him two times before the night you rescued me. Kenneth said if I would not marry the Comming, he would make sure and mark me so no other man would want me."

She studied Alex's face, trying to gauge how he was taking the news. He did not react to her words.

"Go on," he said.

"He had a tool that he heated in the fire while he whipped me."

Alex's jaw clench and he closed his eyes for a moment, but she forced herself to continue.

"After he finished whipping me, he turned me around, and while his guards held me, he held the tool to the skin under my breast. He said he would do it each time I refused him, so that my chest would be completely scarred if I never relented." She wrung her hands as she thought carefully.

Alex turned his face to the heavens and let out a deep breath.

"I was not running from your touch, Alex. I was afraid if you saw my scars, you would not want me anymore." A single tear rolled down her cheek. Her hands shook as she reached up to wipe her face.

Alex held his hand out to her. "Come here, Maddie."

She hesitated, but then walked over and placed her hand in his. Alex led her into the shallower water and sat in the pebbles, where the water reached his chest. He settled Maddie onto his lap, wrapped his arms around her tight, and rested her head on his shoulder. Maddie reached her arms around his back and leaned into him. There was nowhere else she would rather be.

Neither one of them spoke. Alex willed himself to rid the anger from his body. He knew Maddie needed him more. They held each other silently.

Alex, totally undone by the unfairness in the world, could not fight the deep sadness that enveloped his body. How could anyone be that cruel to a helpless woman? Although Maddie was not totally helpless, she could not fight the brute strength of three men. In some ways, though, his wee Maddie was stronger than all three men combined. Her strength was an inner strength, a strength of character. He was so proud of her. After all the pain she had been forced to endure, she still had the most beautiful smile he had ever seen. She was wonderful with the bairns, adored by his sister Jennie, and she always held her head high. He knew many strong men who would let such constant torture defeat them. But not his Maddie.

"Maddie," Alex whispered several minutes later.

"Yes, Alex?"

"Is there anything else you have not told me? I would know everything now, please."

"Nay."

"Are you sure?"

"Aye, Alex. They are not things I would ever forget."

Another minute of silence followed. Alex rested his chin on the top of her head.

"Alex?"

"Aye?"

"Are you going to cancel our betrothal?"

"Nay, Maddie, I am no' going to cancel our betrothal. But I must ask you something."

"Anything, Alex."

"I would see the scars under your breasts. I want no surprises on the day of our wedding. I know this is much to ask, but we need to put this behind us."

Maddie pulled back and gazed at him. He knew this would be hard for her, but he was afraid of the anger that might explode inside him when he saw the marks. Even though he prided himself on his strong control, this wee lass could send every ounce of control he possessed out of his body in an instant. He did not want to spend his wedding night in a fury.

She slowly nodded and reached down to untie the ribbons of her chemise. Covering her nipples, she held each breast up so Alex could see the scars. On each side, a small angry curved welt sat just above the fold where her breast met her abdomen. He leaned down and kissed each one with tenderness.

Alex breathed a sigh of relief. He could handle this. He stood, tugging her shivering body with him.

"I think it is time we head back, you are cold." He dressed and helped her into her gown, then secured the basket on his horse. Once he was mounted, he reached down and scooped up Maddie. As soon as she was settled on his lap, he tied her horse's reins to his.

"Alex?"

"Hmm?"

"I feel better now. I do not have any more secrets."

He kissed her forehead and nudged his horse forward. As they moved away from the loch, his men dropped in behind them.

After they dismounted at the keep, they continued to walk hand in hand, much to the surprise of his clan.

"Alex?"

"Aye?"

"I think I would like to stop at the chapel. I have much I need to be thankful for." She gave him a tentative smile.

"I will go with you, Maddie. I will go with you."

CHAPTER TWENTY-TWO

Jennie and Emma are playing when a sinkhole opens up, swallowing them into the ground. Alex is on patrol, so Robbie waits for his return, but Maddie is unwilling to wait and jumps into the hole to save the wee ones. Maddie grabs another piece of his heart.

THE ROPE WAS finally dangling above them. Emma, still awake, silently sucked her thumb as she clung to Maddie. Standing without much difficulty, Maddie grabbed for the rope above her head, but she could not reach it with Emma.

"More, Alex," she shouted. "I cannot reach it."

He let more of it down.

"More!" she shouted. Finally, it reached her. "All right, I have it now."

"Tie it around your waist, Maddie."

Maddie tugged it a little more and set Emma down. "Just for a moment, sweeting. We are going to get you to your mama." She clumsily tied it around her waist and picked Emma back up with her right arm, holding her tight. There was no other way. Her left arm was dangling at an odd angle.

She tugged on the rope and yelled to Alex. "Ready, Alex!"

As soon as Maddie's feet left the ground, her entire body swayed. The movement made Emma wail and Maddie was forced to grab the rope with her left hand to help steady them. Stabbing pain gripped her, but she refused to let go. *Just a little pain*, she chanted in her mind. She could bear it until Emma was safe. They continued to move up slowly, the pain in her arm relentless.

An image of her mother singing helped her focus, but it was blurry. She switched to Alex, recalling the warm comfort of being in his arms. She pictured his face and thought of everything she loved about him. Hearing her name again, she snapped to attention—they were almost at the top.

"Stop, Alex, stop!" she yelled. "We will not be able to fit through together."

"Hand her up and I will grab her," he shouted.

She found a wedge for her foot and pushed with all her strength. Alex reached in and plucked the bairn from her. He handed her out as the crowd cheered. Moira rushed over and grabbed the lassie, sobbing as she rocked Emma back and forth.

When Alex turned to Maddie, his eyes landed on her arm.

"Maddie, your arm," he whispered.

"I know, Alex. I think 'tis broken."

"It must pain you. How will you hold Jennie? She is much heavier."

"I know, but I can do it. We have no choice."

He turned to Robbie. "Pull her out!"

"Nay," she yelled. She wedged her foot solidly into the side of the hole.

Alex held his hand up to motion for the men to stop.

"Maddie, I cannot allow you to do this. We will dig the hole wider."

"And the dirt could bury Jennie. We have no choice. You clearly cannot fit in here. If you do not agree, I will let go of the rope and jump down again, but then I would risk breaking my other arm. I have to get Jennie out. She needs to see Brenna!"

They glared at each other until Alex turned and motioned for the men to lower her down.

"What is it, Alex?" Maddie recognized Robbie's voice.

"Maddie's arm is broken."

"How can she carry Jennie out then?" Brenna asked. "Jennie is much heavier than Emma."

"You are about to witness just how strong my Maddie is. She can do it." The words sent more strength through Maddie. He believed in her, and it made her believe more keenly in herself.

When Maddie reached the bottom again, she adjusted her arm to relieve the numbness. She attempted to awaken Jennie, but the lass did not budge. The bump on her forehead was no larger, so that was good—or so she thought. She retied the rope around her waist as tight as possible. Her left hand did not want to cooperate, but she did the best she could. Losing control and falling while she carried Jennie was not an option. She gathered Jennie up in her right arm, fighting the lass's dead weight. It took her a few moments to regain her balance with the extra weight. If Jennie had been any bigger, she would not have been able to manage it.

Finally settled, she shouted up to Alex.

"We are ready, but please go very slow to start. I have to balance her. She is very heavy for me."

Alex shouted for the men to pull. She swayed and almost lost her grip on the wee one, but she managed to hold tight. As they ascended, the tie around her waist began to slip.

Halfway up, Maddie yelled, "Hurry, Alex, the rope has loosened!"

Alex hollered at his men to go faster. Brodie's face appeared next to Alex's at the top of the hole.

"Brodie, be ready to grab Jennie when they get close," Alex barked. "I will grab Maddie. Her arm will not hold out for long."

The tie gave way and the full force of their combined weight fell on Maddie's left arm. She groaned in response to the vicious surge of the pain, but managed to wrap the rope around her upper arm and shoulder for extra support, though her whole body screamed at the added stress. Clutching Jennie tighter, she realized she was losing control. "Alex!" she shrieked.

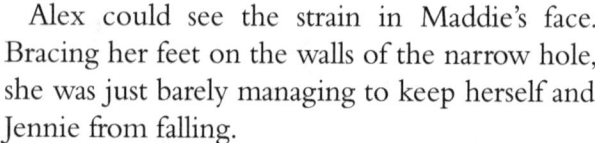

Alex could see the strain in Maddie's face. Bracing her feet on the walls of the narrow hole, she was just barely managing to keep herself and Jennie from falling.

"Hold on, a few feet more and we will have you both. Hang on, Maddie!"

Moments later, Brodie reached into the opening, grabbed Jennie, and yanked her out. He fell backwards on the ground with Jennie on top of him, yet the lass still didn't awaken. The moment Brodie was out of the way, Alex reached in the hole and attempted to grab Maddie's shoulders. Her left hand was no longer able to hold her weight, so he had no choice but to grab her upper right arm, which was still tightly gripping the rope. Maddie twisted away from him as the rope, still partially wrapped around her damaged left arm, held it at an odd angle. Maddie flailed and sobbed at the same time, fighting for her life.

"Alex, Alex!" she sobbed.

"Maddie, look at me! Hold still, I have you."

Madeline's gaze locked with Alex's. There was fear in her eyes and something else. Pain. He glanced at her broken arm and realized the men were still pulling the rope, grotesquely twisting it.

"Alex, help me!" she sobbed in a whisper.

"Stop the rope!" Alex roared. All sanity and calmness left him, and he knew they would not return until his betrothed was safe. He heaved with all his strength and tugged her up through the small opening. Maddie fell across Alex weeping, clinging to him with her right arm.

"Alex, do not let go, please hold me," she whispered into his neck.

Alex carefully cut the rope from her left arm and straightened it as best he could. He held her as gingerly as he could while she continued to weep into his chest.

The crowd fell into a dead silence as they gaped at the odd shape of her arm.

"Look at her arm," someone whispered.

"Her arm is broken!"

"How could she hold on to the bairns with her arm like that?"

"She never screamed or anything."

Slowly, as word passed, everyone started to applaud and cheer Alex's betrothed. He stood cautiously, and—unwilling to cause her any more pain—he cradled her into Brodie's arms and jumped on to Midnight. As soon as Maddie was safely in his lap, he headed back to the keep. Robbie rode some distance ahead of him with Jennie on his lap, Brenna directly behind them with Brodie.

Maddie clung to Alex with her right arm. He kissed her forehead but said nothing.

For Alex, this event had brought clarity to his life. He chastised himself for the doubts he had entertained for the past several days. Maddie belonged in his arms. How could he have doubted it for an instant? The woman had just jeopardized everything for his sister and another wee bairn. She had never questioned whether it was the right thing to do—she had simply done it. The needs of others always came first for Maddie. Long ago, he had thought her timid—a frightened rabbit. Well, timid, frightened rabbits didn't put themselves in danger jumping down deep sinkholes in the ground.

Somehow, he would have to help her bring the same courage to their lovemaking. He probably would still have to be very patient, but they would find a way to make it work.

She would be his wife and he vowed to make her happiness a priority.

Maddie MacDonald had just grabbed another portion of his heart.

CHAPTER THIRTY-TWO

Alex supports Maddie while she's delivering their bairns, a remarkable show of support from a man in this era. No wonder my readers fell in love with him almost as hard as Maddie did.

ALEX, ROBBIE, AND Brodie all jumped when they heard Madeline's scream. Alex and Brodie instantly rushed toward the stairs.

Robbie appeared bewildered. "Where are you going? She is having a bairn. All women scream in childbirth."

Brodie looked over his shoulder at Robbie. "No' Madeline, you fool, she never screams."

Alex reached the door first and pushed on it. It was bolted from within.

"Open the door!" he bellowed. There was no response. "Brenna, open this door or I will kick it in!"

Alex and Brodie kicked in the door, and Robbie followed right behind them with several other guardsmen. Alex froze the instant the door fell. There was a dagger at his wee wife's throat. Kenneth. Time stood still for him. He saw the sweat on her brow, the fear in her eyes, and the fine trembling in her fingers. He met her blue eyes and willed her to be strong. He wanted her to know how much he loved her. He tried to tell her with his eyes, but he felt like a failure.

He had failed his wife in more ways than one. How could she ever forgive him? He had promised to protect her from her stepbrother, and now the man had returned to threaten her and their bairn.

Kenneth was a dead man. Alex's focus returned to him and he stared at his enemy. "What do you want, MacDonald?"

"I want to make you pay for what you did, Grant, and my revenge is just moments away. I lost everything because of you. I lost my friend and all my guards. As soon as this whore drops the bairn, I will kill them both while you watch."

Every muscle in his body tensed and fury coursed through his veins. His eyes turned fiercely dark as he stared at his wife. He willed her to give him what he needed. The next moment, Madeline turned her head and let out another blood-curdling scream right into her stepbrother's ear.

Kenneth started for a second, providing Alex with the only opening he needed. Reaching over, he grabbed Kenneth by the shoulders and threw him as hard as he could against the far wall near the window. Kenneth was momentarily stunned, but he quickly stood up. When he did, he saw the three huge Grant brothers all lunging for him simultaneously.

Kenneth turned and jumped out the window.

He screamed all the way down, but then there was only silence. Everyone in the room froze. "Alex, please!" Maddie huffed out, her face red.

Brenna started to shove everyone out the door.

"Robbie, make sure he is dead!" Alex ordered. When Brenna tried to push him out of the room, too, he stood fast. "Nay, Brenna, I stay!" he insisted. "My wife just had a dagger at her throat." Gazing at Maddie, he strode over to the bed and said softly, "I need to tell Maddie that I love her. That I have always loved her." He leaned over the bed and kissed her soundly.

Maddie gaped at her husband and smiled. "I love you, too, Alex. But right now, I have more important things to do. Your son wants out," she ground out through her teeth as she pushed again.

Alex glanced at his sister, then at his wife, and did the unthinkable. He picked up his wife, sat down on the bed, and settled his wife in front of him. He positioned himself so as not to be in the way of the babe. "I am not leaving, and I do not think anyone here can force me out."

"Then help me push, would you please." Maddie shouted as her body heaved again.

Brenna and Alice lifted the sheet and got Maddie in position for the birth. Each time she pushed, Alex could feel the strain on her body. He wished he could assist her. Marveling at the amount of stamina of his wee wife, he whispered his love into her ear whenever she had to push and let her grip his hands.

"One more push, Maddie, I think." Alice cried. "I can see the bairn's head."

With Maddie's next push, the bairn gushed from her body, and she leaned back against her husband in relief. Alex wrapped his arms around her and kissed her cheek as he wiped the sweat from her brow. They both held their breath until they heard the wee one cry.

"You have a son, Alex! He is beautiful, Maddie." Brenna swiped at her tears as she cleaned up the squalling bairn and handed him to his parents.

Tears flowed from Maddie's eyes as she looked at their son. "Oh, Alex, he is so beautiful, isn't he?"

"Aye, he is," the proud father said.

"You do not mind that he is not a lass?" Maddie pleaded.

"Nay, nothing could make me happier than the sight of our wee lad in your arms, my love." He leaned in and kissed them both.

"Oh, Alex, it's starting again! Oh, Alice, I have to push again!" she announced as her body heaved once more.

Brenna shouted, "Twins! Two bairns. Keep pushing, Maddie."

"Two?" Alex couldn't believe what he'd just

heard. He glanced at his wee wife as she began to push again. "Another bairn, wife?"

A few minutes later, Alex held their firstborn and Maddie held their second son. "I hope I am done now, Alice," looking at their two boys with eyes full of wonder.

After the afterbirth came out, they sent Alex out with one son in each arm so they could clean the bed and get Maddie washed up. They slipped a fresh night rail on her and allowed her to relax on the bed.

"You did beautifully," Alice said as she kissed Maddie's brow. "How I wish your mother could be here."

"I think my mother *is* here, Alice. I can feel her spirit with me."

HEALING
A
HIGHLANDER'S
HEART

BOOK 2

The book that changed all my plans. I received so many emails about Logan Ramsay that I had to add Clan Ramsay to my series.

CHAPTER ELEVEN

Logan Ramsay steals Brenna from her bed on Grant land to save his dying brother. Alex wasn't willing to lose his sister, so he does what he must to bring her home. Alex arrives on Ramsay land with a large force of warriors to retrieve his sister—the beginning of the Grant-Ramsay alliance wasn't so grand. I loved Brenna in this scene because she stood up for what she knew was right, even though it meant going against her brother's orders.

QUADE HEARD THE Grant's battle cry and cringed.

"Grant! By my arrow, give me a moment before you finish me. Every man should be granted a last request. Aye? By your Scottish honor?"

Alex's arm reached across the sea of warriors. Instant silence followed.

Grant nudged his magnificent stallion forward, bringing it within inches of his horse. "You kidnapped my sister, Ramsay. There is no honor in you as a Scotsman."

The Grant was massive and every bit as impressive as he was rumored to be. "Aye, I acted in haste. God's truth, my brother acted in haste because I was on death's door. Your sister has come to nae harm. I ask you to come to my hall and speak to her before you pass judgment on my clan. The actions I took were for my own benefit and no' for my clan's."

Quade's eyes met the laird's. He thought he saw a glimmer of softening there, enough to give him hope he was not about to have his head cleaved from his body in one swoop from the man's giant claymore. Grant's brother flanked him. He had eyes like Brenna, more soulful than the lairds. Quade reminded himself he spoke to the family of the lass he loved, and he would give them as much respect as he gave her.

Grant's powerful warhorse whinnied and pawed the ground, anxious about something, but he couldn't tell what. Then Quade caught the subtle shift of Grant's eyes back toward the keep. What had he seen? He turned his head to look in that direction and drew back.

Brenna.

Brenna flew across the meadow on her horse in all her glory.

He tried to return his gaze to the Grant but couldn't. Powerless against the siren flying toward them, his chest swelled with a strange kind of pride as she galloped toward them. Her hair was unbound, chestnut locks waving in the sun, but she didn't let that stop her. He knew Brenna by now. She never cared about her appearance, whether due to her innocent misunderstanding of how it affected people or because it wasn't important to her, he wasn't sure. Her hair had been back earlier, but it was always in a bit of disarray, so it hadn't taken much for the wind to pull it from its confines.

She was magnificent—glorious in her beauty, steadfast in her strength. Everything about her called to him without speaking. He couldn't let her go, he realized as he watched her, he would never let her go. Beyond her beauty, she was the most intelligent lass he had ever met. She knew things most men could not begin to understand, things *he* couldn't begin to understand. They belonged together. He knew he couldn't marry her, but mayhap he could settle with having her stay in his keep as the healer. He would force himself to use restraint and stay away from her just to keep her near. His people needed her, his children needed her.

He needed her.

He loved her and admired her more than he had ever loved before. That thought frightened him, but he knew he would do whatever it took to make her stay. What Laird Grant wanted did not matter. This called for extreme measures.

She approached their group and nodded to her brothers, situating herself almost between the two chieftains. "Alex, Brodie." She greeted both with a stiff countenance that puzzled him.

"Lady Brenna," Alex greeted her. "How do you fare?"

Her mouth curved a touch. "I am well."

Quade still could not take his eyes from her. She sat her horse as a queen would, regal in her bearing, her brown eyes taking in everything at once. Grant's entire army of warriors stood as still as can be, awaiting any word from her.

"Brenna, move your horse behind mine." Alex barked his order without flinching.

She didn't budge.

"Brenna? Your laird gave you an order." Brodie glared at her.

"Aye, Alex. I heard your order. Excuse me, my laird. I would like permission to speak first." Her eyes bored into her brother's.

Stubborn woman! What was she thinking to deny her laird? Quade wanted to shake her before she made any more poor decisions. He glanced back at Laird Grant and decided he didn't like the menacing look he was giving his sister.

Quade moved his horse over in front of Brenna. "Lass, go behind me."

Brenna paused for a long moment, clearly thinking about her decision and its implications, before slowly moving her horse behind him.

Quade's heart soared. Mayhap there was hope.

A muscle in Alex's face twitched. "You give your life for my sister, Ramsay?"

"Aye, I do."

"You've made your choice." Alex pulled his claymore out, wielding it high enough for all to see.

"Alex, stop! Please listen to me. If you have any regard for me at all, you will stop this nonsense and enter the hall. I have need to speak to you and no' in front of your guardsmen. Quade, you will allow my brothers into the keep for purposes of negotiation?"

Quade's eyes never left the laird's eyes. "Aye, your family is always welcome. As long as I have your brother's word that he will not harm you or force you to do anything against your will."

Alex's eyebrow rose. "I would never harm my sister, but she may no' like the decision I make. I agree, for her sake only, to discuss the situation."

Quade looked to Brenna for confirmation. "Lady Brenna? Is this agreeable to you?"

"Am I allowed to be part of the discussion?" she asked, her eyes pinned on her brother. "Alex, I willnae have important decisions made about my life without my input. You ken how our mother felt about such things."

Alex's mouth quirked before he nodded in agreement. "Stubborn lass. You have my word."

"I welcome you at my table, Laird Grant. You and your brother. We will send food and ale out for your guardsmen."

"Agreed. Brodie, get the men settled and I will see you in the hall."

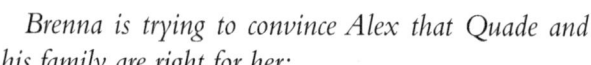

Brenna is trying to convince Alex that Quade and his family are right for her:

She had to call on her reserves. She had hoped it wouldn't come to this, that her brother would listen to reason and do what was best for the Ramsays, but she would have to do what was necessary.

Ever since he had married Madeline MacDonald, her brother's heart had softened. Once she had given him twin boys, his heart had softened even more. His exterior was still a laird's hardened countenance, but he had one weakness and she intended to use it.

When the twins were born, he had hoped for a lass. Alex so loved his wife that he had wanted a lassie with blonde curls, just like Madeline's. He loved his lads with all his heart, but he still longed for a wee lass to settle on his lap, and hoped for one with Maddie's present carry.

He wanted a lass just like Lily. Wee Lily with her long yellow curls and infectious giggle would bring Alex Grant to his knees.

Or so Brenna hoped.

"Alex, I must leave to check on wee Lily. I will return promptly, I promise." She glanced at her brother before heading to the stairs. His forehead furrowed, but he nodded, indicating that she would have time to retrieve Lily before he acted.

A few moments later, she descended the steps with Lily in her arms, the wee lass bubbling with excitement to be allowed back in the great hall, especially to meet someone new.

"Lady Brenna, who is the really big lad? I think he is bigger than my da, and I thought my da was the biggest ever. What is his name? Is he one of your brothers? What are their names? Do you love both your brothers? Who is the biggest? Can I talk to them?" She waved to the group below stairs.

When Brenna set her down in at the bottom of the stairs, she charged over to her father as fast as her wee legs could carry her. Brenna was so proud to see her nearly running—not quite a full run yet, but she was so much improved.

"Papa! I am so happy to be here. See how fast I am now!"

Quade stood up and caught his daughter before lifting her in the air and planting a big kiss on her cheek. "Lily, use your proper manners." He set her back down. "You must curtsy to Laird Grant and greet him."

The plan had worked. Brenna watched as her big brother stood, clearly charmed by the wee lass. Her heart swelled because her instinct had been correct. A smile had broken out across Alex's face counter to his will.

Lily stood in front of him, attempted a curtsy but stumbled. "Good day to you, Laird Grant." Her father helped her straighten and her mop of curls tipped back as she stared up at Alex.

"My, he is big. Why is he bigger than you, Da?" Her innocent grin seemed to hit Alex right between the eyes.

Quade sat and picked Lily up, lifting her into his lap. "Sit, Laird Grant. My daughter is a bit talkative now that she has more energy. I have never seen her this way. I must confess that I owe her good health to your sister. She is the only healer who has been able to determine Lily's problem."

"And I am all better, Laird Grant. Watch me."

Lily jumped off her father's lap and turned to look at him. "Watch how fast I am. Papa, I will run to the other end of the hall and back."

She took off, only stopping once before she came to the other end. "Papa, see? Am I no' the fastest ever? Watch me, Laird Grant! I am the fastest."

They all followed Lily as her little legs churned back toward them, her arms swirling furiously.

"See, Laird Grant?" She stopped in front of Alex. He stared at her wide-eyed and nodded his head.

"Watch me again. Lady Brenna," she tapped her knee, "watch how fast I am." As soon as she was sure she had everyone's attention, she sailed off in the opposite direction once more.

Brenna and Quade both started to laugh, trying to keep quiet about it.

Alex looked at them both in turn. "Brenna?"

"Aye, Alex?"

Four pairs of eyes followed Lily's journey back and forth in the hall, all of the watchers smiling except for Alex.

"Why does the wean run so slow? The lads are much faster than she is and they are quite a bit younger…And why are you two laughing?"

Brenna and Quade glanced at each other and broke into louder laughter. When she was able, Brenna finally answered her brother. "Because she does no' ken she is slow."

Brodie whispered, "I was going to say the same thing, Alex, but I did no' want to hurt anyone's feelings. Why does the lass think she is fast when she is so slow, Brenna?"

"Because this is the fastest she has ever run." Quade's shoulders shrugged as he offered his explanation. "She is the fastest ever in her terms."

Alex stared at him with wide eyes.

"Aye, she could barely walk before your sister arrived. She had been frail for almost three summers. She rarely made it off her pallet, much less out of her chamber. She was too weak." Quade's face stretched into an indulgent smile as his daughter ran back toward them. Brenna couldn't take her eyes off of him. He was so taken with his daughter.

"Here I come again, Papa! Look, I am even faster now!" Her arms swung over her head in her excitement.

They all watched her tear back across the hall toward them, and Brenna and Quade laughed hard enough to make Lily giggle. She stopped in front of Alex and stared up into his eyes, her face beaming with pride. "Do you want to see how high I can jump, too, Laird Grant?"

"Aye, aye, Lily!" Brenna said through her laughter. "We are so proud of you! Keep running and jumping."

Alex continued to stare at the three of them. He finally bent down and patted the wee one's back. "Aye, lass. You are the fastest."

Leaning over, Lily gave him a kiss on his cheek. "Thank you, Laird Grant. I hope you do no' take Lady Brenna away from me. She fixed me. See how much better I am now?"

The big laird was conquered.

CHAPTER TWELVE

Brenna is NOT happy with her brother.

FIVE OF THEM now stood in Quade's solar. Alex's arms were crossed in his laird stance— as Brenna oft called it—and Brodie looked equally serious next to him. Quade and Micheil stood against the opposite wall with Brenna somewhere in between.

Alex spoke first. "Ramsay, since you had your tongue halfway down my sister's throat, I expect you will be agreeable to marrying her as soon as possible.

"Alex!" Brenna could not believe he had said such a thing. Even if it was true, it didn't need to be said in front of everyone. She blushed a dark shade of red. She had blushed as soon as she had seen the look in her brother's eye after he caught her in such a compromising position, but it had been dark in the passageway, even with the torches. Plus, after the way Quade had been kissing her, it was hard to think clearly.

All right, she shouldn't have been kissing Quade, but she wouldn't change it. She had liked it too much. Her whole body would still be tingling if not for her brother's angry countenance. Brodie wasn't any better, except she could see his smirk trying to break out. She knew he didn't dare smile in front of Alex.

Hellfire, what was she to do now? She supposed she could marry Quade. Her feelings toward the lad had grown, especially when he kissed her like that. Whew! How long had they been standing in the hallway devouring each other anyway?

Either way, her brother was just being a big bully.

He had promised their mother she would have a say in who she married, and he had promised her the same thing. Alex would never force her against her will. Would he?

"The marriage will take place in two days' time. Find a priest, Ramsay. I need to get home to my wife." Alex's eyes were pinned on Quade, daring him to argue again.

"Alex, stop!" It was time for her to get involved. She would not allow Alex to run her life. "This was clearly a mistake and it willnae happen again. I promise."

"'Tis too late, Brenna. The damage is done. I did no' notice you pushing him away, so you should be agreeable."

"But I am no' agreeable," she shouted.

"You were agreeable enough to let him run his hands all over you."

"I am no' agreeable to marrying him. I willnae force anyone to marry me."

"I do no' care if you are agreeable or no'. This man, chief or no', willnae shame my sister and get away with it. You will marry him, Brenna."

"Nay! You promised our mother that I would have my say in who I married. And I say nay!"

"Sorry, but it appeared to me you were saying aye when you had your arms wrapped around his neck and you were pushing yourself against him. You will marry him!" Alex's bellow shook the rafters.

Quade stepped forward. "I do no' care if she agrees. I willnae marry her."

Alex strode forward until he was but an inch

away from Quade's face. "What do you mean you willnae marry her? You had your hands all over her. Or is that how you treat every lass, like a common wench?"

Quade did not back down. "Nay, I do no' treat every lass as such. Brenna kens how much respect I have for her. But one kiss does no' force a marriage. I repeat; I will no' marry her."

"You have an odd way of showing your respect, Ramsay. You will marry her at the end of my claymore, if you wish."

"Nay, I will no' do it, no' for you or for anyone."

Brenna suddenly realized what Quade had said. Her brow furrowed. It was one thing for her to deny a forced marriage, quite another for him to react this way, as if marrying her would be the worst fate in the world.

She marched over and stood in front of Quade, her hands on her hips. "What do you mean you willnae marry me? Was everything you said to me a lie?"

Quade gaped at her. "Nay, Brenna. I have never lied to you."

"Lady Brenna to you, Ramsay," Alex barked.

"Aye, Lady Brenna. But nay. I wasnae lying to you. I meant every word I said. Could we nae discuss this somewhere else, Lady Brenna?"

"Nay, now you are insulting me. What is so wrong with me that you willnae marry me?" Brenna's throat constricted on her, but she couldn't stop. "You were going to kiss and run? I have heard of men like you. I thought you had feelings for me." She swung out in frustration and slapped his arm. "How could you?" Tears threatened to fall, but she would not give him the satisfaction. She should have stayed away from him. Never again would she fall prey to a lad's kisses, no matter how they made her feel.

"Stop, will you no'? You ken I cannae marry you. We have discussed this." He reached for her hand, but she pulled away.

"You also said it was a mistake when you kissed me before and it wouldnae happen again. But now it has happened again. What is that supposed to mean? You do no' want me at all? Or do you?" She dared him to deny her again to her face.

Hellfire, she was in a room full of men, each of them trying to run her life. Quade said he wanted her with his actions, but then he insulted her by denying her brother's direct order. What in blazes did he mean? Was he using her? Had he no feelings? When she was in his arms, he acted as if he couldn't get enough of her, but now he could hardly look at her. This lad was making her absolutely daft.

And Alex? Alex just wanted to order everyone about. Wait until she informed Madeline how miserable he was when he was away from her. There was no reasoning with any of the men in this chamber. She wasn't daft, they were. She glanced at her brothers again and narrowed her eyes when she saw that Brodie had finally broken out into a grin. She promptly walked over and slapped his arm. "And that's for laughing. How dare you laugh at me when they are all trying to tell me what to do! You were there when Mama said I was to have a say when it came to marriage."

She squared off with Alex. "And I am going to have my say. He does no' want me and I do no' want him. This was a big mistake and I can promise you, without a doubt, that it will never happen again. You will never see me kiss Quade Ramsay again."

Brenna marched in a circle with her hands on her hips. She had to get out, that was the only solution. She had to leave while she still had an ounce of her mind left. Finally stopping in the middle of the room, she glared at all of them before whispering, "I will no' marry Quade Ramsay and you cannae force me, Alex. And neither can you, Quade Ramsay. I want you out of my life."

"I want to go home. Now."

CHAPTER TWENTY-THREE

And later, a wedding and a reception.
Alex, the gruff chieftain…

BRENNA ATE UNTIL she was stuffed. Logan gave her more than she could manage. The minstrels and musicians began their songs, hoping to get the crowd dancing.

A loud voice interrupted them as a lad made his way over to Alex Grant. "Laird, I would like permission to dance with your youngest sister." The young lad stared at his toes as he stood in front of Alex Grant.

"Nay!" Alex's bellow shook the rafters and the lad scurried away with a sheepish glance at Jennie.

"Alex, how can I enjoy myself if you bark at everyone?" Jennie was close to tears as she looked back and forth between him and her other brothers, Robbie and Brodie. "There must be someone I can dance with besides my own brothers. I am no' a bairn anymore."

Brenna elbowed Quade at the dais to be sure he was watching the show her brother was putting on for all to see.

"Your brother is jesting?" Quade peered at her.

"Nay, he loves to scare off all the lads. He did the same for me. No one dared to come near me."

He kissed her cheek. "Och, I will be sure and thank him. Otherwise, you may have swooned for another and I want you for myself."

She swatted his arm affectionately. "I was never interested in another. It does not mean he has to spoil the special night for her. 'Tis her only sister's wedding." She squeezed his hand before yelling at her brother. "Alex!"

Alex made his way over to her with narrowed eyes. "'Tis only due to your injury and your wedding that I answer your beck and call."

Madeline followed her husband and took the seat beside Brenna's. "Alex, love, you need to ease up and allow your sister to dance a wee bit. There must be someone she could dance with this night."

Alex scanned the room. "Nay, 'tis no one."

Jennie's face fell and her arms dropped to her sides, her lids blinking back tears.

"There is one solution I can propose. Why do you not dance with your sister?" Madeline gave her husband her sweetest smile.

Brenna stifled her laughter as she glanced at her husband, who choked on his ale. Logan stood a few steps away grinning, and Brenna's other brothers were laughing so hard they started to choke. Avelina came over when she noticed the sudden family grouping.

"'Tis impossible, wife, and you ken that. I do no' dance."

"Alex, I know it is not your favorite thing to do, but you are quite capable. Sorry, Jennie, but if he dances, it will be with me." Maddie smiled at her husband. "Besides, if I carry a wee lass and we dance, it will be like rocking her to sleep." Brenna noticed how quickly he softened his demeanor. Apparently, his feelings for his wee wife had not diminished one bit.

Quade spoke up. "May I make a suggestion?" He gave Logan a pointed glance.

Alex barked. "Aye, please!"

"I do no' want any randy lads dancing with my sister either." Avelina's face fell, as though she were imagining an evening empty of dances.

Logan broke through the gathering and held his hand out to Jennie. "Would you care to dance, my lady?" He gave her his best courtly bow.

The girl's face beamed as she waited for her brother's approval.

Quade interrupted. "Seems like a perfect

solution to me, Alex. I have two brothers to dance with Jennie and you have two brothers who can take turns dancing with Avelina. It should suit everyone."

Alex searched the group of faces before giving a gruff, "Aye."

His wife stood up from her chair and stood on her tiptoes to kiss his cheek. "Very wise decision, dearest. Now would you care to escort your wife for one dance?"

Brenna squeezed Quade's arm as her brother's chest puffed out a wee bit more, if that were possible. "I so enjoy watching my brother tamed by a wee lass. He would do anything for Maddie."

EPILOGUE

A small piece but one of readers' favorites.
Alex at his best.

LADY BRENNA RAMSAY stood at the base of the stairs in her brother's great hall, a sense of happiness and peace suffusing her body. She and her sister, Jennie, had delivered her brother's wee daughter the previous night. She had just checked on Maddie and she was sound asleep in her chamber with her maid, Alice, fussing over her.

The scene that greeted her eyes was beautiful. Thanks to the snowstorm raging outside, practically the whole family was gathered together. Jennie and Avelina sat at the table planning the garments they would sew for the wee lass while Brenna's two nephews ran circles around the perimeter of the hall. Lily, Torrian, and Growley scrambled at the boys' heels, their combined laughter bouncing off the rafters.

Brenna's brother, Alex, pumped up like a peacock after the birth of his daughter, paced the hall with his wee one, who was strapped to his chest with his plaid, cooing in the softest voice she had ever heard him use. She couldn't help but giggle. Alex had stayed by his wife's side during the birth, and he was so excited to finally have a daughter to love that he wasn't even disappointed that the lass had arrived with a shock of dark hair instead of Maddie's beautiful blonde curls.

LOVE LETTERS FROM LARGS

BOOK 3

The Battle of Largs drew me in because so little was written about it. But there were tales of a Scottish warrior in a golden helm.

Logan Ramsay became the star of Book 2. The star of this book?

A lad known as Lucky Loki.

CHAPTER FIVE

*Alex and Brodie at court with an obnoxious baron
and a cruel jarl, both wanting to control Celestina.
Alex is the one with the king's favor in the chaos.*

CELESTINA'S FATHER MOVED to strike
her again, and she brought up a trembling
hand to protect her face. "You are a whore, just
like your mother before you. I knew it." Her
eyes closed, but the blow never connected.

A low growl ripped through the haze of her
fear. Her eyes flew open in time to see Brodie
lift her father into the air and slam him against
the wall. Her father's eyes protruded from their
sockets in shock, or so she thought. Then she
realized Brodie was holding him by the throat,
choking his windpipe so that he gasped for air.

Her father swung his fists at Brodie, but his
captor never once flinched. Celestina fell back
against the opposite wall, paralyzed by the sight
in front of her.

Brodie slammed her father against the wall over
and over again, easily avoiding the older man's
attempts to pummel him. "You filthy swine!
How dare you hit your own flesh and blood!
You slapped your own daughter for nothing. No
reason. You will rot in hell, you slime. If you hit
her again, I will kill you with my bare hands. You

should be protecting your daughter, no' hurting her."

Brodie's bellows rang out in the corridor. Celestina heard a flurry of activity headed their way, but she couldn't tear her eyes away from her father and the look on his face. He was demented, beyond furious that Brodie had interfered with his punishment of her. While a part of her cheered for her hero, another part of her wanted to run, afraid of what would happen if her father ever managed to free himself from Brodie's grasp.

"Guards, guards! Save this man from the wild savage who's attacking him!" Her betrothed stood watching the scene unfold from the end of the corridor, spewing lies for all to hear. "The Highlander has gone mad. Stop him!" Hatred and fear poured from him as he stared at Brodie.

The hall soon filled with the king's guards. Her betrothed continued to screech, but she was unable to distinguish any more words in the sound. Three guards surrounded Brodie and the swift sound of metal scraping against metal filled the air as the guards pulled their swords from their sheath, all three aiming their sharp edges at Brodie's neck. Still, he did not release his hold on the baron.

Once Brodie was contained, Ivarsson sauntered toward the group of men. "Now kill him."

"Nay!" Even Celestina surprised herself with the power of her vehemence.

"Kill him, I say." Her betrothed spoke with little emotion, but his face took on a twisted look. "And please make it painful. The lad deserves it."

The guards didn't move to follow the command that Ivarsson had no right to give them. Loud steps echoed down the corridor as the king and his personal guards approached. Her betrothed finally stepped aside to make way for them.

As he approached the melee, the king finally spoke. "You will not kill him, guards, but Brodie, you must release your hold on my baron."

Brodie squeezed a touch harder on the baron's windpipe. The baron's face, beet red, sneered at him. "Your Grace, the man's cruelty to his own daughter is unconscionable to me. The baron has no honor to treat his own lass as he does."

"Surely, you must be mistaken, Grant. I am sure the baron would never hurt his daughter, though now that I look at her, I can see a red mark on her cheek. Did you inflict that on her, Baron?" The king's words held no fury, no anger. He remained in complete control.

The baron wheezed. "Nay."

"Nay, you think no'? I saw you do it with my own two eyes." Brodie said. "Please check his daughter's left arm and you will see more evidence of his abuse."

King Alexander reached out to Celestina and asked, "May I, my lady?"

Celestina held her arm still while the king carefully slid up the sleeve of her gown. Rather than meet his gaze, she cast her eyes downward as her father had taught her to do.

"Child, you may look at me."

Celestina's eyes met his. Her father was not in

her line of sight because Brodie stood in front of him.

"Did your own father inflict these bruises?"

Celestina's father kicked and squirmed in an attempt to get away from the Highlander.

The king turned to him and shouted, "Baron, control your temper." He returned to her and lowered his voice. "Please ignore your father. Did he do this to you?"

Celestina knew she would bear the brunt of this inquisition. Her father could hear her words, but she didn't think he could see her clearly. She nodded ever so slightly, making sure the king saw her signal. He nodded his own head in response. She then spoke loud and clear, "Nay, my king."

Her father relaxed, but unfortunately, he wasn't the only one to miss her nod. Brodie exploded, "Celestina, tell the truth. Your Grace, can you no' see she is afraid of her own sire? He did this to her and who knows what else?"

"Release the baron, Grant." King Alexander whispered his order.

"But...."

"I am ordering you to release him as your king." One of the guard's swords drew blood on Brodie's neck, and he finally loosed the baron, who fell to the floor panting and massaging his windpipe. The swords remained trained on Brodie's neck.

When the baron regained his breath, he huffed out his demand for fair punishment of his treatment, "Kill the savage. How dare he threaten me! He had his hands on my daughter when I came down the corridor. I want him dead, my king. If you wish for her hand in marriage to Ivarsson, kill him now."

"Before anything else happens, I will ask you for your promise that you will not abuse your daughter further." King Alexander stood over Celestina's father, his arms crossed as he awaited an answer.

The baron stood, tugging his clothes in indignation at the king's command. "I do not need to give you such a promise as I have never hurt my daughter." His hand swung toward her in dismissal. "Does she appear abused? She is perfectly fine."

Celestina held her shock at bay, unable to believe her father would lie this way to the king himself.

"Nevertheless, I require your promise...and I will have it before I mete out Brodie Grant's punishment for his part in this situation." The king's chin raised a notch as he waited.

Celestina wrung her hands. Oh, how she wished things had unfolded differently. What a jumble this entire evening had become. Her father's protests told her exactly how angry he was, giving her an inkling of how she would suffer on the morrow, regardless of whatever promises he made the king. The baron's treatment of her did not constitute abuse in his eyes, so nothing would change. And Brodie Grant, her savior, still had three swords at his throat because he'd tried to defend her. Her betrothed's actions were completely out of control, too. He had seemed delighted at the possibility that death might be meted out as just punishment, and in the corridor, no less. What did that obvious violent streak indicate for their marriage?

"Fine," the baron rubbed his throat, "you have my promise, my king. Now in exchange, I expect you to hang that animal."

"'Tis a bit extreme, don't you think, Baron?" The king clasped his hands behind his back.

The baron straightened his neckwear. "No, I want him dead. He almost killed me in a completely unprovoked attack." Clearly agitated, his eyes darted around the room, searching for support among the others.

"Your Grace, the swords," Brodie asked. "I have released the baron, I ask for release in turn."

The man Celestina had been promised to marry stepped in closer, still not venturing anywhere near Brodie—so he was not only cruel, but a coward. "Kill him, my king. If you want our continued support in your endeavor to gain back the Isles, you will kill him for his actions. He is a savage Highlander who knows not how to act properly and respectfully." His voice rose as he spoke. "Kill him, I say. Kill him now for his insult to our station."

"Yes," bellowed the baron. "Kill him now."

"Kill him, King Alexander," Ivarsson repeated. "Kill him and make an example of anyone who wishes to go against your reign. Kill him now to guarantee your win." He would not back down.

Celestina stared at the two men who held her future in their hands, unable to believe the cruelty and unveiled hatred bouncing between them. How could they condone the death of an innocent man? Brodie Grant had stood up for her honor, and the two men who should honor her most wanted him dead. This was all so wrong!

"Nay, please nay." She turned to King Alexander. "Please do not do it, my king. He was only trying to protect me." She had to sway his mind.

Ivarsson barked, "Celestina, close your mouth. A woman's opinion is of no value. We do not wish to hear your thoughts."

Her betrothed's insult neither surprised nor hurt her. He was only speaking to her in the manner her own father had done for years.

"Kill him," her father screamed, his voice so loud in the contained hallway that she had to cover her ears. "He is an insult to all of the Scottish. I say kill him."

"Stop, stop, all of you, please stop." Celestina moved in front of Brodie, as if to protect him. "Please do not do this. He does not deserve to die because of me."

"When will you learn your place, girl?" The baron reached for her but he pulled his hand back when he saw the look on the king's face.

Her betrothed grabbed her around the waist, yanking her away from Brodie. "Get away, you foolish beasom. You have caused enough trouble, and this is not your affair. Leave immediately as this is no place for a female." He twisted her arm.

The king said, "Ivarsson, control yourself." Her betrothed, obviously shocked to have been so corrected, jerked toward the king.

The swishing sound of cold steel filled the air as

the pointed end of a sword fell against Ivarsson's neck. Laird Alexander Grant had just joined the ruckus.

The Grant pressed his weapon forward just enough to prevent the man from moving. "And I say take your hands off the lady."

Her betrothed dropped his grip on her and turned a sad shade of green. "King, kindly call off this ruffian."

"Your Grace, if anyone moves but you or the lady, Ivarsson is a dead man. Believe me, naught would please me more than to spear this spineless waste of a human on the end of my sword."

As Celestina backed away, Brodie's face broke into a grin, even with three swords at his throat. "Took you long enough, brother."

"I was enjoying my oxtail soup." A sly grin caught the corner of his mouth.

"Alexander Grant, always the showman," the king chuckled. "Release the man."

"I would be happy to do so just as soon as your guards release my brother."

"What right does he have to give you orders, King? He should be whipped for his impudence!" The baron's face had turned an even deeper shade of red.

Celestina gaped at the sight in front of her— Brodie Grant with three swords still at him while The Grant's giant blade was just inches away from Ivarsson's throat. She feared for Brodie's life, yet he stood tall. Her betrothed, by contrast, looked as if he was about to lose the contents of his stomach or his bowels. The brashness and vehemence in his countenance had disappeared as soon as the sword had appeared in front of him. How different the two men were, and how she wished their roles in her life could be switched.

The king glared at Laird Grant. "I am requesting you to release him, Grant."

"With all due respect, your guards have my brother at the end of their swords, and from what I have heard, he has done naught but stand tall for a lass's honor. That is what we do in the Highlands. His actions would make my father proud, just as they have made me proud. His king should be proud as well. The lass does not deserve such treatment doled out to her by her sire or her betrothed. 'Tis no' our duty to protect the innocents, Your Grace?"

"Release him and we will discuss this."

Her father's spittle ran down his chin. "What hold could he possibly have on you, my king? Why are you hesitating?"

Laird Grant stared into the king's eyes. "Five hundred warriors. Five hundred warriors to protect his life and my brother to protect his castle. I hardly think he wants one of the Highland's best warriors to be skewered in front of him."

The King of the Scots turned slowly to face his baron. "Your insolence and that of your Norse comrade are about to gain you both a stay in my dungeon. Mayhap a day or two below stairs will remind you who is in charge. I will not tolerate your rudeness any longer." He waited until the baron calmed before pivoting to Alex.

Alex smiled, "Your Grace?"

The king's eyebrows rose as a small smile crept across his face. "Five hundred? Very nice. You have been holding out on me. How have you managed to build such a force, Grant?"

"I treat my men well and they reward me with hard work. I have pulled many from the MacDonalds and the Commings among others."

"You didn't mention that number before, only two hundred and fifty. A small part of your total."

"Many are still in training. I will send you three hundred and fifty. Free my brother with the promise of no retaliation for acting as any Highlander with honor should."

A long pause lapsed before the king spoke again. "Release him, guards."

The guards pulled back and Alex Grant lowered his sword.

The king glowered at the group. "We meet in my solar."

CHAPTER TWENTY-FIVE

Another scene that made Alex Grant a legend, battling in the Battle of Largs with his golden helm and his chain-mailed horse. I tried to stick to history as much as I could, but I love writing about this battle. This is from Brodie's point of view.

SUDDENLY THE GRANT battle cry echoed around him and hope sprang inside him. His gut told him the cry could only have come from his brother, Alex. As soon as he safely could, he turned back to look for his brother. He grinned from ear to ear when he finally caught sight of Alex in all his glory. He rode at the forefront of a group of chain-mailed destriers, his golden helm reflecting the sunlight. Fresh on the field, Alex fought like a man possessed, wounding and killing as he pushed forward, his best warriors fighting with equal fervor at his side. The fighters on the ground tried to take Alex out, but he was nearly invincible with all the gear he carried. Brodie rode up beside him as his brother swung a pole-ax and threw a soldier ten feet backwards.

Alex yelled, "Robbie?"

"Haven't seen him since this morning. He has to be here with Dundonald."

The Grant warriors formed a closely knit line, the mounted warriors in front of their foot guards. Their deadly battle axes and swords finally forced the Norsemen on the mound to turn tail and run toward the beach. Cheers went up amongst the Scots as the group retreated, but then the fleeing Norwegians joined with the forces on the beach.

Had they retreated or just combined forces? Brodie wasn't sure, but the Norsemen made a more formidable group now that they were all together on the beach. As they moved forward, arrows and rocks buzzed by his ears, aimed at the fleeing group. Loki. Though he hoped the lad knew enough to stay the hell back, he knew some of those rocks could only have been hurled from one sling. Celestina would never forgive him if something happened to Loki. He turned his head just for a second and looked toward the left of the mound. He saw a glimpse of the wee lad's shock of brown hair, and then he saw him tumble down.

He charged off to the side, hoping to find Loki and assess his condition. He had to kill three more men to get to the place where he'd last seen the boy, but he finally found him.

"Loki, are you all right?" His sword continued to cut down any Norwegian fool enough to come near them.

"Aye, I just have a wee cut. But it does no' hurt. I am a warrior! I have to keep fighting with my sling."

Brodie had turned to assess the damage of his little friend when he noticed the dark red wetness on his own calf. He looked down and saw blood dripping from a wound there. He recalled a burning sensation in his leg not too long ago; he just hadn't taken the time to stop and look. One wrong move could be your death while in battle.

"Get back!' he barked at the boy. "You don't belong this far in the melee. Stay in the trees like we told you!" Loki nodded and hung his head, so Brodie reined his horse and headed back to the center of the battle.

He fell in line with his brother. Taking in the sight of him, Alex said, "You're cut and bleeding. Protect yourself from further damage."

"I'm fine, Alex. We need to end this." The need to finish the battle burned in his veins; all he needed to do to return to his wife was keep fighting. They pushed and pushed toward the beach until the number of foreign barbarians dwindled, some choosing to return to their ship. Whether they were running for reinforcements or giving up, Brodie wasn't sure. Relaxing a bit as the tone of the battle changed, and more and more of the enemy retreated, Brodie pivoted to search for his brothers. A sharp pain suddenly pierced the side of his thigh. A lone Norwegian was scrambling back toward the galleys, slashing anyone in his path, and he'd escaped Brodie's attention.

As the blood poured from Brodie's thigh, he cantered back to where he'd last seen Loki, lifted the boy onto his horse, and retreated. He found Alex, who ordered him to receive treatment and return home. Brodie refused.

"Have you seen Robbie?" Alex asked.

"Nay, but he is here. If we do no' meet up with him, I'll return on the morrow to search the fallen." Brodie said, though his strength was waning. As he slumped over his horse, he heard Alex tell Loki to take him to the healer's tent in the Grant field.

"I'll save you, Master Brodie, just like you saved me."

Those were the last words he heard before darkness closed in on him.

EPILOGUE

This scene is definitely one of my favorites.
Lucky Loki and Alex Grant.

AFTER THE TOAST to the bride and groom, hugs and congratulations were exchanged across the room. Quiet finally descended as Laird Alexander Grant stepped to his dais and awaited everyone's attention.

"'Tis something else verra important that I must do today. I ask Lucky Loki to come forward, please."

Loki stared at the room full of people from the back of the great hall, clearly unsure of what to do.

"'Tis all right, lad," Alex said, beckoning him forward. "Torrian and Lily will watch the twins. You are needed up front."

As he crept forward, Loki's gaze searched for Celestina. Smiling at him, she nodded in encouragement.

Alex smirked when the lad stopped halfway across the room, staring at the Grant warriors in their plaids, unsure of where he was to go. "Closer, lad."

Once he had passed through the crowd, a group of Grant warriors gathered in a semi-circle behind him. Loki stood in front of Alex, his wee legs trembling.

Celestina's heart broke. Loki looked so lost standing in the middle of all those brawny warriors, especially since he was directly in front of the massive Laird Alex Grant. She worried the poor lad's neck would be sore from looking up at the tall Highlander. She had begged Brodie to allow her to stand next to him in support, but Brodie had refused.

Alex cleared his throat and began, his hands clasped behind his back. "Lucky Loki, do you understand the important code of the Grants, our values of both honor and truthfulness?"

A wee voice squeaked out just loud enough, "Aye, my laird."

"Lad, I have several questions to ask you and I only need you to answer 'aye' or 'nay.' Can you do that, son?"

Loki nodded.

"Is it true you snuck under a cart and rode in a hidden spot to follow Celestina?"

Loki, confused, glanced at Brodie before he answered. "Aye, my laird."

"Is it also true you caused pain to a servant of a nobleman by placing stones in his shoes without his knowledge?"

Loki's eyes widened. "Aye, my laird, but I was just trying…"

"Aye or nay, lad?" Alex barked.

He hung his head before answering, "Aye, my laird."

The laird continued. "Is it also true you ran from my brother's side and followed a cart out of town to find Celestina, without advising anyone of your destination?"

Loki's frantic gaze darted around the room, searching for support. "But, my laird, Celestina…"

"Aye or nay?" Alex's voice boomed through the hall.

"Aye, my laird," he said in a small voice.

Celestina couldn't take it any longer. She started toward the lad, just to let him know he was not alone, but her husband pulled her back and wrapped his arm around her waist.

"Trust our laird, *leannan*."

Celestina swiped at the tears in her eyes, leaning into her husband's embrace, but not before she noticed that Maddie, sitting by Alex's side in front of the dais, had a linen square at her face and was mopping up tears as well. She and Maddie were definitely kindred spirits.

Staring over Loki's wee head, Alex continued. "Is it true you went to the MacLaren keep by yourself, again without notifying anyone of your destination, just to let Celestina know her husband was injured?"

Loki's shoulders slumped, and he hung his head in shame. "Aye, my laird."

Alex's voice softened, "Is it no' also true, lad, that you stood proud and protected the Scots by using your slinger against the invaders?"

Lifting his gaze to meet Alex's, the boy said, "Aye, my laird."

"Is it true that after my wounded brother passed out from battle you managed to get him to the healer immediately?"

"Aye, my laird." His voice was now strong enough to be heard across the hall.

Alex smiled. "And did you no' use your sling to protect my sister-in-law, Celestina Grant, against a group of Norsemen in Lennox?"

The lad nodded his head, sniffling as he stared at Alex. "Aye, my laird."

Alex stepped down from the dais, grasped Loki's shoulders and said, "Well done, lad. You make me verra proud." Then he nodded to Brodie and Celestina, and they came to stand in front of Loki.

Loki's eyes grew big as saucers when Celestina pulled out the red and green Grant plaid made just for him and enfolded his wee body with it. Brodie approached his brother and handed Alex a small sword, then pinned a badge with the Grant crest on the wee lad's chest.

Their parts completed for now, Brodie and Celestina moved back to stand off to the side of Loki, and Alex moved closer to the lad. He positioned Loki where everyone could see him, then held his hand on the lad's shoulder. With his other hand, he touched the sword to Loki's head and began, "Lucky Loki, I christen thee a Grant. I am proud to say you acted as the fiercest Highlander in all the land, protecting the weak and innocent, acting with honor at all times, guarding a member of my family when necessary, and fighting bravely for our country."

When he finished, Alex handed the hilt of the sword to Loki, who took it into his trembling hands before Alex turned him to face the warriors behind him. Alex nodded his head, and the warriors who surrounded him unsheathed their swords at the same time, knelt in unison, each placing their weapon on the floor pointing toward Loki, individually pledging to protect him with their lives.

Celestina's tears flowed freely down her cheeks

as she watched the expression of sheer wonder dance across Loki's face as the warriors knelt in front of him. Her husband wrapped his arms around her shoulders and tugged her in close for a quick kiss. After everything the lad had done for both of them, they were both so glad to see him receive this tribute.

When the warriors finished, Loki turned around, his face lit up with joy. He stared up at Alex and said, "I made it. Is that no' right, Laird Grant? Am I finally a Grant warrior and a member of your guard?"

Alex stood with his hands behind his back. "Nay, lad, that is no' correct."

Loki's face fell and his shoulders slumped. It was time. Brodie strode over to the lad's right side and Celestina to his left. Loki peered up at both of them, unsure of what was happening.

Alex cleared his throat. "Lad, I christened you a Grant, no' a Grant warrior. You will be asked to fight with the warriors, aye, but you are officially christened a Grant, with Celestina as your mama and Brodie Grant as your sire, if you will accept them as your parents in the eyes of Scottish law."

Loki looked first at Brodie, then at Celestina and said, "Truly, you want me?"

Brodie said, "Aye, lad, naught would make us happier than having you as our son. That is, if you want us."

Loki let out his best imitation of a Grant war whoop and jumped into Brodie's arms.

"Aye. I am no longer Lucky Loki."

Puzzled by his declaration, Celestina looked at him as he hopped down and ran to her side to hug her.

"I am Loki Grant," he said with a grin.

JOURNEY TO THE HIGHLANDS

BOOK 4

Alex doesn't quite know how to help Robbie with this woman he fell in love with, but Maddie does.

CHAPTER TWENTY-FOUR

Alex deals with Caralyn and does his best to give her what she wants, but at what price? The similarities between Maddie and Caralyn's situation come out eventually, and our Maddie stands up for her, even months along in her pregnancy.

TWO DAYS LATER, Robbie sat at the table in the middle of the solar while Alex sat behind his desk with Maddie seated close to him. "Why did she wish to see you, Alex?"

"I don't know, but I granted her request. Do you wish to give us a little background on your relationship with Caralyn before she joins us?"

Robbie shrugged his shoulders as he walked over to pull the fur back from the window. "I found her after a Norseman beat her until she was unconscious. She was in bad shape and didn't awaken until the next morning. I brought her to my camp, then went back and rescued her daughters. Tomas and I took them all to the priory near Glasgow right before the Battle of Largs."

"And that's all?" Alex's eyebrows lifted as he watched his brother.

"That's what is most important." He turned back around from the window to face Alex and Maddie.

"Then how did you end up bringing her to our clan?"

"Och, 'tis a long story."

"We have the time." Alex glanced at his wee wife, methodically rubbing her rotund belly. "Is aught wrong, sweeting?"

Maddie smiled. "Nay, I am fine. Just a wee bit tired."

Alex leaned over and kissed her cheek.

"Would you two like me to leave?" Robbie asked.

"Nay! You will stay until you answer my questions." Alex glared at him.

A soft knock sounded at the door.

"Enter," Alex said.

Caralyn stepped in hesitantly before closing the door, pausing for a moment when she saw Robbie standing by the window. "Should I come back?"

"Nay." Alex stood and ushered her over to a chair. "I have asked my brother to attend. Is this agreeable to you, Caralyn?"

She nodded and smoothed her skirts as she waited for a prompt to begin.

Alex settled back into the chair behind his desk and nodded for her to begin.

"My laird, I have come to explain a bit about myself and to ask a favor."

Robbie couldn't guess what she was about. Nervous, he started pacing in front of the hearth.

"I have two things I wish to discuss with you, if I may."

"Go ahead, lass."

"My mother always taught me to be honest, so I feel the need to give you an explanation of my background. I don't know what Robbie has told you about me." She glanced from Robbie to Alex Grant.

"Verra little. You tell us whatever you need to tell us," Alex said.

Caralyn's hands gripped her skirts before she started. Robbie wanted nothing more than to walk over and hold her in his arms before she started, but he could tell how much it had cost her to come here to speak with Alex, and he needed to let her stand on her own.

"I have a verra different background. While I was married for a time, for the last five years I have been a mistress to a man who sometimes gave me to his friends."

Robbie barked. "What are you doing? They don't need to know this."

Alex held his hand up to his brother before taking his wife's hand. "Maddie, would you like to leave?"

"Nay, Alex, I am fine."

"Continue." Alex nodded to Caralyn.

Caralyn glanced up at Robbie before she spoke. "I realize it may not be best for me to be around all your weans due to my background, so I wanted to be completely honest with you. I would like to stay at your keep, if possible, but I realize I'm an imposition. Still, I wondered if you might have a cottage near the loch where I could stay with my daughters."

Robbie stopped pacing and crossed his arms.

"I apologize if this upsets you, but I can't change who I am." Caralyn kept her eyes fixed on Alex Grant as she spoke.

After taking a moment to reflect on her words, Alex cleared his throat. "Is this what you wish to do? Do you wish to continue to be a mistress to someone while you are at the Grant keep?"

"Nay!" Caralyn bolted out of her seat, but then sat down again. "Your pardon," she whispered.

"Was it your choice to be this man's mistress?" Alex asked.

"Nay." Caralyn shook her head adamantly, then bowed her head. "I was forced. We were desperate for food, and the man made his price clear. Then he held my daughters and threatened to hurt them if I didn't comply with his instructions."

"Then I don't see its relevance to this discussion."

Caralyn's head jerked back up, and she glanced from Alex to Maddie.

Maddie stood and walked around the desk to her, grasping her hands in hers. "It does not matter to us what you have done in the past. I disagree with you. You *can* change who you are. What would you like to do to contribute to the clan?"

"Well, 'tis part of my problem. The only thing my husband taught me before he passed was how to fish. I thought if we lived near the loch, I could catch and clean fish for you. Ashlyn loves to fish, as well."

Alex nodded his head. "I see. And the second thing you wished to discuss with us?"

"The person who forced me has been searching for me. He followed us out of Glasgow, but Robbie and his men fought off his men. He was able to escape back to Glasgow. I fear he may come for me and I don't wish to risk any of your clan being hurt by him."

Alex turned toward his brother. "Robbie, the man got away?"

"Aye, he threw Caralyn on his horse while we fought off his guards. By the time I followed, he was far enough ahead to force me to use my arrow. I struck him in the shoulder and he pushed Caralyn off his horse down an incline. I had to make a choice, and it was more important to me to make sure she wasn't in danger."

Alex quirked an eyebrow, then returned his attention to Caralyn. "If he comes for you, you are safer here inside the keep than in a cottage."

"But I don't wish to endanger anyone here." Her voice was firm.

Maddie returned to her chair in time to hear Alex whisper to her out the corner of his mouth. "Hmmm, where have I heard that before, wife?"

Alex stood. "Thank you, Caralyn. I will give some thought to your request. Until I make my decision, I expect you to stay in the keep."

CHAPTER TWENTY-SIX

Maddie and Alex give Robbie advice on how to help Caralyn adjust to Clan Grant and Robbie.

LATER THAT NIGHT, the Grant brothers sat around the hearth drinking ale, along with their brother-in-law, Quade. The only female present was Maddie, fast asleep in Alex's lap, resting in their favorite chair together, the one Alex had made special for them. He kissed her forehead and she sighed and cuddled closer to him.

"So, Robbie, do you want to tell us exactly what this lass means to you?" Alex asked.

Brodie smiled, "Aye, I see a bit more interest than is usual with you. Most of the time, you just ignore the lasses until it suits your needs. Your eyes follow this one everywhere."

Robbie sighed. "'Struth, I am interested in her. But her past has been so difficult that I don't know if we will ever suit. Her life is focused around her bairns, and I don't know if she wants another man in her life."

Maddie sat up, brushing the sleep from her eyes. "Your pardon. May I, Robbie?"

"Och, aye. I was hoping for your input, Maddie. I seem to say and do all the wrong things."

"Based on what she has said, my guess is she won't want to be touched for a while. She was forced for so long, she probably wants no part of a man's touch right now."

"She isn't afraid of a man's touch. But I don't think she understands the way things should be between a man and a woman. Again, her experiences have tainted her view of the world."

"Aye, because all she has learned is wrong. It has

been five years for her since her husband passed. The years since sound like pure torture. I know this is hard, but you will have to be patient if you really wish to pursue her."

He paused for a moment before he admitted the truth. "Aye, I do."

Quade said, "Are you ready to be involved in her daughters' lives? I think that would be important for her. She needs to see you interact with her wee ones."

"Gracie accepted me right away, long before Caralyn did. So she isn't an issue. I guess I am not sure about Ashlyn. They are so tied up with their new friends, I haven't spent much time with them."

"You must court her," Alex said.

"What do you mean?" Robbie asked.

"Start from the beginning and do the things she has never had done for her. Take her for a walk, go for a picnic, go for a boat ride in the loch. She needs to know life with you will be different."

Maddie nodded. "Aye, she has to learn what a good relationship is all about."

"Mayhap we can set her up in a place so that she feels she has something of her own. What about the cottage by the loch? We could fix it up for her." Robbie looked at Quade for support.

Alex said, "The family cottage is still there and it needs fixing up, but she can't stay there alone until the issue with Murray is done. I don't think it will be long before he'll be here, so go ahead and work on it if you wish."

Quade said, "I'll help. Will give me something to do while we wait for our new niece to be born."

"Nephew," Maddie said.

"Another lad, wife?"

"Aye, another lad. I can tell from the way he carries. No blond-haired lassie yet, Alex."

"Hmmph. Then we'll just have to try again," he said with a smile.

CHAPTER TWENTY-NINE

*Alex in the birthing chamber again,
this time for Connor...*

THE DOOR BURST open and Alex flew in, tugging Caralyn off the bed so he could climb up behind Maddie. "Sorry, lass," he gave Caralyn a sheepish look. "This helps when my wife has to push the bairn out. 'Tis all I can do for her." He began to massage Maddie's shoulders and Caralyn stepped back.

Robbie stood in the doorway, winked at her and said, "See you later, lass. Time for me to leave."

Time flew by over the next hour. Maddie worked hard to deliver her bairn, and Caralyn helped where she could. She forgot about everything they had discussed, devoting all her focus to Maddie and Brenna. Alex was a delight to watch as he took care of his wee wife, cradling her between pains, encouraging her when she needed him. He mopped her forehead and kissed her cheek. She had never heard of any man staying through a birthing. This was definitely something she would have to ask Robbie about.

Sometime in the following hour, Brenna yelled, "I can see the bairn's head, Maddie. Push now, push hard." Brenna pulled Caralyn down next to her and pointed to the babe's hair. "I think 'twill be yellow haired, Maddie. Push for your husband." Jennie popped her head in at the last minute and Brenna beckoned her inside. The lass stared at everything in wide-eyed wonder, but she knelt down on the floor to watch.

Alex held Maddie up while she pushed, her hands locked behind her knees for leverage. The bairn's head came closer to being ejected, but it fell back when Maddie took a breath. While Maddie relaxed, Brenna told Caralyn and Jennie about the life cord that came out with the baby, and showed them what she would use to tie it and then cut it when the time came. They waited for another wave of pressure to prompt Maddie into pushing.

When it came, Maddie pushed with all her might. Finally the head popped out and Brenna cradled the bairn's wee head in her hand, using a cloth to wipe off the wean's face. "Come on, Maddie, the head is out, you need to push and get the shoulders out."

"I cannot, I have no strength left." Maddie panted in exhaustion.

Brenna cleaned out the inside of the babe's mouth. "Alex, she needs to push. Get her to finish this."

Alex sat her up and when a new wave of contractions assaulted Maddie, she pushed until her face was beet red. The bairn's shoulders slipped through the small opening, and Maddie fell back against her husband, sighing in relief.

Brenna caught the wee one and Caralyn reached down to help her. The healer had just set the babe in Caralyn's waiting hands when he let out a loud yelp and turned bright red.

"You have another lad, Alex! Maddie, 'tis a beautiful lad. He has light hair and he is hopping mad right now. What a strong laddie!" Brenna's joy was contagious.

The bairn let out a feisty scream as he wiggled, his wee hands fisted with all his might, and they all smiled. Caralyn only realized there were tears streaming down her face when her vision blurred. She watched Brenna tie off and cut the life cord and wrap the bairn in a soft plaid before settling him in his mother's arms. Maddie cried when she saw her new wean and Alex kissed her.

Alice, who stood by Maddie's side, cried rivers and, in between, managed to say, "Four, my word, child, four healthy bairns. How I wish your mama could see you now."

MY DESPERATE HIGHLANDER

BOOK 6

Alex has to help his cousin Diana find a husband.

CHAPTER TWO

Alex has the responsibility of taking care of his cousin, Diana of Drummond, who is presently betrothed to a less-than-admirable baron, while she only wishes to find her knight.

MICHEIL'S EYES WIDENED, and Diana's reaction was swift. "Do you not see, Robbie? I cannot marry the man."

"Alex will be the judge, lass, not me."

Micheil thought carefully about commenting about what he knew of Gow but decided to wait to hear more about their plan before he shared his thoughts. Thankfully, Alex returned.

Alex grasped his shoulder. "Come, we have a nice dining area to ourselves where we can feast and relax for a few hours before we continue on with our journey. 'Twill be good to catch up."

Once they settled inside, Alex ordered meat pies, cheese, bread, fruit pies, and ale.

As soon as everyone found a place, Diana said, "Tell me, my lord, what hear you of Baron Gow?"

Micheil froze. She stared at him with the deepest green eyes ever, eyes that seemed to dig into his chest and touch his very soul. Lying, he said, "I know little of the gentleman." Gentleman is hardly the word he would use to describe the man. The baron's cruelty was well known throughout the area, primarily because three wives had predeceased him. Many in his employ believe the baron had played a part in each of the timid ladies' death. And his treatment of horseflesh was known to be horrendous. Micheil would have to find an excuse to speak with Grant privately about the matter. It was hardly appropriate dinner conversation.

"Surely, you must have heard something." Her eyes bored into his, searching for the truth.

"I do not know him. I have never met him." At least this was not a lie.

"'Tis bad, is it not?" She glanced at both Alex and Robbie. "Do you see? I cannot marry the man. You cannot make me follow through with this."

Alex leaned back in his chair. "Cousin, we are charged with ensuring your prospective husband is suitable before the marriage takes place. Do not pester us all the way there. Do you not trust Robbie and me to have your best interests in mind?"

She leaned forward over the table. "Aye, perhaps you do and you are well-meaning. I am trying to show you there is no need for us to visit the baron at all. Take me to Edinburgh and I'll find my own husband." Micheil was so shocked he felt his mouth fall open.

Robbie said, "You want us to allow you to walk the streets in Edinburgh until you find a man you deem suitable?"

"Father is too ill to see reason, but I would prefer anyone to that cruel, smelly old goat. Do you truly intend to sentence me to such a life? Besides, I am quite sure my knight is there."

Micheil hid his smile. So Diana Drummond was a wee bit dramatic, or perhaps she had a secret lover in Edinburgh she planned to meet.

She switched her attention from her cousin to Micheil in a second. "And you. Stop looking at me like I am daft. I am not spoiled just because my father wished to allow me to choose my own husband."

Robbie said, "Now, Diana. Your father did permit you to do many things most women are denied."

"Irrelevant." She glared at Robbie. "Now will you take me to Edinburgh, or must I find someone else to help me?"

Alex said, "Diana, we will carry out the plan we agreed upon with your sire. We promised him to take you to Falkirk to your betrothed, see if the two of you are suited, and see you married if you are. We will not bend from that, so cease begging. Your constant demands may have worked on your father until now, but they won't sway me. I will do what I pledged."

A range of emotions flashed through Diana's glorious eyes as she stared at Alex. First Micheil saw anger, then self-righteousness, fear, and finally a spark of determination. Her voice trembled when she spoke. "As you wish." She turned to Micheil. "Just to inform you, I may have been spoiled by a man's definition, but naught was done for me that wasn't done for you, being a male. Were you taught to ride a horse?"

Micheil nodded. "Of course."

"And to hunt?"

"Aye."

"And to read?"

"Aye." He knew he could not pull his gaze from hers if he tried. Something about her was absolutely mesmerizing.

"And I am the only Drummond heir. As such, I am no different than you or either of my cousins. Just because I have a woman's shape does not mean there is aught wrong with my mind."

Micheil nodded in agreement. Yet there was naught wrong with her body either. Her delicious curves were just the type he favored in a woman.

"And I am verra good with numbers, so I will be able to run a keep with no problem. Just because I am as capable as a man does not indicate I am spoiled. I am well-trained. Now, since my cousins refuse," she stared directly at Micheil, "will you take me to Edinburgh? I am in need of an escort." Then she raked her glance over the three of them, making it clear that her next words were intended for all. "And if he denies me, I'll go on my own. I will not allow my betrothed to touch me."

CHAPTER THREE

Alex Grant, the savage?

LATE IN THE afternoon, their destination appeared on the horizon. Diana's stomach did somersaults, almost bringing her to the point of gagging.

Diana rode between Alex and Micheil. Robbie brought up the rear, along with three other guards, and her cart was being drawn behind him by one of his men. Alex had directed the other forty-some guards to stay back until he beckoned them, though Diana did not comprehend this tactic. As they approached, she noticed a small party leaving the castle gates, headed in their direction. The closer they came, the more her stomach churned. The party was comprised of six horses, and as they came near, she realized she had no idea which of these men she was intended to marry.

The two parties halted, a small distance separating them. The man in the lead of the baron's party was tall, gray-haired, and thin, though not unattractive. She had been told by a stable boy that Gow had a paunch, but this man did not. He held himself with an air of superiority that Diana did not like. Could he be her betrothed?

The gray-haired man spoke first. "Alexander Grant, I presume. You escort my betrothed, Diana of Drummond?"

Diana glanced at the Grant, who was Laird and Chieftain of his own very large clan in the upper Highlands. Alex's demeanor changed as the man spoke, his shoulders drawing back, his hand drawing toward the hilt of his sword. It was a subtle move, but she was close enough to detect it. Perhaps she could trust her cousin after all.

"I am Laird Alexander Grant, and aye, I am

escorting and protecting Diana of Drummond."
His chin lifted at the end of his sentence. "I must
see Baron Gow."

The gray-haired man's gaze narrowed, never
meeting her gaze or acknowledging her presence.
"I am Baron Gow. And if you are in charge of my
betrothed, why is she riding a horse? A woman's
place is in the cart." He pointed to the cart as if
to emphasize his argument.

"Diana prefers to ride," Alex answered, his face
void of expression. Alexander Grant was a huge
man, much larger than Baron Gow. The fool had
to see that, did he not?

Several seconds passed as the two leaders stared
at each other, the others waiting with bated
breath. Baron Gow moved his horse toward
Diana, but Micheil inched his mount closer to
her right side and Alex stayed firmly seated to her
left. The baron reached out for her and snarled,
"You will get off that horse, woman, and take
your proper place. You do not belong alongside
men."

Diana gasped and backed away from him,
clenching her reins in both hands as two swords
swooped down in front of her, one from the
Grant, and one from Micheil Ramsay. She had
never seen anything happen so quickly.

Alex spoke, "The lady is under my charge. You
will not touch her until she is transferred to your
charge." His voice radiated with authority.

"Release her to me and be on your way. I did
not promise accommodations for all your men.
I will see to the lady." The baron stared at her

cousin, waiting for a challenge, his men behind him poised to attack.

Alex smiled without budging from his position. "I am sure you would love to have her released to you, but as I just said, she is in my charge, and I will not leave her in your care until I deem that care to be appropriate for a lady of her station."

Gow's mouth twisted in a sneer that made Diana want to vomit. She prayed frantically that her cousins would not desert her with this man.

The baron turned to glare at her. "And who is going to prevent me from taking her now? You and your friends? I think not. She is mine, so she will do as I say. Her land belongs to me. It should have been mine years ago, but my ancestors were fools. You will not stop this from taking place. I have waited too long for this."

Alex whistled and his forty guards galloped full force behind them. Diana released her breath, not realizing until that very moment that she had been holding it. "In the Highlands, honor requires a man to offer a night's stay to parties on the road that are traveling a distance. No honor at your castle, Gow?"

The baron backed off and gave a grim smile. "This move to you, Grant. I will accommodate you and four others. The rest shall remain in the bailey." He nodded to Alex. "I can wait to get my hands on my betrothed. When the time comes, she will learn a wife's proper place." He turned his horse around and headed toward the castle, his five men trailing behind him.

Diana glanced at Alex and whispered, "My

thanks, cousin." He nodded in response, his brow furrowed. Emotion welled up inside her, threatening to unseat her.

Robbie spoke up from behind her, though whether he addressed Alex, Micheil, or both was unclear. "This is not going to go at all as I expected. Things will get interesting, will they not?"

The Grant smirked and quirked an eyebrow. "Och, so they will." He then glanced at Diana, who was losing her fight to hold in her tears. "Do not fret, cousin. You remind me of my mother. Protecting you will honor her memory, so 'tis not a duty I will shirk. If you have need of anything, you will come for me. Understood?"

Diana nodded, unable to speak for fear of bursting into wrenching sobs. She would maintain her composure in honor of her mother and his. The look of concern on Micheil Ramsay's face did not go unnoticed. Perhaps she did indeed have an ally in him.

As they entered the gates of the castle, Diana could not help but notice all the threatening glances sent her way by her betrothed. She decided the only way to she could handle her situation was to refrain from looking at him at all. As they walked up the steps to the great hall, she felt an arm brush across her back. She whirled her head around to see her betrothed was touching her, the taunting grin on his face an implied threat. Micheil stood back and gathered her in front of him, for which she was eternally grateful.

Once inside, the baron summoned his servants

to feed their guests. Not wanting any more to do with him, Diana said, "My lord, if I may, it has been an exhausting trip. I would like to rest." She wished for anything to get away from his presence.

He smiled at her, "Of course, my dear. Allow me to show you to your chamber." He held his arm out to her so he could escort her.

Diana panicked at the thought of being alone with him and glanced wildly at her cousins. She had hoped there would be a maid to attend to her.

"I would like to see my chamber as well, Baron," Alex said.

"Of course." He led the way up the staircase and down the corridor. He stopped and pointed down the passageway. "Your chamber will be the second on the right, Grant." He stood aside, awaiting the Grant's leave. When the big man did not move, the baron gave him a questioning glance.

Alex stood there for a moment, then headed down the corridor. A moment later, the baron stopped in front of a doorway, motioning for Diana to do the same. "Your chamber, my dear." He opened the door for her and stepped inside. "I'm sure this will please you. It was my former wife's chamber."

As soon as he finished his sentence, Alex, who must not have walked very far down the passageway at all, forced his way into the chamber and searched the room with his gaze. "Where does the door lead, Baron?"

Baron Gow, clearly appalled to be questioned, leveled an intimidating expression at Alex. "As I said, Grant. This was my wife's chamber. The door connects to mine."

Alex grabbed Diana's elbow and ushered her out the door. "Then Diana will not be staying here, and I am offended you would seek to risk her reputation in such a way."

Alex moved down the passageway, but Baron Gow bellowed after him. "Cease your interference. She is to be my wife in less than a sennight. The marriage will happen, whether you approve of it or not."

Alexander Grant turned around slowly, his height and posture even more impressive when he was off his horse. Diana glanced at his face and wanted to take a step back, but she was delighted to see he was in complete control of the situation. The baron could not hope to best such a man. "That is where you are wrong, Baron Gow." He dropped her hand and stalked toward the baron until he was nose to nose with him, although the Grant had to bend over to do so. "She is my charge, and I will do what my kin has requested of me. The future Drummond will *not* marry you without my approval. And if I need to put my sword through your black heart to prevent it, do not doubt that I will." Alex never moved.

The baron spewed hatred. "You are every bit the savage you are reputed to be. Highland savages, all of you. I hated being given land so close to the Highlands. Put her in your chamber if you'd like. She'll be in mine soon enough." He spun on his heel and headed down the passageway, hitting the wall with his fist and growling as he passed.

Alex directed her into his chamber, holding his finger to his lips to encourage her not to speak until they were inside.

"Alex, my thanks, but please remove me from these premises." Diana had progressed to sheer panic after witnessing her betrothed's behavior with a man of Alex's stature. "He frightens me to no end."

"Diana, I cannot just remove you. I must have justification. This union received the king's support, so we cannot break it without a good reason. I will find it, but it will take some time. In the meantime, you will sleep in my chamber, and I will post guards outside your door. Take your rest. He will not bother you today." He kissed her forehead and headed out the door. As soon as it closed behind him, Diana fell onto the bed and cried herself to sleep.

CHAPTER TWENTY-NINE

You'll find one of my mistakes in this scene. While a fair-haired Connor could have changed to dark hair as he aged, the opposite rarely happens. Here I have Jamie as dark-haired, but he was the fair-haired.

Micheil Ramsay found his love, Diana of Drummond. When they finally arrived on Ramsay land, she had a special treat. The very first Ramsay festival, and another situation where a lass outdoes a lad, my favorite.

THE DAY OF the Ramsay Festival had finally arrived. The sun shone bright on the late autumn day, making it warm enough to be outside. Diana was excited to finally be allowed out of the castle, but yet she had no wish to watch her husband joust. The day before she had walked inside the keep to see if she was better, and there were no problems. Brenna was confident she could walk out to the fields as a judge.

Micheil strolled alongside her, carrying a fur and an extra plaid to keep her warm. Torrian and Logan had already taken a cartload of stools and benches to the field for the ladies to sit on. Even Micheil's mother had promised she would come out to watch.

Quade had made sure everyone in the clan understood they were to come to the festival rather than working. They had planned a large feast for everyone in the courtyard after the event.

The first competition was for those under ten. Micheil and Diana were to be judges, and Quade and Torrian had everything arranged. There were ten entrants of various ages, including Alex's twins, Jake and Jamie, Lily, Maggie, Molly, and five other members of the clan. Ten separate lanes had been set up to accommodate all of them. The course was mostly as Torrian had described to her, and Micheil and Diana assigned two guards as backup judges to assist them at the end in case all ten competitors ended up throwing their hazelnuts at the same time.

The ten lined up as their parents screamed their encouragement. At the last minute, Alex held his hand up to Micheil.

"What is it, Grant?"

"Just need to make this a bit easier on everyone." The youngest competitors were his two boys, and they stood at the end of the line, shoving at each other in the hopes of getting a head start over the other. "Lads!" A loud bellow stopped all the chatter, including the twins' squirming.

He marched down the line, picked up dark-haired Jamie without uttering a word and carried him under his arm down to the opposite end of the lanes, moving all the contestants down one to make room for him. Once he had settled Jamie in a different lane, he turned to the event coordinator, Quade, and nodded. "Mayhap they will not kill each other with eight others between them. They are a wee bit competitive." He made his way off the field to the good-natured guffaws of the spectators.

"One, two, three, go!" Ten pairs of legs flew across the logs, and a couple of entrants fell right away. Micheil followed the course with them as judge, but Diana remained seated at the side with her family. Hoots and hollers followed their trail through the obstacle course. By the time they reached the tent, Jamie and Jake and another boy were way ahead of the rest. Molly was ahead of Maggie, and Lily spent too much time giggling to progress very far or fast.

The three lads hit the beginning of the long field where the race would take place ahead of the rest, but Molly was gaining on them. Logan shouted, "Come on, Molly. Show the lads who's the best." He wrapped his arm around Gwyneth, who was holding Sorcha on her hip, biting her fingernails as she watched her eldest daughter compete.

Molly was three strides behind the lads, but as soon as she hit the field, the spectators all took their eyes off the leaders to watch her race.

"Logan, she runs like the most beautiful deer I have ever seen," Gwyneth said.

Diana was in awe. "Gwyneth, I have never seen anyone so graceful. What a lovely sight." She couldn't help but pull for a lass sent out by her own sire.

And indeed, Molly sailed across the field with elegance and strength that gave her speed way beyond the others, her long strides powering her to the end way ahead of the boys. She picked up a hazelnut and flung it, missing the target by a long shot.

Logan shouted, "Come on, Molly!" He glanced at Gwyneth. "Wife, could you not have taught the lass how to hit the broad side of a stable?"

She had thrown three nuts and missed each one by the time the lads caught up with her. She had one left and flung it as hard as she could, finally hitting the very edge of the target. Micheil declared Molly the winner, while Jake came in second and Jamie won third place.

Logan ran over and tossed her into the air after they announced the winner and pinned a ribbon on her. Molly could not stop smiling.

THE
BRIGHTEST
STAR
IN THE
HIGHLANDS

BOOK 7

I loved Aedan Cameron for being different. He and Jennie were perfect together. The only two who could love the treasure. Many in the land sought the reputed treasure, but no one would have been as pleased as Jennie to see what it was. Inside the box were two items: a book with diagrams of human anatomy and a box full of a new material no one had seen before—paper.

CHAPTER ONE

*Jennie struggles as a healer, frustrated with
all the wounds she must tend. Alex is assisting his
neighbors in an attack, but he begins to see Jennie
in a different light, though he will always have
a soft spot in his heart for her.*

HEARING SOMEONE APPROACH, she
stood and turned, expecting to see Caralyn.
She froze mid-motion. Just the person she had
hoped to see stood not ten feet away from her.
The large form of her brother, Laird Alexander
Grant, filled the doorway, blocking anyone from
moving in or out. The brother who had been
like a father to her stood there shaking, sweat
pouring down his brow, his hand always at the
ready to grab his giant sword.

"Alex? Are you injured?" She glanced from
head to toe, but saw no fresh blood.

He shook his head. "I'm fine. How many?"

"How many what?" she crossed her arms in
front of her as she moved toward the door.

"How many dead, lass?"

His eyes bore into hers, his entire countenance
casting the intimidating laird aura over the
room. Her brother, renowned as one of the best
swordsmen in all of the Highlands, renowned for
fighting the Norse and sending them scurrying

back to their ships at Largs, could frighten almost anyone.

Anyone but her. "Two dead, Alex. Many injured…so many I am unable to count. This must stop." Her hands settled on her hips as she moved closer.

"Jennie, I'm exhausted. I will discuss this with you on the morrow. I need rest."

"On the morrow?" she barked. "And how many more injured will I have to treat by then? How many more widows must I hold up after informing them of their husband's death? This is too much. You cannot continue to do this to your clan. 'Tis wrong." Her fingernails bit into her palms.

Brodie's gentle hands descended on her trembling shoulders once more. "Jennie, do not speak to our laird so rudely."

She jerked away from Brodie's grip. "I'll speak to our laird any way I wish. You are no better than a murderer, Alex. A murderer! Our men are dying out there."

Alex's eyes narrowed. She could see the tic in his jaw, a sure sign of the fury that he usually kept controlled around her. "I did not start this fight," he responded through clenched teeth.

"Then who did?" She glowered at her brother, wanting him to listen to her. Just once, just this once, could he not back off from being the powerful Alex Grant?

He hissed through clenched teeth. "I know not who began this foolish warring, but I refuse to leave our neighboring clans defenseless. The attackers wear no tartans and they claim no clan. They wreak havoc wherever they go, and I mean to stop them, Jennie, whether you approve or not. I will not desert our neighbors." He gave her his back and stalked toward the great hall.

One of the men groaned, and she turned to check on him but he'd just rolled over in his pallet.

She raced to the door and held onto the two sides of the frame. "Alex! You must be the peacemaker. Stop hurting, stop fighting." Tears slid down her cheeks as she braced herself with both hands. "It *must* stop." Her voice dropped to almost a whisper as sobs overtook her small frame. "I cannot listen to the wailing any longer. I simply cannot. Please, Alex—" she crumpled toward the floor, "—no more."

Brodie picked her up in his arms and settled her on the empty pallet, covering her with a worn plaid. She rolled to her side and closed her eyes, wishing the specter of death would leave her alone.

She had to make Alex stop.

CHAPTER TWO

Jennie and Alex discuss her issues, but it does not go well. She requests an escort to Lochluin Abbey.

AS SOON AS they entered the great hall, the little boys went running off to the kitchens. Jennie headed for the dais, where all three of her brothers, Alex, Robbie, and Brodie, sat with their porridge, deep in conversation.

"Good morn to all," she dipped her head before she sat on the bench.

Alex quirked an eyebrow at her. "Have your spirits improved this morn, lass?"

She took a deep breath before she continued. "Alex. I'm sorry I lost my temper with you last night, but I meant what I said. This needs to end. There are too many wounded."

They were the only ones in the hall presently, except for the few servants cleaning the trestle tables from the early meal. Alex sat up in his chair before he answered. "I wish it were that easy. If I could end this by nightfall, I would, but every time we quell one attack, another one pops up somewhere else. I know not who is behind this offense, but 'tis neither the usual reivers nor the typical Highland manner of overtaking land. 'Tis a new group—and a young one, at that. Worries me."

Jennie persisted. "Why must we get involved? 'Tis not on our land. Why not let each clan handle their own problems? Then our men would not be dying and losing limbs."

Robbie drilled his fingers onto the table. "And if we do that, the attackers will win our neighbors' land. And once they are larger, they will move on to attack *us*. We cannot allow these marauders more power. Besides, our neighbors are good clans. And other than the Camerons, they are able fighters. We should not have to do much to send the invaders back whence they came."

"Where do they come from?" Jennie looked at each of her brothers in turn, but naught came forward.

Finally Alex spoke. "We have not discovered their origin or their purpose, though the few we have caught have told us they wish to dominate as much land as they can. None will discuss their leader."

"Alex, please." She folded her hands in front of her on the table, hoping it would give weight to her plea. "Can we not end our part in this? We need to be at peace. I can't handle this pain."

"I do what I must. I've vowed to protect my clan and my neighbors, Jennie. I'll not go back on my word." Alex reached over and squeezed her hand. "My apologies, lass, but our help is needed and welcomed."

Maddie entered the hall with Nicol's two lads and two bowls of porridge. Once they were settled at a separate table, she told them, "Here, lads. Eat up and have some goat's milk." She patted each tousled head and made her way to the dais. "I couldn't help but overhear, Jennie."

"Maddie, do you not agree? In a few years, it could be Jake and Jamie going off to battle. This needs to stop. Alex loves to fight too much."

Alex growled, but he held his tongue as they all waited for his wife's response. Though he was laird of their clan, capable of making decisions for all of them, Maddie was the one person whose wishes and thoughts he never ignored. Jennie should have thought of this tactic before. Maddie would definitely agree with her. She held her breath and waited for the set down his wife would surely give him.

Maddie reached for Jennie's hand and held it tight in hers. "Jennie, I don't agree with you. I don't want these invaders to come any closer to our home. I'm sorry that men are hurt, but 'tis exactly why Alex and your brothers require the guards to train in the lists for days on end. They must be able to protect themselves and their clan. 'Tis not just their job, but their duty. They must protect the young, the feeble, and the infirm."

"But Maddie, have you not seen the blood and gore that has come through that door lately?" Jennie could hardly believe her ears.

"Aye, I have. There has been an occasional injury, but you're very talented and can heal the men. 'Tis your gift. My husband's responsibility is to protect this clan, all of us, and he does what he thinks is best."

Jennie stared at Alex for a long moment and then turned her attention to her other two brothers. "Do you not agree with me, Brodie?"

Brodie shook his head. "If you saw the deranged attackers, you wouldn't ask such a thing. I protect my clan, my family, and most importantly, my wife and sons."

Her gaze turned to Robbie, but he nodded before she could ask him. "Lass, you don't have weans as we do. Now that Brodie and I have bairns, it changes everything."

"It shouldn't." Tears welled in her eyes. "You should not enjoy killing others."

Alex's booming voice shook the rafters. "Who

said we enjoy it? You mind your tongue, lass. Do not insult us when we fight so hard to protect you and everyone else here."

Jennie jumped to her feet, tears now running in rivers down her cheeks. "I appreciate all you have done for me, Alex. You've been like a father to me, but I can't condone this violence. I wish to be taken to Lochluin Abbey."

"What?" Robbie asked, his eyes wide.

"I cannot continue on here as the clan's healer. Please arrange for my escort to Lochluin Abbey."

Maddie gripped Jennie's shoulders. "You know not what you ask, lass."

"Aye, I do." She spun around to face Maddie. "I need to get away from here. I want no part of battling, of wounds, of bandages. I am finished with this. Do you hear me? Finished!"

Alex whispered, "And what if one of your brothers is wounded, lass? Will you turn your back on them, as well?"

Jennie closed her eyes, unable to believe what she asked. Perhaps she was wrong to leave. They were her family, her clan. Even if her nightmares persisted, and the pain in her head worsened, she needed to stay to heal her family. "All right, I shall stay. Alex, do all you can to end this. Please, I can't handle it much longer."

Alex stood and moved to her side, wrapping his arms around her and tucking her head under his chin. "I promise to do what I can to end this. I wish it were that simple. We need your talents during such times."

"I know." Tears drenched Alex's tunic.

His finger lifted her chin. "Is there naught you can do for your head pains and your nightmares?"

She shook her head. "I know not what to try. 'Tis hopeless, Alex, but I will stay."

CHAPTER NINE

Jennie struggles to find her purpose, causing strife between her and her beloved brothers. Here she is forced to leave Cameron land and learns the meaning of Alex's words the hard way.

THEY TRAVELED UNTIL dusk, stopping only for necessaries. Brodie found a clearing and set up a tent of furs for Jennie. After they ate roasted rabbit, Jennie headed off to the stream with some linen, intent on washing her face and taking care of her needs.

As soon as she was ten feet away, a booming voice echoed behind her. "Jennie!"

She turned to stare at Alex. "Aye, my laird?" she ground out through clenched teeth. He would not even allow her some time alone.

"Not too far. 'Tis not safe in the woods until we are on Grant land."

Her eyes narrowed to slits. "Alex, I need my privacy."

"You heard my orders. See that you do as you're bid."

"Of course, my laird," she said as she turned away, "whatever you say. I always do what I'm bid.

I'm a good lass. Aye, my laird." She didn't bother trying to hide her sarcasm.

"Jennie…" Alex snarled. "Do not push me. These are dangerous parts. I see evidence of others in the area. Be agreeable for once or I'll come and watch you."

She spun around. "You would not!"

"Aye, I would do it to prevent you from being kidnapped. There are plenty of vagrants about, and a laird's blood sister is valuable. Tread with care." He turned and stalked away.

Alex couldn't see her glare from behind, so she ended it and headed to the spot she had spied before. He would not order her around like one of his guards.

A few minutes later, she headed back from the creek. She hung her head, unable to forget that she was separated from Aedan—from her one opportunity to truly fall in love. And now he was in danger. She thought of that eve on the hill, how special she had felt in his arms. At least she had experienced a kiss and more. She smiled at the beautiful memories.

A second later, the pounding of a horse's hooves echoed through the trees and shouts of warning met her ears, but to no avail. A strong arm lifted her up by her waist and flung her face down across a horse's saddle, the rider shouting with satisfaction at his prize. He reined in his horse and took off in the opposite direction. It happened so fast she could do naught to fight or run away. She was caught.

Jennie's ribs bounced against the horse, taking

away her ability to speak and seriously impeding her ability to breathe. The stench from the man invaded her nostrils and she fought to keep from vomiting. She pushed down against the horse in an attempt to move and caught a quick glance at the man behind her. His hair and long beard were stringy and dirty, and he was missing half his teeth. When he grinned, a wave of dizziness hit her and she thought she would empty her stomach for sure. Desperate to escape, no matter how badly it injured her, she tried to push herself off the horse, but she stopped when he slapped her bottom. "Stay there, wee fool. Ye're mine now, and ye'll do as I say."

She closed her eyes, saying a swift prayer for Alex to come for her even though he was probably furious. The hand rubbed her bottom now, and she swung her fist at the man's leg. He barely seemed to notice. He caught her chin in his hand and said, "Ye sure are a pretty one. My friends will take care of the rest of you, but I got the real prize."

Jennie heard the bellows and shouts in the distance, a good gauge of how fast they were moving. At first, she could hear every sound as sword met sword. Grunts and screams echoed, and she prayed her brothers would dominate.

Jerking her head away, she heard her brother's war whoop in the distance and seconds later, her captor flew off his horse. Jennie managed to climb up and grab the reins, fear clenching in her gut.

Alex grabbed the reins of the horse and turned her to lead her back to the clearing. As soon as she had the horse under control, Alex nodded to her and took off toward the melee he had left behind. He pointed to the side and bellowed, "Dismount and get off to the side."

This time, she didn't argue. Tears slid down her cheeks as the enormity of what had almost happened sunk into her. She had been stolen just as Alex had said. Had he been any farther away, the horrible man might have succeeded in abducting her. She dismounted and slapped the horse's hindquarters to get him away from her.

After finding a hiding place behind a group of bushes, she sat down and hugged her knees to try to stop her trembling. Behind her shallow cover, the clash of steel, the screams of pain, and the death continued. One man fell after another, and she couldn't pull her gaze from the fight. Alex fought like a man possessed. He rode Midnight as if the two were one, his sword arm cutting down invader after invader. She heard high-pitched screams, and only then realized they were *hers*. The screams came each time a sword slashed near her brother. He was too quick for any of them, and he easily ducked and dodged each blow. If anything happened to her brothers, she would never forgive herself. All this fighting was too much for her, but she was beginning to recognize how important it was to have someone who would fight and protect her at all costs.

Alex's body was covered with sweat and blood as he swung and swung in a fury, his hair free of its tie, long and wavy. Satisfied that he was safe for the moment, she searched the area for Brodie and breathed a sigh of relief when she found him on the opposite edge of the skirmish, his sword delivering death blows as frequently as Alex's.

But Alex was different: possessed, powerful, unrelenting until the last of the invaders realized their battle was lost and took off. The Grant men broke out into smiles as they realized they were the victors. Swords pointed to the heavens, Grant war whoops abounded, and all celebrated except for one rider.

Alex. Alex spurred Midnight off into the distance following the last of the attackers, letting out the longest and deepest Grant war whoop Jennie had ever heard. Her heart pounded in her chest as she wondered where he was going. Would he come back and wale on her? Was this her fault for not doing as he'd asked? Would he tie her to his horse so she could never wander again?

He finally turned Midnight around and headed back toward their camp at a full gallop, slowing only once, so his steed could rear up on his hind legs in a celebration of the victory. Alex's arm seemed to reach to the heavens before Midnight settled and came back to the ground. Her brother brought him straight to the creek for water. There was one difference between Alex and the other men, Jennie noticed—there was no smile on his face.

Actually observing him in battle taught her something. Mayhap he didn't enjoy it as much as she had thought, and he deserved more credit than she had been willing to give him.

Her gaze followed him through the woods. He dismounted and crooked his finger at her. She took one look at the sweat on his body and the look on his face and ran to him. Wrapping her arms around his waist and sobbing into his chest, she choked out an apology that felt so inadequate. "Alex, I'm sorry. I'm so sorry. Forgive me."

Alex wrapped his arms around her and said, "'Tis not your fault, lass."

"Aye, I didn't do what you bade me to do. I wandered too far." She sobbed so hard her breath hitched.

"Jennie, those men would have fought us anyway. You were an extra prize."

"But where would I be now if you had not followed me?"

"Hush, lass, 'tis over. They are gone and will not return. Mayhap you understand why I could not leave you behind with the number of men headed toward Cameron land. This was a small group of reivers, naught more. Cameron is in for much more than what we just experienced."

She continued to sob as Alex guided her back toward the clearing, one arm wrapped around her waist. Aedan's words returned to her, advising her that she had been well protected up until now and had no idea what real danger was. Aye, he had the right of it, she had never seen her brothers in battle before.

The implication of what Alex had said finally sunk in. If these were just reivers, then Aedan's land was destined for something much worse than she had envisioned. Perhaps it was best she not be there to be a burden to him. Mayhap she had better do as she was told during these turbulent times. "Thank you, Alex, for protecting me and for leaving men with Aedan."

"Jennie, you are my sister, almost a daughter to me. I will always protect you. You may not like all I do, but I do it because I love you."

"I know, Alex. I'm so sorry. I have acted like a spoiled bairn."

"Nay, you are a woman who is trying to find her place in the world. 'Tis not easy." He kissed the top of her head and settled her on a log as he moved to check on the rest of his men.

CHAPTER TEN

Alex admits one of his greatest weaknesses…
Jennie…

JENNIE CAME DOWN to the great hall for the evening meal with butterflies in her belly, scared to death to meet the two men who had been brought here for her perusal. How did one go about seeing if a stranger would suit as a spouse? Was she supposed to quiz them both? One at a time or together?

She controlled her wish to chortle. Mayhap she should ask Alex if she should kiss each of them and decide which was better? What exactly was his plan for this foolish venture? She had almost made it to the steps of the great hall when Alex strode up behind her and ushered her into his solar. All cleaned up in his red dress plaid and his hair tied back, her brother was still an imposing figure. Many a lass still gazed at him, even though everyone in the clan knew he would never stray from Maddie's side.

She gave him a questioning look as soon as she noticed they were alone in the chamber. "What is it, Alex?" she asked after he closed the door behind them.

Alex paced the room twice before he stopped. "Maddie told me she has made you aware of the two men I invited to our keep." He settled his hands on her shoulders.

"Aye, but why did you make plans about suitors without asking me?" She adored her brother, always had, but his commandeering ways tested her patience.

"'Tis my job, lass, to see you married. I made a pledge to our parents. While I have not wanted to admit 'tis time for you to consider marrying, Maddie reminded me that you are of age."

"But Alex…"

"Let me have my say, Jennie, then you may chastise me as I know you are wont to do."

She nodded and he ushered her to a chair in front of the hearth while he leaned on the mantle. "I know 'twas not easy for you to lose Ma and Da so early in your life, but I have tried my best to raise you well. I was not so good at it early on, but with Maddie's assistance, I have improved. Brenna was also a great help, and I admit I felt lost when she left us. I am grateful she has invited you to their castle so many times."

Jennie stared at her brother. Laird Alexander Grant, renowned for fighting off the worst enemies, a grand swordsman, was struggling to find words.

He crossed his arms. "I have not told you this, because I did not feel there was a need, but there have been several who have sought your hand in marriage before now. I have rejected them all."

"But why?" She wanted to know why he had kept this from her, why he had ignored her needs so completely.

"Why did I reject them, or why did I not tell you?" He tugged on his ear and started pacing in front of her.

"Both."

"Because you were not of age yet. You were not ready."

"Aye, I am." Well, she was of age to marry, but her heart had already chosen another.

Alex stopped in front of her, his hands clasped behind his back. "All right, you will force me to admit it. I am not ready yet. I became quite fond of the wee lass who sat on my lap for all those years, and now that you are old enough to leave, I find I am not ready to lose you." He turned his gaze away from hers, an expression on his face Jennie had never seen before. Embarrassed? Sad?

"And who asked for my hand?" She hated to push him, but she needed to know the answers. She thought it only fair.

He hung his head, his arms now crossed in front of him. The way he moved told her he was uncomfortable with this conversation. But she was even more uncomfortable, and this was her life.

Alex took up most of the front of the hearth, his arm muscles bulging from the continuous practicing he did with his mighty sword. He finally let his breath out in frustration. "Lass, do you not see? None of them were good enough for you. You are like my first born. You had such a difficult time after we lost our parents. You were still sucking your thumb on rare occasion at almost nine summers."

"I was not! You are creating tales to make yourself feel better, Alex." She crossed her arms in a huff, unable to believe what he had just said to her. True, she had taken advantage of her older brother by using her age to get what she wanted, but suck her thumb? Never.

He quirked his brow at her. "You never did it for more than a few moments, but, aye, you did. We lost both our parents within a short time. 'Twas tragic for you, at the verra least."

She ran a hand down her face as memories of that difficult time flooded her thoughts. Aye, it had been hard—almost unbearable—but she refused to believe she had sucked her thumb.

"Alex, 'twas a trying time for all of us, yourself included."

"But I was old enough to become laird, and you were still a wean. When I look at my bairns, I cannot imagine how they would fare if they lost either of us at such a tender age. The twins would be lost without their mother, and you know I pride myself on how fierce they are."

Dead silence settled over them. Alex rubbed his chin, then whispered. "The point is this…I have come to accept this truth. Maddie has forced me to accept that I must let you go, much as I wish to keep you here."

Jennie was surprised to feel her eyes mist at Alex's declaration.

"So my apologies if I have waited too long, but I have arranged for two of the lads who expressed an interest in you earlier to come to our keep to meet you. There is to be no pressure on you. Do not let them insist on any time frame. If you are interested in either, so be it. If not, so be it. This matter is entirely up to you. I have looked into their backgrounds, and unless I see entirely different men here at the keep, I expect they will be acceptable to me. But they must be acceptable to you. I promised our mother."

Jennie could see how difficult this was for him. She strode over to her brother and wrapped her arms around him, though they didn't begin to go around his large frame. "My thanks, Alex, for loving me so. But I don't know if I am ready either."

He kissed her brow and said, "You let me know after you meet the two lads. They will be here for less than a sennight, but please keep me advised."

"I will. My thanks. Shall we go now?"

Alex wrapped his arm around her and escorted her toward the door. Before he opened it, he stopped and turned toward her. "Aedan Cameron. Did I detect something between the two of you? Or did I imagine it?"

Jennie coughed. "Aye, well…I am interested in him. He said he would come after the skirmishes were ended, but I am not sure it has progressed to thoughts of marriage. I don't know if he would offer for me, but…"

"Say no more. Your expression tells me all I need to know. But there is naught wrong with checking to see if you are interested in others. I fear I have been lacking in this duty to you. Please be tolerant, for me?"

Two suitors arrive, but one is sent away quickly by Alex and Jennie both…
The fool made the mistake of disliking Alex's bairns…

ALEX SAT BETWEEN her and Maddie at the table, while Coll sat to her left, and Donnal Boyd sat across from her. The others were spread out around them, except for Celestina, who did not feel well and was not at the meal. Brodie had left to check on her.

Loki sat a distance away with the other weans at a small table. The young group was a bit boisterous, but Jennie loved to listen to their chatter. She smiled at them, wishing she could join their table and escape her duty.

Donnal dominated the conversation. "Lady Jennie, I hear you have great skills as a healer."

"Aye, I have worked…"

"Do not fret, lass. You will not be required

to do work of any kind at my keep. We have two wonderful healers. You can just direct the servants, relax, and of course, tend to my needs." He flashed a wicked grin at her. Jennie glanced out of the corner of her eye to see if Alex had heard his comment.

Judging from the scowl on Alex's face, he *had* heard.

Coll spoke up. "We would be very grateful for your skills, though we also have two healers on our lands. I hear you have a fresh outlook on healing that differs from the ways of the old wizened healers. Is that true, my lady?"

Jennie was pleased to answer this question. "Aye, my mother taught me..."

Donnal interrupted. "If it pleases you, Laird Grant, I would like to insist on a wedding before the next moon, as we are in need of some organization at our castle. Seems our staff have become quite slovenly and lazy. We need someone who can crack the whip, shall I say?" His smug expression did not speak well for him.

A small commotion took place over in the bairn's area, so Maddie promptly got up to tend to them.

"Truly, Laird," Donnal said, glancing over his shoulder at the unruly group. "Is there a reason you have the weans nearby? Are they not too young to act appropriately around guests?"

"Aye, there is a reason," Alex said gruffly. "They're my weans and I want them here. They'll learn to act appropriately in time."

Jennie stifled a giggle, wishing she could hug her brother over his declaration. He was a good sire and a good leader.

"Mama!" Braden screamed. Maddie whispered something soft in his ear, then sent Loki away with him.

"You see. They are too young." He nodded his head, apparently in affirmation of his previous statement, but no one volunteered to agree with him.

"That wean is my brother's first born lad, and I prefer to have him here. Please do not concern yourself, Boyd."

Donnal let out a loud belch and excused himself. "Must find the garderobe."

Coll reached for her hand under the table. "My apologies for his rudeness. 'Tis unforgiveable. I love weans and hope to have many."

Jennie turned to look into his kind eyes—he was such a better lad than the other suitor—but she still pulled her hand back. She noticed Donnal was headed in the same direction as Loki. Her intuition told her to follow them so she excused herself and did just that, trailing him toward the passageway that led to the tower rooms where Brodie and Celestina lived.

Once she left the great hall, she caught sight of Donnal a few steps behind Loki, who was desperately trying to manage an unruly Braden.

"Here, lad. I'll handle the wee twit." Donnal reached for Braden, but his wee protector was faster.

Loki pulled his small sword from his sheath.

The weapon connected with the skin of the suitor's hand and drew a drop of blood, causing him to yank it back. "You will remove your hand from my brother, my lord. No one touches him without my permission."

"Why, you ungrateful cur."

Jennie rushed up to them just as Donnal was about to wrest away Loki's sword. "Leave him be, my lord. They are not bothering anyone."

He spun around to glare at her. "They're bothering me. Weans should not be heard from. They should know their place."

Jennie nodded to Loki. "Why do you not continue and take Braden to his mama."

"Nay, I will not leave you unprotected with this brute, Lady Jennie." His chin came up and he squared his shoulders, just like his sire did so many times, his sword still drawn at his side. Braden had stopped crying and was staring at the stranger with wide eyes.

Jennie smiled. "My thanks, Loki, but I can handle myself."

Loki nodded and continued on his way, tugging a whining Braden behind him, but he watched Jennie over his shoulder. Loki had grown quite a bit over the last couple of years, and he was mighty protective of his adopted family.

Once he was gone, Donnal took a step closer. "Aye, 'tis much better to be alone." He reached for her and pulled her close enough so his lips could descend on hers. One quick taste of him was all Jennie could tolerate before she shoved against his chest to push him away. He didn't give up easily, but he finally stepped back. "You needed a taste of how wonderful our lives could be together." He winked at her.

Quite sure Alex would support her, she made a bold move. "Forgive me, my lord, but I have no interest in you as a husband. Please feel free to spend the night at the keep to gain a restful sleep, but I would like you to leave immediately after breaking your fast on the morrow. Good eve to you."

She had turned around to head to the great hall when she felt a hand on her shoulder. "How dare you tell me what to do? We are not done, and *I* will decide if we suit, not you. Do you not understand a woman's place? You are to do as you are told and let the men decide your fate. You have no right to reject me."

A booming voice echoed down the passageway. "'Tis where you are wrong, Boyd. Remove your hand from my sister. I expect you to do as she requested. You are welcome until the morn, but then I will expect to see the last of you. You have offended both of us. My sister will not be marrying you, and that is *my* final decision."

Donnal Boyd left in a huff, heading down the passageway, his footsteps echoing on the stone.

"Jennie," Alex's hands settled on her shoulders. "My apologies. I should have spoken to him first."

"My thanks for respecting my opinion, Alex. Even you must realize many men are completely different around lasses. Mayhap he would have been quite gracious with you."

"Aye, but I will do anything to save my sister

from a life of drudgery and servanthood. I believe
'twas his plan for you."

She hugged Alex and they ambled together
toward the great hall. But her mind repeated the
same expression over and over.

One down, one more to send away.

CHAPTER FIFTEEN

This pregnancy is not the same for Maddie,
and Alex is undone.

A SHLYN CAME BARRELING down the
stairs and ran over to her mother, Caralyn,
and whispered in her ear. Caralyn got up and
motioned for Jennie to follow her.

Rising so quickly he knocked his chair over,
Alex bellowed, "Where are you off to? Is aught
wrong with my wife?"

"Nay, Alex. We would let you know if there was.
Womanly issues. Do not concern yourself." Jennie
hurried up the stairs behind Caralyn. Maddie was
carrying again, bairn number five, and she was
having more trouble with this one. Up until her
departure for the abbey, Caralyn and Jennie had
worked together as healers for the Grants, and
they'd delivered Braden, Brodie and Celestina's
son, and Connor, Alex's third son. Alex was quite
sensitive about anything concerning his wife. He
would move heaven and earth for Maddie, no
one doubted that fact.

Once they reached the passageway, Caralyn said

to Jennie, "Maddie's cramping terribly this morn. Will you take a look for me?"

They guessed her to be about two moons away from delivery, but they didn't know for sure. Jennie knocked on the door and walked inside to find Maddie curled up in bed, clutching her lower belly.

"Maddie, tell me what you are feeling," she said.

"Jennie, something is not right. I have so much cramping with this bairn. How do I stop it?"

"Will you allow me to check your progress?" Jennie brushed Maddie's hair back from her sweat drenched forehead. She knew Maddie never expressed it when she was feeling pain, so the sweat told her how difficult this was for her. Jennie had to use her best healer's skills with Madeline.

"Aye, go ahead. Do what you must." Maddie repositioned herself in bed to give Jennie access to do what she needed.

Once she finished her exam, Jennie covered Maddie up with several blankets. "I don't see any cause for the cramping. The sac seems to be in place, and there is no blood, so you appear to be fine for now. But I would suggest you be extra careful and stay in bed for a few days, getting up for your needs only.

"But I must talk to Cook, and then…" Maddie's hand rubbed her forehead.

"Nay, Maddie. You'll stay here. We'll see to everything." Caralyn rubbed her shoulder, attempting to soothe her.

Just then, the door flew open with a bang and Jennie and Caralyn both jumped. Alex stood in the doorway, his hands on his hips, concern etched in every line in his face. "Maddie? Why are you still abed?"

Jennie stood up and said, "Alex, Maddie will be staying abed for a few days. She's having some womanly issues and I have recommended that she stay flat to make sure the bairn is fine."

The color drained out of Alex's face in an instant. "Maddie?" He rushed over to the bed and sat on the edge, cupping Maddie's cheek in his big, callused hand. Jennie loved to see her brother like this. The great swordsman of the Highlands could only be brought to his knees by one thing—his wee wife.

"Alex, I am sure I will be fine and the babe will be fine, too. I need some rest. I am tired with this one. Please take care of the lads for me? Jennie and Caralyn will watch Kyla." She leaned her head against her pillow, and within a few moments, she was fast asleep.

"Maddie?" He leaned over and placed a tender kiss on her forehead and covered her with furs, tucking them up under her chin.

Her brother looked so lost. Maddie had been healthy as a horse for her other pregnancies—on her feet until the day she delivered and up again in less than a sennight. He gave Jennie a look that broke her heart, but she held firm. "Alex. Your wife has taken care of all of us for many years. It's time for us to take care of her for a wee bit. She's a strong woman, but she still needs her rest."

Alex turned and left the room with a dazed expression that Jennie guessed would not leave him for a while.

CHAPTER SIXTEEN

Oh, the storybooks. Maddie is missed by many, and Alex has to do story time for his bairns.

THE GROUP SAT around the dais with a sense of loss. He (Aedan) sat on a bench at the end of the table near Jennie. Maddie was not with them, and everyone could feel Alex's tension. At one point, their three lads, Jamie, Jake, and Connor attempted to sneak up the stairs in pursuit of their mama.

A booming, "Lads!" caught them in the midst of their journey, and all three stopped instantly.

"Papa," Jamie whispered. "We want our mama."

"Lads, you will not bother your mother. She is ill and abed, and you will stay here."

Jake turned to look at his father. "But Mama reads one of her storybooks to us every eve."

Alex pointed to the bottom of the stairs and all three of the bairns rushed back down the stairs, their hands clasped behind their backs as they gazed up at their da. Kyla strolled over and grabbed her sire's hand. "Papa, you can read us the story tonight. Please?"

Aedan watched with bemusement. He leaned toward Jennie, "Maddie has storybooks?"

Jennie nodded. "Aye, she makes them herself, drawing pictures. They are quite beautiful. She has read from them for many, many moons. All the bairns of the clan love them."

All of Alex Grant's bluster had been taken out of him by his four bairns and his wife's illness. He didn't know what was wrong with Maddie, but this couldn't possibly be the first time she had been abed.

Connor tipped his head back as far as he could as he stared up at his sire. "Please, Papa?" he asked in a small voice.

"Please?" Jamie added. "We do so love it when Mama reads to us."

Jake nodded his head.

"Connor, you shall choose the book." Alex strode over to the hearth and sat in his chair while three of his bairns followed him and Connor scampered off to choose a book. Gracie, Robbie and Caralyn's daughter, followed with Roddy in hand, and Braden toddled over on his own.

Aedan found himself glancing at Jennie to see how she was reacting to the scene. He most enjoyed catching her unaware. Jennie couldn't help but smile when her brother's booming voice echoed through the room. The tale was about some monster, and Alex's interpretation had all the weans staring at him with wide eyes. He noticed Loki had made his way over a bit closer so he could hear the story. He was quite sure that Maddie would have told the tale differently, and the weans would probably beg him to read many more books to them in the future if they managed to survive the night without haunted dreams.

Aedan moved over and took the seat next to Jennie. "Your brother is lost without his wife, I see. She has never been sick before?"

"Nay, never. She has the constitution of a horse, and if she is forced to bear any pain, she never lets on. Maddie has been invincible up until now."

"She'll get better? 'Tis not some unknown sickness?"

"Aye, she'll improve in a few months, after she delivers the bairn. Mayhap this will be their last."

CHAPTER EIGHTEEN

*Jennie sneaks away from Clan Grant
without telling her brother.*

JENNIE FILLED ANOTHER saddle bag and snuck down to the stables. She waited until Mac was alone. "Mac."

The old man jumped at the sound of his name. "Jennie. What is it? I'd not heard you."

"You must help me."

"Aye, anything, lassie."

"I need a horse, and I need a few guards to travel with me to Cameron land. Who can I trust?"

Mac let out a slow whistle. "Lass, if you do this thing, you will be taking your life in your hands two different ways."

She scowled at Mac, unsure of his meaning.

"One, there are many reivers about. Two, you will be sneaking out without telling Alex. I take it he has refused your request for escorts?"

"Aye, but I must go. The abbess at Lochluin Abbey told me 'twas divine intervention that brought me there in time to save Aedan. Now he is going into battle again, and he could be dying. I'll fret terribly until I see him with my own eyes." Her eyes misted at her confession.

Mac stared at her for a long moment before walking over to a horse and saddling him. He spoke to a stable lad and sent him off in the opposite direction. "I have five guards who will protect you. Get yourself set. You'll need to leave in a hurry."

Jennie had only been traveling half a day when the rumble of horses' hooves met her ears. She motioned to her guards to move off the regular path and hid in a copse of trees, waiting to see who was approaching, quite sure it had to be a group of Grant warriors because there were so many. Hellfire, but she was not going back—no matter what her brothers said.

As the horses drew near, her heartbeat sped up. What if it wasn't the Grant warriors? She could be in danger if not. She thought of what Brodie had said about how war drew the most unsavory of men.

Suddenly, the rumble came to a halt. It was still a good distance away, so she crept out from her spot to see if she could determine who was approaching. As soon as she stepped out from hiding, a throat cleared off to the side. She jumped and whirled around in time to see Alex standing in front of her, his arms crossed as he leaned against a tree.

"Handfasted? You handfasted without seeking my permission?"

She tipped her head back and bellowed to the heavens. "Brodie! 'Tis the last time I ever confide in you."

Brodie came up on his horse, his grin wide. "Sorry, lass. Mac and I both consider your safety a priority. You didn't think Mac would let you go without telling his laird, did you?"

Alex pointed back to her horse. "Mount up. Cameron is under attack and we need to get there soon. You're lucky we are too far for me to send you back. I will not split my men, and we need all the guards we have to help him. You will go to the abbey while we join the battle. 'Tis expected to take place tonight."

Alex whistled for Midnight.

"But Alex, who is the traitor?" Jennie stared at him as he mounted the horse, hoping he knew the answer.

"Hmmm…my own sister did not trust me enough to tell me that she handfasted *or* that she was in love with the Cameron, and now you wish for me to share my news with you?" Alex galloped ahead of her, leaving her in his dust without a backwards glance.

Hell, but Alex was angry, and he had every right to be. She found a log and mounted her horse so she could follow in his path. Aye, he was stubborn, but she would be relentless. If there was one thing she knew to be true, it was that her brother loved her. And that meant he would forgive her. Eventually, she was able to catch up with him. "But Alex, you were so distraught over Maddie that you wouldn't have listened. If you recall, I did tell you I had feelings for him."

"Would I not? And you know that how?" His gaze bore into hers and she finally knew how it felt to be under attack by Alex Grant.

Jennie didn't answer; she couldn't answer. Somehow, she knew she had failed her own brother, and it hurt. How could she make it up to him? She hung her head and fell in behind him, her eyes misting.

He yelled at her over his shoulder. "You will go to the abbey as instructed, sister, and if I must tie you to a tree in front, I will. You will not impede this battle in any way. Understood?"

Jennie whispered, "Aye." They rode hard, and she spent a good portion of the time sobbing. She had disappointed the man she loved like a father.

What should have been the happiest day of her life had turned into a disaster.

The Grant men arrived in the middle of the night, stopping at the abbey on the way for just long enough to leave Jennie there before they continued onward. Before they left, Jennie moved over to Alex's horse and gazed up at him. "I'm sorry I failed you. But please help Aedan. Do not allow the attackers to win. You must save him. I love him, Alex."

She would not fight Alex in this. The Grant

warriors were here, and Aedan needed them most.

She had gotten this far, now she would just have to wait.

———∽∽∽———

CHAPTER NINETEEN

And when Jennie thought her husband was dead,
Alex was there for her too.

JENNIE VOMITED TWICE before she cleaned her mouth and climbed onto Drew's horse. He had to be lying, he just had to be. As they rode toward the castle, Drew continued.

"Fletcher ran him through. We were wrong. We all thought the traitor was Hamish, and we left Irvine to guard Aedan at the rear. Only Irvine turned on him and drove his sword through his belly. He died instantly. I'm sorry, Jennie."

She clung to Drew from behind and leaned her head into his back, sobbing and wailing uncontrollably.

But it didn't make sense. If he were truly dead, where were they going?

"Where are you taking me?" she asked through tears. "If he's dead, I do not want to see him. Have Fletcher and the Englishmen taken over the castle?"

"Aye, they have taken over, but your brother is here with his men and they guard Cameron's body for burial. Fletcher's men tried to take him so they could put his body on display for all to see, but your brothers got him back."

She refused to believe it. The Lord would not do such a thing to her. He would not take her husband from her within a few days of their marriage, would he? Her stomach churned even though there was naught inside. She would never eat again, never. How could her intuition have been so wrong? She had come, just as she had been told to do. The Lord had told her she was needed by her husband, and here she was. She had trusted in God just as the abbess had told her to do. Had he lied to her?

Trying her best to hold everything together, she slipped into the same inner zone that helped protect her heart and her soul when she treated wailing men, torn and slashed and bloody from battle, though it had failed her of late. Drew helped her to dismount, and she glanced to the center of the gathering, where a man lay unmoving on a Cameron plaid. Brodie ran toward her.

"Jennie, nay. Do not come any further. We wanted you here safe, but please do not look at him." Brodie held her back. "'Tis not a memory you wish to keep."

She glanced toward the body, her eyes taking in the blood that covered it from head to toe. Something swelled in her body, something from deep in her belly, and she couldn't control it. Aedan. It was Aedan, she would know him anywhere. Aedan lay dead on the ground in front of her. All thoughts of it being a lie fled, and reality set in—a horrible reality of which she wanted to part.

"Nay!" She screamed over and over again, pushing and shoving against Brodie, raking her nails down his skin. He held fast. "Nay, he's my husband, let me be. Brodie, let me hold him, please. I love him."

She sobbed hysterically for what seemed like an eternity while ironclad arms held her back. "Please, let me hold him one more time. I did not have enough time with him. I need to hold him…once more is all I ask." She crumpled against her brother, clinging to him. "Let me be, please, Brodie."

She fought against Brodie, kicking and screaming, until he finally let her go. But before she could make it to her husband's dead body, someone grabbed her from behind. Alex picked her up and cradled her like a babe, carrying her away from her husband. "Nay, Alex," she screamed, "let me love him once more. Nay, nay, nay."

"Shush, Jennie." The same calm voice that had soothed her after the loss of her parents settled her just a touch. She turned into Alex's chest and cried until she had no more tears, allowing his familiar voice to wrap around her like a blanket once again. She thought of the day her mother had died and how she had listened to her father cry at the ceremony, of the day her father had died six moons later. Now her husband was dead, too, and her brother still held her as he had done before, allowing her to grieve but holding firm.

Alex carried her over to Logan, kissed her

forehead, and said, "I'm sorry, Jennie." Then he settled her on the other man's horse. "Get her out of here." Logan grabbed onto her and spurred his horse.

Jennie collapsed against Logan, sobbing her heart out, still unable to accept the horrible truth. As soon as they were a distance away, Logan whispered, "Shush, lass. 'Tis a ruse."

Jennie stilled instantly. "What?"

She pulled back and stared at Logan.

"Nay, do not stop your crying. 'Tis important no one knows," he whispered.

She leaned against him and cried again, wondering if she had heard him wrong. Was it possible? Could her husband be alive after all?

He brought her to the abbey, then carried her inside. Once they had arrived, she said, "Repeat what you said, Logan Ramsay."

He tugged her inside a chamber and said, "Aye, 'tis a ruse. We need Irvine to think Aedan is dead. We must wait here one hour, then Gwyneth will take you to him while we distract the traitors."

"Truly?" She swiped at her eyes, her breath hitching so much that she started coughing and could not stop.

Logan fetched a cup of ale and brought it over to her. "Here, drink, lass." He set the cup down and clasped her shoulders. "Gwynie will come to you within the hour and take you to Aedan. You must dress as a poor lad. You are to wait here and speak to no one except the abbess. She will assist you. I must return as part of the ruse. Trust me, we are being watched."

She gulped and nodded. "He is well?"

"He has only a small injury, I think to his left arm. I came upon him just as Irvine was about to spear him, but the traitor turned tail at the last minute. Our plan 'twas the only way to discover the true traitor. Aedan's small injury helped us in two ways. It revealed Fletcher, and it also fooled the blackguard into thinking Aedan was much more severely injured than he is. He rolled when he hit the ground, so Fletcher knew not where he struck him. Take what you need to tend his arm." He kissed her forehead. "My apologies, but we had to do it this way to be safe for all."

"My thanks, Logan, and my apologies for drenching you with my tears." Relief spread through her with such a force, she almost fell to the ground. Thanking the Lord her husband was alive, she promised Him never to be deceitful again. Aedan was alive, her husband lived.

He gave her a sheepish look. "Do not worry. At least you did not score me as you did your brother. We all said you would be wild with grief. 'Tis one of the reasons we wanted you to stay back on Grant land. But you are stubborn, as your brothers promised." He headed out the door of the abbey, but stopped at the last minute. "You are much like my Gwynie, Jennie. Strong, intelligent women have strong emotions."

CHAPTER TWENTY-TWO
*Alex Grant totally undone and
not by any threat of war…*

A RUMBLING COULD BE felt in the ground from nearby. A group of riders was headed straight toward them, though Aedan couldn't yet determine who they were. But soon he caught sight of the Grant plaid and heard the familiar war whoop.

While he dreaded telling Alex the news of his sister, at least the extra men would be able to assist in their search. Many of his men knew Dermid's land well. They'd find her, they had to locate her. This failure he would not accept.

As Alex approached, Aedan could tell from the look on his face that all had not gone well at court. He mounted his horse and moved to greet him. "All is not well with the king?"

"Nay, all is well, but word has come to me that Maddie's wellness is at risk. There could be serious problems with the bairn. I have come to fetch Jennie and invite you to our home. I need her there. I cannot lose my wife."

Aedan had never seen Alex Grant in such a state. His color was ashen, his hands fisted, and his jaw clenched. He looked more relaxed in the midst of a battle than he did at present.

Aedan realized he felt the same way about his wife, and they had been married less than a sennight.

"My sister. Where is she?" Alex's eyes bore into his.

Aedan returned the stare. "I know not. She was kidnapped. Dermid MacLean stole her and planned to rob the coffers of the abbey, using her as a bargaining chip."

"Is that MacLean on the ground?"

Aedan nodded. "Aye."

"Did you get the information you needed from him before you killed him?"

Aedan took a deep breath and let it out slowly. "Nay, I did not. He wouldn't release the information. I suspect that she is well hidden on MacLean land."

Releasing a bellow that shook the branches in the trees, Alex clutched his horse's reins so tight that Midnight reared up, as if he were connected to his rider in some way.

Aedan turned his horse around. "Follow me, I have an idea of where she is. We can split into groups when we get close."

CHAPTER TWENTY-THREE

*Alex confesses what he thinks
is causing Jennie's nightmares.*

JENNIE VOWED SHE would go help dear Maddie, but what if the wailing returned? She was just so frightened to try working as a healer again, too happy with her new life. She squeezed her husband's hand as she followed Alex over to a rock, grateful Aedan had insisted on coming with her.

Once at the rock, Alex pointed and said, "Sit. You will hear me out."

Jennie nodded and sat down. She loved her brother and would listen to what he had to say, though unsure of what he wished to tell her. She loved it at Aedan's. The wailing in her dreams had stopped; the wailing that disrupted her waking hours had stopped. If she returned to healing, she was sure the wailing would return. The haunting cries had driven her almost to a permanent state of daftness, and it had grown worse with every passing day she spent on Grant land.

"Jennie, are you upset because of the wailing?"

"Aye." She peeked up at him, unsure of what he would say next.

"I brought you to the abbey because we thought you needed to come to this on your own. 'Twas Brenna's idea, but…I cannot wait any longer. Maddie's life is at stake, so forgive me, but I must."

"Alex, I know not what you are about. Where are you going with this?"

He paced in front of her, his hands clasped behind his back. "Do you recall the day our mama died?"

"Nay. I recall the day Papa died, but not Mama."

He turned to gaze into her eyes. "Because you will not allow yourself to remember."

She frowned, still confused. "I still do not understand."

"I will remind you, and I think you will understand. Please be patient. When Mama was ill, Da was away. When he returned, he was in complete shock to find her near death.

I remember standing in her chamber when Da came in, and you and Robbie were with me.

"Brenna had many candles going, not of the typical lavender scent that Mama loved, but a medicinal type that was to help her lungs. Mama had accepted her fate, but she hung on for a long time with her fever, hoping she would be able to say good-bye to Da. She was lying in the bed, and the candles were lit, but she would not awaken. You and I were standing opposite the bed, and Robbie was standing next to it, singing to her because she loved it. Da came into the room and took one look at her and wailed harder than I have ever heard any man, falling across the bed and throwing himself into her arms."

Jennie stared at Alex, bits and pieces falling into place. She hung her head because all of a sudden, the memory was returning. She could smell the candles, could almost hear Robbie singing.

"Brodie and Brenna were not there, just you and me and Robbie. There was a small pillow on the bed and you grabbed it when Da came in, though I know not why." Alex paused and stared up at the night sky. "'Twas a terrible moment in my memory, so I do not know how it could be anything but bad in yours." His hands fell to his sides and he turned to gaze into her eyes.

"The wailing you hear at night is our da's. Da yelled and hollered and sobbed like I have never seen any man do before. He lay on the bed and sobbed his eyes out, cradling Mama on his lap. Robbie stopped singing, and I froze, unsure of what to do, and eventually walked out of the room."

"But where did we go?"

"*We* did not go anywhere. You and Robbie stayed. I was in such a rush to get away, I left you there. When I remembered and returned to the chamber, Papa was still wailing." He sighed.

"And Robbie and I?"

"Robbie was holding the pillow against one of your ears and his hand against your other. You were screaming."

"What was I saying?" She did not need to ask, because she *knew*. The memory of grabbing onto Robbie and telling him to make it stop, please make it stop was so vivid it was as if she were living it again. Was that how Alex remembered it?

"You were screaming at Robbie to make it stop."

Tears flooded her face and she leaned into her husband. "I said it over and over again, did I not?"

"Aye, and the two of you hid."

She sobbed as she clutched her husband's hands. "In the corner. I tried to hide in the corner under the table. Robbie climbed under there with me and kept holding my ears, but I wouldn't stay still for him. And Papa just kept wailing. 'Twas horrible."

"Aye. I am so sorry I left you behind. 'Twas only a minute or two before I remembered you remained in the chamber."

"But then you came in and picked me up. And you took me away from the wailing. Just like you have always done." She stood up and fell against her brother, wrapping her arms around him. "You have always been there for me, always protected me, always held me when I needed you. Alex, I'm sorry." She clung to her brother, but then took a step back.

She swiped at her tears and turned to her husband. "'Tis true. 'Tis my father's wailing I hear at night. 'Tis not the men's, 'tis my da's. I do not know why."

Alex whispered and kissed her forehead. "I do. Because the wailing of the wounded men has brought you back to the memories of that night, I am sure of it. You chose to forget it, and it worked for many years. But now, I think it needed to come out."

Jennie kissed his cheek, then her husband's. "Come, we mustn't wait any longer."

Alex let out his breath. "Good. Because if anything happens to my Maddie, I will wail much louder than Da ever did."

~~~

When they arrived at the Grant keep, Aedan helped her down and said, "Go. I'll take care of our things."

She gave him a quick kiss and ran up the steps to the great hall, then headed straight up to Maddie's chamber. When she stepped inside, the first thing she noticed was how pale Maddie was. She was still alive, but her breathing was shallow and she had most definitely lost quite a bit of blood.

"How long has the bairn been trying to come out, Caralyn?" Poor Caralyn was exhausted, even though Alice and Fiona, Maddie's maids, were both there to assist her.

"Three days. I cannot make the bairn turn. The babe comes feet first, and I have found one foot, but cannot locate the other."

Alice was near tears. "Can you do something, Jennie? Please?"

Jennie walked to the chest and washed her hands and her face. The bed was soaked in blood, and Maddie was covered in it as well. All of a sudden, Maddie grunted and sat up. Just as she did, Alex bolted into the room.

"Jennie, I have to push again and naught happens. I do not have the strength. Let me go. I am too weak."

Alex climbed into bed behind his wife and pushed her into a sitting position.

"Alex, I cannot do this. I'm sorry, but I cannot continue." She shoved at her husband with what little energy she had left.

"Aye, you will continue, Madeline. I always give in to your requests, but no' this one. You will push. Do you hear me? And I will help you."

"Alex, please. 'Tis too painful, too hard…" She drifted off and closed her eyes. "I'm too tired."

"Maddie!" Alex shouted in her ear.

"Alex, give her a few minutes rest. Allow me to check her over."

Jennie spread Maddie's legs apart and inserted her fingers to see what she could feel. Just as Caralyn had said, she quickly latched onto a wee foot. She moved her fingers as far as she could, but could not find the other foot.

Maddie suddenly leaned forward and began to push again, so Jennie said, "Alex, help her bear down. She needs to push the baby in this direction. Caralyn, lean against her belly right here and see if we can twist the bairn just a bit while she's pushing."

Jennie could feel the powerful pulse of the womb pushing on her fingers, but she kept searching. Just as she was about to give up, Caralyn pushed in the right spot and something seemed to give way.

"I've got it. I think I have the other foot." She waited for Maddie to slow so she could move her hand and grasp the extremity a bit better. The look on Maddie's face told her she was hurting, but she continued, knowing that her brother's wife had a high threshold for pain.

She finally had a good grip, so she waited until Maddie felt the need to push again. As soon as she moaned, Jennie said, "Alex, push on her belly, too."

While Alex, Maddie, and Caralyn all pushed, Jennie pulled. A moment later, the bairn slid out in a rush of water, and Maddie moaned with relief. Alice was there to help her get the bairn breathing and clean, and it seemed to take forever, but the wean let out a weak cry, though it was strong enough to improve her color. Alice and Jennie cleaned her up, then handed her to Caralyn.

"Alex, congratulations. You finally have your

yellow haired daughter. She's a wee one. You must keep her verra warm." Maddie fell back on the bed and was fast asleep while Alex reached for his new daughter, cooing soft words to her. As soon as she nestled into her sire's warm arms, the bairn quieted.

"My thanks, Jennie." Alex whispered, unable to tear his eyes from his new daughter. "Will Maddie be all right?"

All of a sudden, Jennie said, "Caralyn, I need your help. Alex. Outside." Alex looked at her as if he wanted to argue, but he took one look at the blood on her hands and left the room.

She and Caralyn worked and worked, though Maddie never moved. A few hours later, she finally had things back in order. They had changed the bed and cleaned Maddie up, so Jennie stepped out to see Alex.

Her brother gave her a look of worry that shot straight to her heart, but she had to be honest with him. "Alex, I am sorry, but I don't think Maddie will be able to have another bairn. There was a problem with what came out after. My apologies."

His face was gray. "But Maddie will be all right? I don't care about more bairns, Jennie. We have five. 'Tis plenty, but my Madeline?"

"I think she will be in good shape in a moon or so. 'Twas much more difficult for her, and she is weak, but with time, she should come back hearty. You must allow her to stay abed for a while. She can nurse the bairn, but that is all. Someone else must mind the other bairns."

"We can handle that. We are a family. The whole clan will band together to help. My thanks." He gave his new daughter to Alice and hugged Jennie. "May I see her?"

"Aye, but allow her to sleep when she needs it."

Alex hurried into the room, and Jennie moved over to peer at her new niece in Alice's arms. "She is quite a beauty. She looks just like Maddie."

Caralyn came up behind her. "Thank goodness you came when you did, Jennie. This could have been disastrous."

"Nay, you are a wonderful healer, Caralyn. You kept her going until I could get here."

Caralyn hugged Jennie, then stepped back, holding her at arms' length. "I have much to learn, and I work hard, but I do not have the gift you do, Jennie. You are the gifted healer."

Alice nodded. "Aye, I hope you will continue to heal. 'Tis your nature, lass."

Jennie thought for a moment before declaring, "It is my nature. I agree with you. I hope that the wailing will end so I can return to my life's work." Working on Maddie had settled a few things in her mind. Seeing her niece delivered and the look of gratitude on her brother's face convinced her that she was indeed in the right vocation.

Alice winked at her as they all gazed at the newest Clan Grant member. "Wait until a laddie tries to get near this one."

HIGHLAND
HARMONY

BOOK 8

The Ramsays, the Grants, the Camerons, the Menzies, the Drummonds.

And the beginning of the sapphire sword.

This is the true start of the fae in my books. Avelina, the first seer.

CHAPTER TWENTY

Alex, leading his family to Ramsay land to support Brenna, sees the truth of what is about to happen.

LAIRD ALEX GRANT led his guards across the valley. When they made it to the other side, he held his hands up to signal for those in the front to wait for the rest to gather. They all knew this was the toughest area to traverse in all of the Highlands. Trekking down this next mountain was slow going. Rocks and pebbles and steep drops that could catch the horses' hooves threatened to slow their progress. But at least it wasn't winter.

This was a rare journey for them, one they had never made before as a family, which was why Alex was taking such care. He had two hundred guards with him, but he needed them all. His dear wife, Maddie, rode in a cart behind them with Celestina and the Grant bairns.

After receiving the message about his sister Brenna's loss, he'd made the decision they would go as a family to offer their support to the Ramsays. Most of his clan had traveled out of the Highlands at some time or another except for Maddie, and she had asked him if he would take her to see dear Brenna.

The entire world knew he was unable to turn his wife down. He still adored her as much as the day they'd married, nay, even more. He glanced over his shoulder at the cart. There she sat with their youngest, Eliza, in her lap, next to Celestina, who was cuddling her newest daughter, Catriona, on her lap. Maddie had been telling the little ones stories, but she had stopped short.

Alex didn't like this one bit. He had never seen such a sight. His mother had always sworn that the land was controlled by the fae, who would come out every so often to shake up the land. He hadn't seen it happen yet. But this vision in front of him had him wondering whether this was exactly what his mother had warned them about. The fae came when there was trouble, she had said, and they would help a worthy human, a chosen one, lead the land in the direction they desired, in the direction of good.

He recalled Brenna's question to their mother at the time. "What do you mean, direction of good? Where else would we go?"

They'd waited patiently for their mother to answer. "Sometimes there are evil souls who try to wrest power for themselves," she had said, smoothing back Brenna's hair. "But remember that the fae are always watching us. You will know when they step in to provide us with their protection."

"How?" Alex had asked.

"There will be a strange cast over the land. At first, you'll just think the day is different, yet you'll know not why. You will continue, and you'll feel as though something is there over your shoulder watching you, but there'll be naught there. Even the clouds and the rain will be different—darker and heavier. You'll know it when you feel it. Trust me."

His mother was right. He could feel it.

His gaze narrowed as he searched for any clues, but there were none. They were more than halfway to the Ramsays. His gut told him not to turn back. His sister and her bairns were near the Lowlands.

His decision finally made, he gave crisp instructions. "Once we get to the bottom of the next mountain, Brodie, you'll take the cart, all the bairns, and one hundred guards. You are to head to Ramsay land using the peripheral route that curves away from Cameron land. Robbie, you'll come with me and we'll take the rest of the guards to Cameron land to see if Jennie is safe."

He didn't like it. There had been many skirmishes in the Cameron's land not long ago, right before Jennie and Aedan married. Lochluin Abbey, full of riches, sat near the keep. Apparently, the skirmishes were not over.

Loki, Brodie's eldest son, rode up behind Alex. "My laird, I'd like to request to travel with you to fight. I think my skills would benefit you."

Alex turned slowly to address him. Aye, Loki was a clever, cheeky lad, but he lacked good judgment as of yet. And Alex did not like being questioned.

Brodie barked, "Loki, apologize to your laird."

Alex's hand came up to stop him. He turned his attention to his nephew. "Loki, are you telling me that the job of protecting my bairns and my wife is not important enough for you?"

Loki paled and stuttered, "N-nay, my laird. Forgive me."

"You'll follow the cart and the horses, watching the rear for any threats. I have five bairns that need protecting, and many nieces and nephews."

Jake and Jamie, his twin lads, growing up so fast it frightened him, spoke up. "Da, we can protect…"

"Silence!" His stare raked across the group. "I know not what we are up against, and you are all to do what I say without question. And when I am not with you, you will do as Robbie or Brodie instruct you. Understood?"

A sea of heads nodded, but Alex's youngest, golden-haired Eliza, just a wean, began to cry. "Papa, up?" she asked, outstretching her arms to him from the cart.

Alex turned and gave directions to Robbie and Brodie before they all continued on down the mountain. He couldn't look at his daughter right now. The thought of anything happening to her made him not furious, but ill, quite ill.

He didn't like this one bit. The tales his mother and father had told him of the fae had conveyed one lesson.

Visits from the good fae came when evil threatened to overtake part of the land.

And what he saw in front of him looked purely evil.

CHAPTER TWENTY-FIVE

Alex, the festival, and the tree…

A FEW DAYS LATER, Alex clasped Quade's shoulder as they headed out of Quade's solar. Both came to a sudden stop in the middle of the Ramsay great hall.

"Where is everyone?" Alex asked, his gaze searching the empty space.

Quade's mother came down the stairs with several plaids slung over her arm. "They are hoping to tire the weans out by spending the afternoon at the loch. Brenna is excited to show off the improvements Quade has made to try to compete with the famous Grant loch. I've heard much about it, though I have yet to see it. Come, walk with me. I am bringing out more plaids for the bairns for when they get out of the water. 'Tis a lovely day."

Alex followed Quade and his mother out the door and down the hill toward the loch. "Did it take much work to adjust your loch for the bairns to use?"

Quade took the plaids from his mother before he rolled his eyes. "Nay, not to make it as you have arranged your loch, but it took a bit more to please my wife. Aye, creating a gentle slope for the weans on one end and removing the grass was not difficult, and we were pleased to find a

soft sand mixed in with the stones. But Brenna
came up with a few more things she wanted. And
my brothers had their own ideas." Quade clasped
his shoulder. "You'll see what I mean. Your sister
is like you in many ways. And I'm sure after you
leave, she'll have even more ideas for me."

Alex smiled. He and the Ramsay laird had
always been a wee bit competitive. He couldn't
wait to see how the Ramsay loch compared to
the Grant loch. It had not been difficult at all to
create a comfortable area at the opposite end of
the loch from where Robbie and Caralyn lived,
and the swimming spot had, in fact, become a
clan favorite. Many a clan member spent the
warmest days of summer out by the loch.

Quade continued as they drew near. "As you
can see, my men had to build stone benches for
seats, and we also put a dock out in the middle
of the loch as you did. I admit the dock island is
a favorite with the older bairns. But Brenna did
not stop there."

Alex noticed the edge where all the weans
were splashing. "Why do you have rope across
the loch?"

"Och, you're catching on to your sister's
thinking, are you not? The rope is the limit for
the wee bairns. They cannot go beyond it until
they learn to swim. 'Tis Brenna's idea. And Molly
is gifted at teaching the youngest ones how to
swim."

Alex nodded. "I suspect Maddie will be having
me create the same as soon as we are home."

A giant old oak leaned gracefully over the

water in the middle of the loch. Alex stopped in his tracks and turned his head to the side. "What the devil is that?"

Quade chuckled. "I see you've discovered Logan's contribution to the loch. After watching him try to toss my son and daughter from the lower branches of the big oak tree, I agreed to allow him this instead. But 'tis all Logan's creation. As you can see, the older ones enjoy it."

As Alex watched, Loki grabbed the knotted rope that hung from the highest branch of the oak, pulled it back as far as it would go, then ran down the grassy slope leading to the loch, jumping up and lifting his feet to the knot at the last minute. As soon as he sailed over the water, Loki threw himself into the air and did a flip before landing in the water with a huge splash.

Alex applauded Loki's achievement and watched as all the lassies giggled and collected around the lad as he climbed out of the water, his chest puffed out with pride.

"Do a double flip, Loki," Torrian yelled.

Lily shouted, "Nay, do a backward flip."

But before he could do any of those things, Logan came charging toward the tree, grabbed the rope, and ran back as far as he could, stopping at the top of the slope with a huge grin on his face. "Are you all ready? I'll give you a challenge. This will be the biggest splash ever. Then we shall see if all you wee bairns—" he pointed at Loki, Torrian, Lily, Ashlyn, Molly, Jake, and Jamie, who were all standing around watching, "—can beat me."

Logan flew down the slope and launched himself into the air, letting go of the rope at the last minute to fly out over the water. Landing at an odd angle, Logan created a huge splash that spouted like a fountain, saturating those who were standing nearest to the edge of the loch. The spectators shrieked at getting wet, but all laughed and applauded when Logan climbed out.

While Alex stood to the side, Brodie came running past him from the end of the loch with a grin on his face. "I take up the challenge," he said, grabbing the rope. "We'll see who can make the biggest arsewhacker of all."

Brodie did his best to beat Logan, but he did not quite make it. Micheil followed with a hoot.

Maddie ran up to Alex, who was still watching the display, and flung her arms around his waist. "Alex, is it not wonderful out here? Have you seen the swing? And look at how Quade chopped a tree down and cut off pieces to be used as seats around the loch. And we have to add a rope to our shallow section for the bairns, just as Brenna did."

Quade chuckled just as Alex gave him a pointed look over Maddie's head. "Ramsay, the next thing she'll have me doing is planting an oak tree next to our loch."

"But that would take too long, Alex," Maddie pleaded. "I'm sure the men would be happy to transplant one from another spot. Just choose your strongest men." She gave him a sweet smile as Quade guffawed.

Alex kissed the top of Maddie's head just as

their daughter, Eliza, tottered over, all wet, and lifted her arms. "Papa, up?"

Alex picked her up, kissed her cheek with a resounding smack, and then hoisted her up onto his shoulders.

"By the way," Maddie said, "you know the wee lads have been waiting for you to play the tree game, Alex. I promised them 'twould happen." She gave her husband a hug, and Alex rubbed his thumb across her cheek.

"Did you, now? Hmmm…that could cost you later, sweeting."

Quade said, "Alex, play a tree? I'd like to see that."

Alex passed Eliza off to her blushing mother, then made his way over to the shallow end of the loch where the bairns all splashed in the water. As soon as they spied him, the wee ones all ran over yelling, "Tree, Uncle Alex. Please, be the tree." Celestina held her youngest, Catriona, while Caralyn held her wee lad, Padraig.

Maddie smiled up at her husband. "See how they love you, Alex?"

Alex strode into the water up to his knees, holding both arms out to the side, and shouted in his deepest voice, "Watch out, a storm is a brewing." The bairns giggled and ran toward him, each of them reaching up to grasp his enormous arms.

Gregor was last, chasing the older ones into the water. "Dabin, wait for me!"

Once they were all hanging from his arms,

he started to swing them back and forth, "Here comes the wind."

The bairns started to swing and squeal, some of them landing in the water with a splash, others hanging on for dear life.

Maddie yelled, "Be careful, Alex. Do not hurt them. There are so many hanging on your arms."

Once all of the bairns had landed in the water, he climbed back out and headed over to greet his sister, Brenna, who was standing off to the side on the hill overlooking the water.

"All is well, Brenna? Is this not too hard for you, watching all the bairns?"

Brenna's eyes teared up. "Nay, 'tis wonderful. You know not how happy you have made me by bringing the family to support me. Alex, look at our clan and all it's become."

As Alex stopped to stare out over the loch, Jennie and Aedan came to join them. "I know," he said. "'Tis hard to believe they are all part of our clan. I wish Mama and Papa could see us now, how we've grown." He wrapped his arm over Jennie's shoulder and kissed her cheek.

"I know, but I believe they are watching." Brenna swiped away a tear as Brodie and Celestina joined them, and Maddie came over to hug her husband. "How could I be sad about losing one child, when we have so many strong bairns?"

"You'll have another someday," Maddie whispered. "Alex and I lost one before we had Eliza."

Silence settled over the siblings, but the solemn moment was broken when Logan came running at them from the tree, followed by Robbie. Before he reached them, Logan first chased over to Gwyneth, who was sunning herself on her plaid, and proceeded to drip water all over her.

"Logan, you'll pay!" She jumped up and chased him back to the tree.

All the older bairns chased after the two to see what they would do next.

Logan flung himself into the water from the swing, yelling, "Come catch me, Gwynie." He landed with a big splash almost as loud as his first. Gwyneth used the swing next—after flipping in the air, she kicked her legs straight up and landed in the water head first, with her arms leading overhead, not far away from Logan. Dressed in her leggings and a sleeveless tunic, she hardly made a ripple in the water.

"How did she do that?" Robbie whispered, Caralyn right behind him with their babe on her hip.

"Are those two always so playful?" Celestina asked.

Micheil and Diana came over, holding their two lads, David and Daniel, both a bit overwhelmed by everyone. "Aye, Logan loves to tease Gwyneth," Micheil replied.

"But Gwyneth enjoys every moment of his teasing," Diana added.

Celestina said, "I love to see the strong friendships among the cousins. Look at Bethia and Kyla, and Gracie and Sorcha. Roddy and Braden are inseparable until they come here, and then they love spending as much time as they are able with Gavin and Gregor. Those four lads are all within a year of each other, are they not? And look at Molly and Ashlyn, they're so dear together!"

Moments later, Logan and Gwyneth climbed out of the water laughing, arms wrapped around each other.

YULETIDE
ANGELS

BOOK 9

*A beloved story of Alex and Maddie, when they both
meet their grandbairns…
Dyna, Alick, and Alasdair.*

CHAPTER ONE

I wrote this with the idea that it was before Elizabeth and Connor were born.

Obviously, I wrote it after Highland Swords, so I admit the timing could be confusing.

This is such a great story of Alex and Maddie's relationship. Readers often think of Alex as being the perfect husband, laird, and lover, but he did have a habit of yelling a bit.

My apologies, but this is my favorite Christmas story.

Kyla's personality comes out at a young age.

THE DOOR OPENED as if on cue, and Alex filled the doorway, stomping his boots just outside the door. "What will Alex agree to do?"

"Travel to Ramsay Castle for Christmas," Logan said. "You're all invited. You, Brodie, Robbie, and your families. Maddie tells me Robbie would stay here. Even so, with Jennie already with Brenna, you will nearly all be together." He glanced at the large man filling the doorway, also chieftain of the clan. "Brenna's fixing to make room for all of you while I'm gone. She's already set Quade to building all kinds of furniture. But my brother would do anything for his new wife, as you know. He adores Brenna. Mayhap he'll be adding a tower or two by the time I return."

Alex removed his mantle, placing it on the peg by the door and grabbed an ale from the sideboard. "As enticing as that sounds, the Norse presence remains heavy in the Highlands, and they search for travelers to take their anger out on. I don't suspect we'll be going anywhere with the bairns for at least another year."

"Year?" Maddie asked, stopping the organizing she was doing in the hall. She had moved away to begin preparations for their departure during Logan's explanation, believing they'd likely set off tomorrow. Alex's words shocked her. "Not for a year? Surely you do not mean that, Alex. A year is a verra long time."

Logan snorted in agreement. "I understand your concern, Grant, but 'tis the holiday, and if I don't bring you back, I'll have to answer to that new ornery mistress of my castle."

Alex set his goblet down and settled his hands on his hips. "Would that ornery mistress you refer to be my sister?"

Logan chuckled. "You know I jest. She's verra dear to me, but 'struth is there are others asking."

"Who?" Maddie asked, sitting in a chair near the hearth, handing a toy to Kyla, who ignored her and waddled over to her father.

"Upsy?" She stared up at him, her hands waving in the air over her head.

Alex leaned down to pick up his daughter, kissed her cheek, and said, "I'm sure I can guess. The only two Logan cannot refuse."

Maddie gave her husband a perplexed look.

"Wise arse," Logan replied.

"'Ise arse," Kyla mimicked.

"Logan!"

"Mayhap she may not—"

"'Ise arse!" Kyla grinned at Maddie's groan, wrinkling her nose as she giggled.

Logan looked chagrined and said, "Sorry, Maddie." Then he took Kyla away from her father and swung her high into the air. "You wee trickster. You got me in trouble."

Kyla giggled with glee, and as soon as he set her back down, Kyla looked at him and said, "'Ise arse."

Alex barked, "Kyla, you'll not be talking like a reiver."

He picked her up and set her on his shoulders, one of her favorite places to be. Then he spun in a few circles, Kyla weaving back and forth in the air a bit as he moved. She laughed louder and louder, hanging onto her father's long dark locks.

Maddie said, "Alex, be careful."

Alex shot her a grin but dutifully set Kyla down before settling himself into a chair in front of the fire.

As soon as the wee one's feet hit the floor, she took off toward the spot in the corner where her father kept his extra swords. Though the swords were well-protected from the bairns inside a wooden case it was still their favorite place to go, their wee fingers trying to reach through the narrow space between the slats. "Alex, I fear someday she'll manage to reach inside there. You must find a better place to keep your weaponry, a place none of them can reach."

"Maddie, they just need to learn not to touch them. 'Tis no' a difficult concept to teach them."

"Since 'tis not difficult, then I'll settle this task on your shoulders, Alex. Please teach the bairns not to try to take your weapons all the time."

Alex gave a low grumble as he chased after Kyla. "You wee troublemaker. Now I'm in trouble because of you." He swung her back into the air, her feet flying over Alex's head, and she carried on with such delight that everyone in the hall stopped to watch the interplay between the large Highlander and his wee daughter.

<hr/>

CHAPTER THREE

*Alex and Maddie's first true challenge
as husband and wife…*

"ALSO, I'D LIKE to know what you all have heard from patrols about Norsemen in the area."

"Why? Is there a new threat?" Robbie asked.

"The threat is Maddie. Or mayhap Logan. It depends how you wish to see the situation. Logan brought the message that Brenna invites us all to Ramsay Castle for Christmas."

All three nodded their heads, waiting to see what Alex would say. When he said nothing, Robbie finally spoke.

"I'll volunteer to stay and protect the castle. Ashlyn and Gracie say they're never leaving Grant land again. I wouldn't put them through it just yet. Mayhap when they're a wee bit older and trust that I'm not going to give them back."

"Give them back?" Brodie asked.

"I heard Ashlyn speaking with Gracie. The lass told her sister that if they were still here at Christmas, then I probably wouldn't be giving them back to the bad man. Caralyn can't quite convince them I'd never do such a thing. Time will prove it."

"But if you stay, Robbie, then you'd be here alone while we all went to Ramsay land. We've always tried to spend Christmas together," Brodie countered.

"We won't be all together in any event. Even if we all stay here, both Brenna and Jennie are on Ramsay land. Jennie will be upset if the rest of you don't go." Life had been mostly calm in the Highlands, but the war with the Norse had changed much for their family. Now four of them had spouses, so Jennie, the youngest, split her time between the two clans. "My family are looking forward to their first Christmas in the Highlands. Nicol and Inga will be here, and others. We'll be far from alone." Robbie gave a convincing argument. Nicol was Brodie's best friend and assistant throughout the war and had married Celestina's maid not long ago.

Alex nodded. "Before I make my final decision, I'd like to know what your patrols have found over the past week. And what are they hearing from our neighbors? Any trouble? Any reivers foolish enough to come this far north of the borders to try to steal cattle?"

Robbie scratched his head. "We have not seen many Norse. No reports that I'm aware of. They're probably closer to the firths so they can jump back in their galley ships quickly if the weather takes a turn for the worse."

"But we did catch signs of reivers in the area. 'Twas a sennight ago. Naught since."

Alex ran his hand along his jaw. "Then there remain some threats out there. Send another patrol out with a focus on reivers or wandering Norsemen or anyone in the area who doesn't belong. I want a full report this eve."

"Aye, Chief." As second-in-command to the laird of Clan Grant, it was Robbie's job to see that Alex's instructions were followed. "There is always some kind of threat in the Highlands. You know that, Alex. But you have plenty of warriors to protect them all. What say you? What did you say to your wife?"

Alex rubbed his hands together to warm them up, then turned away to pace in a small circle. He knew his brother's words to be true. There would always be danger, and he had a great many men. Yet no matter how he tried, he couldn't rid himself of the vision of reivers closing in from all sides, attacking his wife and his beloved bairns, while he was unable to defend against their numbers.

"I made no promises yet," he finally said. "At first I said nay because I'm worried about the number of Norse still looking for revenge after the Battle of Largs. I told her we'd go next year."

"And?" Brodie leaned forward, the question had them all waiting for his answer.

"She asked me to think on it. I said I would, but

I am of a mind to still deny her. She'll accept it in time. I know she'll be disappointed, but Maddie trusts my instincts."

Mac snorted. Brodie grinned. Robbie hung his head.

"Do you have something to say, Mac?" Alex bit out.

Though his anger flared, he'd trusted Mac's opinion on courting Maddie on multiple occasions, and he was loath to admit that the man had always been right. His brothers hadn't always known, but Mac knew exactly how Maddie's mind worked.

Mac took a step back. "Now don't be getting upset with me, Chief, but you know I'm an honest man, and I've been on this world a bit longer than you have, and I have a wee bit more experience with the female mind, particularly with your wife's."

"Aye, you've known Maddie many years. What of it?" Alex set his hands on his hips.

"Well, I know your lovely wife to be a stubborn woman, and she will not give the idea up easily if it's truly what she wants for Christmas." When Alex narrowed his eyes, Mac quickly added, "But I'm certain you can convince her."

"And you two? What say you?"

Brodie glanced over at Robbie before he spoke. "Maddie can be persistent."

"Aye, 'tis a good word," Robbie said. "I'd just give in to the lass now if I were you, Alex. It will make your life much simpler, aye? She'll wear you down. She usually does."

Robbie arched a brow at him as if challenging Alex to deny his beliefs about his and Maddie's marriage.

Alex couldn't believe his ears. Maddie always did what he said to do.

She loved him, trusted him. She would do what she was told as a good wife should. He did his best to discuss things with her, and he allowed her to speak her opinion inside their bedchamber, but when it came to battle and warriors, she would never question his decision.

What were Mac and his brothers talking about?

He felt they'd set a bit of a challenge to him. He'd be glad to prove them wrong.

CHAPTER SIX

*Alex begins to learn more about
his wife from his brothers.*

"WHAT THE HELL do you mean she left?" Alex's roar could be heard across most of the Highlands, if he were to guess, though they were still in the great hall. He only hoped it reached Maddie's ears.

Logan said, "She's been gone for hours, is my guess. Are you going to stand here and holler or go after her?"

"Mayhap I should allow her to go alone. See how well she does." He paced in a circle. "And I'll kill Mac."

"I wouldn't do that. He went along to protect

her, I'm sure. Would you rather he stayed back? You married a stubborn lass, Grant, and she was going one way or another. Her plan had been for me to leave and for her to follow if you did not come around. I did not argue, as I knew at least I could keep an eye on her that way. Why she decided to leave in the middle of the night, I don't know."

"You knew of her plan?" Alex snapped, his rage climbing.

Logan returned his stare without any fear. "I knew that nothing would stop a woman with that look in her eye. Telling you would have done nothing. And someone needed to be reasonable enough for her to trust him with her confidence. At least I know her plan—something you don't know. You yelled at her, not me."

Brodie came across the courtyard and held up a sack. "I've gathered enough food in case your wife forgot." He had a sack in his other hand. "Oh, and extra plaids. The storm will bring the winds up."

Robbie was directly behind Brodie, hiding his face from Alex. "And why are you hiding, Robbie? Are you grinning? I don't find this amusing at all."

Robbie stuck his head out and said, "We tried to warn you, Alex, but you didn't believe us."

"Of course I did not. I never thought my wife to blatantly disobey my order. She'll pay for it, you can be certain."

"Your order?" Logan guffawed. "Say that word

to Gwynie, and she'll knock you down with a fist."

Alex scowled, trying to understand Logan's words. "A wife's job is to obey her husband. The church commands it."

"Mayhap you're correct, but I don't order Celestina around," Brodie said.

"Why are you afraid to give your wives orders?"

"'Tis not fear, Alex," Robbie said, "but respect. Caralyn says giving her orders all the time reminds her of her former life."

"Celestina says the same. Her father never allowed her to question his commands. Ever. She cries if I bark an order at her. She said it takes her back to being held prisoner by her own father."

Alex hadn't considered that before. Would Maddie feel the same about any order? His orders weren't cruel or inhumane as Kenneth's had been, so he'd felt they were acceptable to make. It was the way of marriage. But Maddie had compared him to that terrible man yesterday. At the time, he'd thought she'd spoken only in anger, but perhaps his ordering was too much of a reminder for her.

"And you'll not be going after Mac," Brodie said. "I heard your threat earlier. I'll stand by his side, and you know why."

Alex did know why. In truth, he thanked the Lord above for Mac. It'd been Mac that had sent him that message years ago that the bastard Kenneth beat his sister. Without it, he might never have returned to MacDonald keep, and Maddie would not have grabbed a piece of his soul with one glance.

Brodie had been with Alex when he'd received the letter that spurred their return to the castle, and he knew well Mac's role in it. He'd always respected the man for that.

"I know, Brodie. I recall it well. Mac's only protecting her. I spoke through rage."

"Aye, but we need to move, Grant," Logan said, grumbling while he paced. "There's a storm on its way."

Alex nodded, shifting to strategic thought. He had to be prepared for any circumstance. "Robbie, you're willing to stay back? If they've gotten to a certain point, we'll go on to Ramsay land and not return until after the Yule."

"Aye, you know we'll stay here."

"I'm leaving now with twenty warriors. Send another two score behind us, but have them bring two carts, just in case 'tis needed."

———— ✸ ————

CHAPTER SEVEN

Alex's thoughts along the way, and a wee lass who has already grabbed a piece of his heart…

THEY HEADED OFF toward the ravine, the wind swirling flakes in their face. He was glad he'd allowed his beard to grow for the winter. It was rough against Maddie's tender skin, but Kyla loved it, giggling and squealing with delight every time she touched it.

He'd told his wife as much only a sennight ago, while holding a giggling Kyla.

Maddie had rolled her eyes and smiled. "I know it keeps your face warm in this weather. I'll survive."

Then she'd kissed his cheek while Kyla giggled even more.

"Kiss," the wee lass had said, touching his lips.

He'd kissed her as carefully as possible, not wanting his beard to scratch her delicate skin, and she'd still broken into a fit of giggles.

After she'd calmed, she had pointed at the door and said, "'Side," with the quiet confidence of a child who knows her request will be met.

His daughter loved the outdoors even at such a young age.

He'd cast a glance to Maddie, who had nodded, so then he'd done his favorite task of all: wrapped the lass against his chest and headed out to the stables, her favorite place. He loved having her wrapped so closely against him so he was able to inhale her sweet scent as he carried her to see the horses.

Another gust of wind and snow brought him out of memory and back to the ravine.

They'd find them. They would find them all, and all would be well, and his sweet lassie would be against his chest again.

He couldn't consider the alternative.

Chapter Eleven

*Alex's anger turns into fear,
and he meets his grandbairns.*

HE HADN'T THOUGHT that making a decision would upset Maddie, but he hadn't discussed it with her at all. His fingers rubbed across his jaw. He had a faint memory of promising his wife to discuss any major decisions with her.

His father had told him it was the man's job to make decisions and the woman's job to follow them. But Alex vaguely remembered his mother standing behind his father with her arms crossed and an angry expression on her face when he'd said it.

Was Logan right? Did all women feel as Caralyn and Celestina did?

If so, if his decision had brought Maddie back to her previous life with Kenneth, the memories it conjured for her would not be sweet. In fact, all he had to do was think about the first time he'd seen Maddie, and his blood reacted fiercely, shooting through his body fast enough for him to clench his fists in reaction.

Her body would react more strongly to that memory than his own. Now he understood. She'd made the decision to leave Grant land out of a combination of fear and anger.

A poor combination for decision-making. Perhaps he needed to calm his own thinking before he found his wife.

If he found her in time. That thought made him break out in a cold sweat, certainly abnormal for these weather conditions. He had to find Maddie, Mac, and the twins, and quickly. His anguish grew so great then that he stopped his horse near a clearing on a hill, tipped his head back to stare up at the gray sky filled with snow clouds, and let out a roar unlike any he'd ever released before. He unleashed his pain, his guilt, his worry over his family. He apologized to Maddie over and over again for failing her.

Then he started. Another rider approached him, but Midnight did not startle, instead remaining calm, as if he knew the rider. Still, Alex reached for the hilt of his sword.

"I'm not here to fight you," the man said, chuckling.

Alex paused. He had never seen the man before, though he looked vaguely familiar. He had long black hair, gray eyes that locked onto his, and a strong profile. It was almost as if Alex were looking at himself at a young age.

"Who are you?"

"Alasdair is my name. You've taught me something just now. I know where I get that tendency to yell when I don't know what else to do," the man said, smiling.

Alex felt his brow furrow. What was the man speaking of?

"What do you want? I cannot waste my time

with you," he said, tugging the reins so that Midnight led him away from the odd man.

"I know where she is," the man spoke as Alex prepared to gallop away.

Alex paused. Had he heard him wrong? "Who?"

"Maddie. I'm here to take you to her. You do not have much time." The man crossed his arms; he had an impressive presence.

Alex ignored him, unable to believe the man knew his wife. He turned his horse around and left the man, but it wasn't to be.

A few moments later Alasdair was riding abreast of him. "Maddie. I know where your wife is. I'll take you to her if you'll stop being stubborn and listen."

A blonde woman with a bow across her back suddenly appeared not far away from them, her eyes as blue as Maddie's. "Alasdair, we must hurry."

Alex stopped his horse and stared at her. "Where did you come from?"

He swore that she had not been there the moment before.

"We don't have time for this. Follow us to your wife."

Alex turned back to Alasdair. "Who the hell are you, and who is she?"

"He'll not budge until we tell him, Dyna. You know he's infamous for his stubbornness."

The woman—Dyna—sighed and merely replied with a "Hurry."

Alasdair turned back to Alex. "We are your grandchildren, and we are acting as guardian angels. We were allowed to come and help you because Dyna wishes to be born and I wish to know my grandmama. If you don't hurry, Dyna will never exist. She's to be the daughter of your yet unborn son."

Alex just stared at Alasdair, unable to comprehend the words he'd spoken. Grandchildren?

"Jake will be my sire."

His three-year-old son Jake? That's exactly who Alasdair looked like. Jake. The eyes were the same. Alex did not understand how this could be. But suddenly, it didn't matter. He had to find Maddie.

"Come," Dyna said, as if hearing his thoughts. "We cannot wait. You must follow us."

"Where is she?" He followed them because he knew not where else to go.

Alasdair said, "She's in a cave, dying. We sent illusions of your horse to pull Mac and the lads to the same place. Hopefully, they'll arrive about the same time we do."

Alex did not understand half of what they said, but he had to trust his gut on this one. And it told him that these people could take him to his wife. "Take me there and hurry."

Alasdair glanced over his shoulder at him. "You should know you were not wrong, Grandda, about refusing to travel to Ramsay land. There will be a big avalanche from this snowstorm. Had you agreed to come and left in a few days with Logan as planned, it could have buried you all. 'Tis why Grandmama—Maddie—followed her gut and left on her own so suddenly. She felt it her only window of opportunity—and it was."

Dyna smiled and said, "Do not blame her

overmuch. We pushed her to leave then, knowing that she'd win you over in the end."

He'd lost his mind, if he were to guess, staring at these apparitions in front of him. But then, he'd been in desperate need of guidance, and there were some things a Scot never questioned.

They flew across the landscape, and he didn't pass another soul along the way, so he had no way of knowing if the two with him were real or not. He supposed it did not matter as long as they brought him to his wife.

A short time later, the lass led them off the main path toward a hidden cave. "She is in there."

She dismounted, pulled on the reins of Alex's horse, and tied them to a bush. He dismounted and rushed into the cave, Alasdair behind him.

"The others will be here soon. They've gone off to direct the others here. Your lads are grand. It is Grandmama you must help."

There Maddie was, curled up by a dying fire, looking small against the backdrop of the cave. Alex knelt in front of her, Dyna behind him, as Alasdair attended to the fire. His hand went to his wife's cheek, and he was surprised at how cold she was. Should she not be warm near a fire?

He set his hand on her neck to feel for the rhythmic pulse of her heart, but he couldn't find it. He tried the other side of her neck and thought he felt just a wisp of a pulsing beat. "Is she dead?"

"She will be soon if you do not help her. We cannot keep her alive. You must. All we can do is guide you in the right direction. She is too cold. Even the fire is not helping her. Something is going on inside her mind—something we cannot tell—so tread carefully with your words."

"I don't understand what that means." Alex would do anything at this moment for his wife, but he didn't wish to hurt her more, either. He needed guidance.

"She's losing her strength, her will. The will to live is everything. Speak to her. Bring her back."

"Maddie," he whispered, then said it louder when she didn't respond. "Maddie."

Still no response.

"You must give her your heat."

"What?"

"Pick her up. Take her into your arms," Dyna said. "We built a fire, but she needs your heat inside, too. It is why she has not warmed enough."

He did what Dyna said, picking up his wife, the fear of losing her gripping him so hard that he would believe anything these apparitions told him. "Help me. Tell me what to do. Anything. I'll do anything."

"Warm her. She needs to know it is you. You are much of her strength. It comes from you."

Alex wrapped his arm around Maddie and held her tight, closing his eyes to take in her scent. "I'm so sorry, Maddie. Do not leave me yet. Please. Wake up. Yell at me. Anything. I promise I'll listen to you always. I may not agree, but we'll compromise. Please."

Nothing.

"Tell me what to do," he said to Dyna. "I don't know what else to do."

"Give her your heat. Your breath. Your verra

will in that breath. The storm drained her will. She is tied to you. Only you can bring her back."

He stared at her, not sure he understood.

Alasdair moved next to Dyna. "Hurry, we don't have much longer. We are only given a short time to do our work."

"Dyna?"

"Place your lips against hers. Part her lips and kiss her so she knows it is you. Your bond should do the rest."

He did what she suggested, setting his lips against Maddie's cold ones, tears filling his eyes at how limp she was, this woman who could be fire in his arms, who could light up his entire being with just a look, whose sweet touch could shoot passion through him as nothing else did.

Limp, nearly dead, not responding.

Alasdair stepped back. "We have to go, Grandsire, but don't give up. She's fighting on the inside."

Dyna reached for Maddie's arm and grasped it tightly, her body taking on a glow and a warmth that made Alex sit back to stare at her, her gaze locked on his. "Don't stop. She will come back to you."

Then Dyna and Alasdair faded away right in front of his eyes.

Alex was frozen for a moment, staring at the empty space where they'd been, before he startled into action. He set his lips against Maddie's again, but she remained limp.

He shifted, holding her tight against his chest as the sobs he'd been holding inside burst forth. He'd only cried like this one other time in his life, and it felt as if the emotion would swallow him whole.

He buried his face in her hair, crushing her against him as he slid closer to the heat of the fire Alasdair had built. "Maddie, Maddie, please . . . come back to me . . . please, Maddie. I love you, I need you. We have more bairns to bring to life. Bairns and grandbairns and more love to give."

He put his lips to hers again, willing her to wake.

He thought he felt a movement against him, so he stilled. After a moment, he set his lips on hers again, willing her to breathe.

This time her lips did move, slowly melding against his, and the joy in his heart burst inside him. She pushed against him, and he lifted his head, looking at her, praying she would awaken and be strong enough to return. Her eyes fluttered open.

"Alex?"

"Aye, I'm here. I love you, Maddie. Wake up, please."

Her eyes opened but then fluttered shut again.

THE
HIGHLAND
CLAN
THE SECOND
GENERATION
1280

LOKI

BOOK 1

*Alex knows Loki's value,
but the younger man does not.*

CHAPTER FOUR

Loki was adopted as a child, but now that he's grown to adulthood, he begins to question his value. Does he truly belong at Clan Grant? Did he deserve someone like Bella?

It's Alex who sees his struggles for exactly what they are, and forces him to do something he doesn't wish to do.

THE NEXT DAY, Loki stood in the middle of the solar, tapping his foot as he waited for the inquisition…or whatever this would turn out to be. He'd rather be back in the forest trying to fight off five reivers than standing in front of these five people.

His da stood at one end of the room with Laird Alex Grant and Uncle Robbie, while Uncle Logan and Aunt Gwyneth stood on the other. These were five of the people he admired most. He'd do anything rather than disappoint them.

Was the day finally here? Had his welcome faded from Clan Grant? It was what he had always feared.

Loki's mother had tried to nurse his wounds before he was called into the solar, but he'd just pushed her away. He could not allow himself to be coddled anymore.

He kneaded his hands in front of him to try to hide the slight tremors.

Alex, still the tallest and most braw warrior in the clan, spoke first. "If you want the lass as your wife, lad, just say the word."

Loki stared at the floor and clasped his hands behind his back. "My thanks, my laird, but her sire does not consider me an acceptable husband."

"I do not care what her sire wants. I'll see that it happens if 'tis what you and Arabella want."

Loki gritted his teeth. "I wish to earn her sire's respect, and if I cannot, then we shall not marry."

A voice came over his shoulder from someone he had not seen enter the solar. His mother. "Loki, I know you have felt the need to prove your worth to your clanmates over the last few years, but you do not need to prove it to us. We all know your worth."

Brodie added, "None know your worth more than we do, lad. They've not seen you in action. We have. Everyone in this chamber has seen what you can do. You are deserving of the lass, but if you do not act soon, she will probably seek another."

Loki didn't answer, mostly because he couldn't. He wished to say so many things about how unfair and unreasonable Bella's sire was, but it was impossible to do so with his mother in the room. He would never, ever disrespect her. When he had nicknamed her missy angel in his youth, he'd had no idea how close to an angel she was.

Now he did.

"Do you have feelings for her?" Alex asked. "Or is there another?"

Another? Shite, nay. Remembering his mother was near, he replied, "Nay, there is no other."

His sire asked again, "So your feelings are for Bella?"

Feelings? How the hell could he answer that? Of course, he knew what his uncle meant, but a part of Loki was not sure what to say. He'd spent the first seven years of his life with no feelings at all. The only thing he'd ever felt was hunger. He recalled almost every moment of his life in that wicked crate. He'd lived with rats and mice and bugs, and dug through the trash thrown out of tavern windows… But Bella, Bella made him wish for all the things he wasn't quite certain he deserved.

"Loki?"

Not knowing how to express himself, he mumbled, "I do not have feelings…"

Alex made his pronouncement. "Then it's settled. We'll not question you anymore about this. But you are to stay away from Bella. Understood? She's free to choose another. You've had your chance and you've turned it away." Immediately, he heard the door close behind him. His mother had left. His sire soon followed. Loki stayed rooted to the floor. He had no wish to see his mother cry.

Logan moved over to his side of the room. "Then we'll take him in training for the crown if you are agreeable, Laird."

Alex's narrowed gaze focused on Loki. "Aye, take him. His hot head will get him in trouble. Loki, before you go…" Alex tipped his head toward the door. "You know how you've hurt your mother. I expect you to mend this. I recall how foolish young lads are. 'Tis why I'm ordering you to say goodbye to your parents before you leave."

Loki frowned. "I'd be happy to pen her a note."

"Loki, you did not hear me. You will speak to her before you leave. Lad, I know you've not had the easiest life, but no one could care for you more than Brodie and Celestina do." His voice softened. "I believe you know that, but you're young, and my guess is you must work through this in your own way. I'm forcing you not to be too heartless along the way. You'll speak kindly to your mother before you leave, or I swear, I'll hunt you down. Understood?"

Loki swallowed before answering. "Aye, my laird. My thanks for all you've done." His uncle was the last man he wished to anger.

"Do not thank me, thank your parents. They are the ones who brought you home. And this *is* your home, lad. I trust you'll discover that in your own way. There will always be a place for you in Clan Grant."

Logan turned to Loki. "Go see your parents. We'll be leaving before first light on the morrow."

JAKE

BOOK 4

The twin most like his father.

CHAPTER FOUR

★This scene stuck in readers' minds. It's the twins and the stones, and the pain in their mother's eyes. I loved that when Jake matured, he asked his father why he stopped his mother from striking them, but that scene comes later...

IT HAD HAPPENED over six summers ago, back when Jake and Jamie were five and ten summers. Their uncle, Robbie, had warned them to make careful decisions, but they were young and giddy and three other lads had found some of the best liquid the Scots could make and hidden it for a special occasion. The "breath of life" that the Scots brewed and aged had a reputation like no other. They'd each had their times with too much ale, but this was different.

They'd decided to hide the bottle of whisky and celebrate with it on a special occasion. Ewan, Roy, and Douglas had told him they'd talked two lassies into baring their breasts for the lads. Like most lads that age, the twins had developed a keen interest in lassies and their bodies. Though it shamed him to think back on it, Jake had been stirred by the mere thought of such a show.

Jamie had tried to talk him out of going, but Jake had insisted, knowing that his brother would follow him anyway. So they'd planned the occasion carefully, choosing an isolated place in the stables, setting sentries outside to watch for them, and bringing food and drink for all. Jake had been as excited as if they were attending a jousting match or a fair, but the evening had not unfolded as he'd expected.

The lassies had changed their minds.

When Jake stepped into the stall at the far end of the stables, the two lasses were struggling with his three friends against the wall. Douglas was trying to rip open the one lass's bodice while Roy held the other lass and Ewan had his hands all over her breasts.

"Stop, please, Ewan," she said through tears. "I've changed my mind."

Ewan exploded. "Then why in hell are you here? You should have stayed home. When you walked through the door, you agreed to show us your titties."

"But Roy said I could kiss Jamie if I came. 'Tis all I want. Leave me be." She struggled against Roy's arms.

The other lass cried out, "I've changed my mind, also. I do not want to do this anymore."

"Too late," Douglas said. "You'll show us now. You cannot be a tease." He pulled on the ribbons at the front of her bodice, causing one breast to fall out of its confines, and the lass screamed in response.

Jamie yelled, "Leave them be. Douglas, take your hands away."

When Douglas did not answer him, Jamie rushed over and tugged his hands away from the lass. Jake took off toward Ewan. But Ewan was the quicker of the two, and he took a swing at Jake, catching him in the jaw, before he turned back to the lass. He grabbed her breast, and the only thing Jake could think to do was grab the lad's hand and pull it away.

Unfortunately, that was the exact instant the twins' mother had flung the door open. Jake's hand was on the lass's breast and Jamie's hand near the other lass's bare breast. The look of pain and anger on his mother's face was one he'd never forget, but it was almost eclipsed by the fury of his sire, who stood behind her.

Hellfire, he glanced at Jamie because he knew they were in the worst trouble they'd ever been in.

Maddie Grant shot across the room and raised her hand to slap each of her sons, but Alex stopped her, attempting to remove her from the stall altogether. Instead of her sons, she grabbed Ewan and Roy by the arms, yanking them away from the girls. Alex managed to pull her to his chest before she could go after Douglas. Having never seen his mother in such a tirade, Jake was stupefied.

"Mama, we were trying to stop it," Jamie cried just as his mother came after him again.

"Do not dare to lie to your mother on top of what you've done." Alex hauled Jamie away from Maddie and tossed him across the stall as if he weighed no more than a feather.

Jake saw his sire coming toward him, so he ran, but his sire—big and bulky and surprisingly fast—got to him first and tossed him out the stable door. Jake looked up from the ground and saw his two uncles coming toward them along with more guards. Uncle Robbie looked down at him and bellowed, "Do not dare to move from that spot." The sentries they'd posted outside the stall to keep watch had been hauled off to the side, where they were being watched by two other guards.

Jamie came flying out of the stall, landing next to Jake on the ground, and the brothers just stared at each other wide-eyed.

"*Mo chreach*," was the only thing Jake could get out. "We're in the worst trouble ever."

Jamie rubbed his face as if his mother had actually slapped him. "I know. Mama almost hit me. I've never seen her hit anyone."

Jake whispered, "And now she's sobbing."

Maddie came out of the stall, an arm around each lassie's shoulder. Celestina had just arrived, and she came forward to help Maddie with one of the lasses. They walked past the twins as they headed off toward the lassie's huts, passing close enough for Jake to see the tears running down his mother's cheeks. There was something else that bothered him more. She refused to look at either him or Jamie.

This was not going to be good. His sire sent Ewan, Roy, and Douglas off with the other guards, though Jake and Jamie did not know where they were headed. They waited an eternity for their father to step out of the stall. When he finally did, his head was down as if he couldn't stand to look at either of them.

He barked orders to his brothers. "Get them up and meet me out at the rock pile."

"But Da…" Jake tried to defend himself, hoping to explain that they'd tried to stop the other lads.

"Silence!"

Uncle Brodie said, "Are you sure you do not wish to lead them out?"

Alex Grant lifted his head to stare at his sons. "Nay, I said I'd kill anyone who put that look on my wife's face again, and I do not wish to kill my own sons. If I touch them, I will."

Uncle Robbie grabbed Jake and forced him to stand. "Consider it done."

Their uncles led the way to the rock pile, and Jake didn't dare speak until he noticed his sire was staying behind, pacing.

"Do not get your hopes up, lads. He's waiting to be sure your mother is all right. Once he tends to her gentle sensibilities, he'll come for you."

"But Uncle Brodie, we were trying to stop it," Jamie cried out as he stumbled along the pathway.

"Aye," Jake added. "The other lads lost their senses."

Uncle Robbie said, "So you're saying you'd heard about their plans and were only there to stop it?"

Jake frowned, wondering how to explain everything. "Not quite."

Jamie sighed. "Mayhap it doesn't matter. We'll be in less trouble if we just shut up and accept our punishment. You know that's what Da has always said."

"But Jamie, we *were* trying to help." He glared at his brother. There had to be a way to convince their father that in the end, they'd made the right decision.

"Aye, 'tis true, but 'twas not why we were there, and you know it." Jamie had whispered low enough so his uncles wouldn't hear him.

Jake opened his mouth and snapped it shut. He couldn't argue with that, and besides, he'd talked Jamie into going. He'd have to thank his brother later for not tattling on him.

"Wise move on your part, lad. Lying will get you in worse trouble." Uncle Brodie narrowed his gaze at his nephews.

"But they said they wanted to show," Jake said. "That's all."

"According to the expressions on their faces, they were not willing." Uncle Brodie spat off to the side. "Hellfire, lads, but you're putting me and your uncle in the worst of spots."

"Why is that?" Jake asked.

"Because your sire is in a killing rage. Could you not have pished off someone else?" His uncle glanced over his shoulder to see if anyone was behind him.

Uncle Robbie shook his head. "Lads, I'm only going to give you one warning. Keep your mouths shut and accept responsibility for the deed you've done. 'Twill go better for you."

Uncle Brodie added, "Robbie's right, 'tis the only way. Your sire is coming this way, and he does not look happy."

Laird Alexander Grant strode over to stand

in front of his sons, his feet apart and his hands clenched into fists so tight Jake expected to see blood dripping from his palms at any moment.

"Lads, do you not recall the several conversations we've had about respecting females?"

"Aye, Papa, but we…" Jake started.

"Silence!" His sire glowered at him and took two steps forward, opening and closing his fists several times. "You're trying my patience, lad. Do you know who you hurt the most with your actions?"

Jamie squeaked out, "Aye, Mama…"

"Aye, your mama. As you know, I've said any man who put that look in her eyes again would be a dead man. Do you know your only good fortune?"

Jamie shook his head; Jake said naught.

"Your good fortune is I made a promise to your mother that I would not flay you both alive. And do you know why I agreed?"

Jamie shook his head again.

"Because your mother says ten and five is not the age of a man grown. She says you are still lads. And since the look in her eyes would be worse if her eldest sons were dead, I'll not touch you. If I touch you, I fear I'll lose my temper. So you will move that pile of rocks from that spot—" he pointed to the mountainous pile they used for various purposes in the clan, made up of rocks and boulders of all sizes, "—and you'll move them over there." He pointed to a spot way off to the right.

Jamie stared at his brother, a green look in his

face. The pile of stones stood taller than either of them. "All the way over there?"

"Aye."

"Fine, we'll start at sun up," Jake said through clenched teeth. After all, his sire hadn't even allowed them to explain. True, he and Jamie had decided not to tell the whole story, but he could have *asked* them.

"Sun up? Nay, it will be finished by sun up. You'll start now. And if it takes all night, so be it. You had plenty of energy to be randy, you'll have enough energy to move boulders."

Jamie emitted a groan, but then squelched it.

Jake wouldn't give his sire the satisfaction to see him upset about his task. "Fine. I'll get the cart." He walked past his father and headed back up the hill to retrieve a cart from the bailey.

"Lad," his father bellowed.

"Aye?" Jake halted, his hands on his hips.

"No cart. With your hands." Alex finished his statement and spun around to head to the keep.

"What?" Jake yelled after him.

His sire came back and stood face-to-face with Jake. "I said no cart. You have until dawn. If you decide to quit, I'll settle your punishment with my fists, and I'll be sure your mother will not see your bruises."

Jake murmured a few cuss words after his sire left, but then returned to Jamie's side. "Come along. We need to get started. 'Tis not a big concern."

Brodie and Robbie snickered.

Jamie asked, "Why are you laughing?"

"If Jake thinks moving all those rocks that far by hand is not an issue, then he's a bigger fool than I thought." Uncle Robbie chuckled as he cast a sideways glance at Brodie, who had his hand over his mouth. "Were we that foolish at their age?"

"You'll see by day break," Jake said as his uncles headed back toward the keep. He reached down to pick up his first rock. "This will not be that difficult."

Jamie followed him. "Somehow, I think you've just made a big mistake."

By morning, Jamie and Jake were barely moving. They'd almost finished when his father, Uncle Brodie, and Uncle Robbie came along to check their progress. Uncle Robbie whistled when he saw how hard the two of them had worked all night. Barely moving due to exhaustion, they continued until they had moved the last stone. His hands trembling, his muscles twitching from the stress, Jake wiped his sleeve across his forehead, then nodded to his sire before making his way back toward the keep.

"Jake, I did not say you were finished yet." His father's booming voice would awaken everyone in the keep.

He turned back in bafflement. "We moved the rocks just as you said. Now I think after that chore that we both deserve to break our fast."

"No breakfast. I'll have water brought out to you."

"What must we do now?" Truth was, he hadn't thought he was capable of doing anything else.

Alex's gaze narrowed as he stared at his firstborn,

his hands held behind his back. His voice came out as a whisper. "Move them back."

Jake could not believe that he'd heard him correctly. "Move them back? Those boulders? All those ones we just moved?" He thought his head would explode from the rage coursing through him. His father had to be jesting.

"Aye. Do you have a hearing problem?"

"Nay. I just cannot believe you would tell us to do something so ridiculous. It took us all night to move those boulders, and now you want us to move them back?" Jake's voice had almost become a roar.

But his sire roared louder. "Aye, 'tis what I said. Now get started."

That was all it took for Jamie to run over to the pile and pick up two boulders.

Jake shouted to his brother, "Nay, Jamie. I'll not do it."

"What did you say?"

The look in his sire's eyes told him to run, but he stayed rooted to his spot, vowing to stand up to his father.

Jamie froze as his father rushed up to Jake and lifted him into the air. Squeezing Jake's throat, he bellowed, "Repeat what you said, son!"

Jamie came to his brother's defense. "Papa, we were trying to help them. Aye, we'd agreed to the plan at first, but when we saw the lasses had changed their minds, we tried to pull the other lads away from them."

Alex did not move, still holding his son in the air, though Jake was now big enough that he had to use his other hand to keep him balanced. "Jamie, you are excused, return to the keep."

"Papa, I'll stay and help him. I want to."

"Jamie, your laird ordered you to go to the keep."

Robbie and Brodie brought a horse over and helped Jamie onto the horse. Jake had always been a little stronger physically than his brother, and he was so physically exhausted he could barely walk. They left the area with him.

Jake, red in the face, ground out, "I'll do it. And I'll hate you for the rest of my life."

His father let him down and spun on his heel to go back to the keep.

Fortunately, the day was cloudy, and by mid-afternoon the rain came and drenched the sweat off his body, but the slippery rocks did not make his chore any easier. He could tell he had pushed himself too far because his thinking had become hazy. Uncle Robbie had brought him water on two occasions, but other than that he'd seen no one. Apparently, his sire had kept everyone at bay to prevent the chance of him being fed by onlookers who might have felt sorry for him.

Darkness fell and he continued on, finally noticing that the pile was dwindling. He could barely feel his legs moving, but they functioned on their own, dragging his body from one place to another, barely able to carry one rock at a time. He slipped several times in the mud, picking himself up before he continued. His father would not win this one. He'd show him how strong he was, that he could not beat him. He'd move every last stone.

When he had the last two stones in his hands, he slipped again. This time, he couldn't get up. He lay face down in the mud and closed his eyes. A pair of arms picked him up and tossed him over a shoulder with an oomph from him. He knew it to be his sire.

"Foolish lad."

"I did it, Papa."

"I know you did. Stubborn lad. I hope you'll remember it."

"You needn't have done it. I learned my lesson before moving all those rocks. But I wanted to prove to you how tough I am."

His father snorted. "I had to come up with a way to make it sink into that thick skull of yours. When you're older, your mother will never survive it if you attack a lass or disrespect one. How did you learn your lesson? What got through to you?"

"Mama's eyes. I never want to see that look in Mama's eyes again either. You could have asked. 'Twas worse than moving the rocks. How can I ever make it up to her?"

CHAPTER EIGHT

Jake learns how his father handles his anger.

JAKE PACED THE lists. Every once in a while, he'd swing his sword at one opponent or another, but then he'd return to his pacing.

His sire came along mounted on his horse and said, "We trust Ashlyn, or we would not have sent her."

"Aye, but can I not go after her? She should be on her return voyage by now."

"Nay, 'twould endanger her cover. I have a job for you." He tossed the reins of a second horse over to him.

"Now?" Jake gritted his teeth as he stared at his sire. He wished to go against everything his sire had just said, but he could not.

"I need a few trees cut down."

He motioned for Jake to follow him, so he did. They moved out through the forest, moving in the direction that Ashlyn had gone, which only made him even more eager to ride out to greet her.

He galloped behind his sire, feeling the wind in his hair, something he did love, so that helped a bit. His sire brought him through a maze until he finally came to a stop in a clearing. Jake dismounted, staring at his sire. "This is where you go to chop trees when you are upset?" It had long been his sire's habit. Alex always went alone. The twins had oft begged to go along with him, but he'd always denied them. He'd return a few hours later with a smile on his face. Now his sire had finally brought him here.

Jake was stunned, completely stunned, taking everything in about the special place.

"Aye," his father said with a grin. "Do you not approve?" Once he dismounted, he walked over to a large, flat rock that sat atop a hill overlooking Grant land, quite a steep drop beneath them.

Once Jake stood next to his sire, he took a deep breath, shaking his head at the beauty. He'd never seen anything like it.

Alex Grant pointed at all the tree stumps in the clearing. "I judged this to be the best vantage point on our land, and there are plenty of trees to handle my anger when I feel the need." He glanced at his son. "Did I judge well?"

Jake stood next to his father, looking him straight in the eye. "Papa, when did I get to be as tall as you?"

"Och, you've been the size of me for a while, lad. What do you think of my clearing?"

Jake whispered, "Brilliant and beautiful, Papa. All this time, you came here?"

His sire nodded, a smug smile on his face. "Aye. I learned long ago that my bark was too loud for your mother, so when I could feel it building inside me, I came out here. It took me a year to find the exact spot, but ever since then, I've come here to trim trees." He nodded toward all the stumps in sight. "I always go back with a smile on my face. This location also has another advantage—it gives me a perfect view of anyone who's fool enough to try attacking my land. 'Twas time to invite you along. Your mother wouldn't allow me when you were a laddie because of the steep drop."

"I could spend hours here," Jake commented, almost in a trance as he took in everything about the place.

His sire clasped his shoulder as they stared out over the land, and Alex pointed. "My eyes are not the same anymore. Do you see anyone on the rise?"

Jake glanced beneath them, at the path that wound through the forest, across the stream, and through the meadow where Uncle Robbie and Loki had fought Malcolm Murray. Memories flooded his mind, and all fell into place at once, but then he noticed something. His hand shot out, pointing at a spot in the trees down below. "I think I see several horses there. Aye, 'tis Ashlyn."

"Well, then grab an axe. She'll not be here for another hour, and I need a few more trees felled. I like to keep your mama warm in the winter."

Jake smiled as he doffed his tunic and grabbed the axe. Choosing a tree on the other side of the clearing, he swung and swung, the only other sounds being the crack of his father's axe on a tree and the birds in flight over the treetops through the stir of the turning leaves. Hellfire, he had a few more things to learn from his sire yet.

"Papa?" He wiped the sweat from his brow once his first tree fell. "I think we should build a bench or two out here." Glancing at his father's powerful body, he wondered if he'd ever have the same strength.

His father stopped for a moment, then broke into a broad grin. "A bench? Nay, your sire is getting too old. I need a chair with a back to it."

"Papa, you are not that old. We could take the time to relax after we finish our work. And if we leave a few stumps up higher, we'll have a table." Jake waited to see if his father would approve of what he was suggesting. "Do you ever come out here with Uncle Robbie or Uncle Brodie?"

"Nay. Neither shares my temper, but 'tis the best way to release it." He scanned the area, apparently considering Jake's proposal. "I like the idea of having an ale or two with my son after we're done chopping wood."

"And Jamie, too?"

"Probably not. He would be welcome, but he does not share my temper. I'm afraid you and I are the only ones with it. You have to have it to appreciate this place and its purpose."

Jake couldn't stop himself from staring at his father's creation, taking in the beauty and the quiet of the place. "I feel better already. I'd like to build the chairs. If I get the opportunity, it will take my mind off Aline until she returns."

His father quirked a brow at him. "You mean if she returns?"

"Aye. She'll return. I know not her purpose in wanting to go back to that place, but I'll discover it one way or another."

"There's only one other lad who has the same

temperament as we do, the type who would both enjoy and understand this place."

Jake was puzzled, unable to think of anyone at the moment.

"Do not think too hard. I believe he's almost here, ahead of Ashlyn. We missed him before." Alex tipped his head toward the path beneath them, closer than the one Ashlyn had been on.

Jake yelled, "Uncle Logan!"

His sire smiled and said, "He'll fit right in."

CHAPTER FIFTEEN

*Alex knows when to give in to his dear Madeline…
and Maddie knows when to speak her mind.*

THE LADS ALL stood outside the chamber talking, mayhap sensing that Maddie wanted a private word with her husband, but Alex was already inside the room and behind the desk. Maddie walked into the room with Jake, then shut the door before moving in front of Jake, facing Alex. He expected his mother had followed his sire's cardinal rule—never question him in front of the clan. He would listen to all she had to say behind closed doors.

"Maddie," Alex said. "I know you wish to clean his wounds…"

His mother held her hand up to his sire, lifting her chin a notch. With a smile on her face, she spoke with a strength Jake recognized, and his sire listened, as he always did. Jake could feel a weakening starting in his legs, so he locked his knees to stay upright.

"Husband, may I take this moment to remind you of what we both went through to bring this lad into this world. I would also wish to remind you of what your dear mother's first teachings were to your sister, and…" Her breath hitched with emotion, and she stopped speaking for a moment to regain control.

Jake's sire moved out from behind the desk, his gaze on Maddie. "And?" He brushed a stray lock of hair back from her face, tucking it behind her ear before his thumb rubbed her cheek.

This is when Jake had learned the most from his parents. Their respect for each other amazed him. Alex Grant would stop speaking for only two people—his wife and his king.

"And I'd like to remind you of dear Kyle Maule's sire, bless his soul." She leaned toward her husband and he caught her, one hand on her hip and the other on the back of her neck.

Kyle Maule's father had died from complications from a wound that had never been cleaned.

His sire settled his lips on her forehead, then leaned back and said, "I see no reason why we cannot converse with him while you cleanse his wounds. We shall follow you." And just like that, Alex Grant changed his plan, giving in to his wife's tender needs. He explained the new circumstances to the others, and then Maddie pivoted and led them into another chamber used for healing.

CHAPTER TWENTY-ONE

And here is the sign that Jake has matured.
Alex's response surprises him but is a terrific
example of true love.

"WHY DID YOU stop Mama from hitting us that night in the stables? I almost wish she had." If she had, he may not have been so foolish out in the rock field.

"If I had been worried about you, I would have let her hit you. You deserved it. But I was worried about *her*."

Jake turned sideways to look at his father. "What? Why?"

"Because if she had connected with your face, she would have had to deal with the guilt of becoming violent. She would have considered herself no better than an abuser. I couldn't allow her to go through that."

"You thought of all that in such a short time?" Jake was astonished at his father's insight.

"When you love someone, you understand how their mind works. She only cried twice for *almost* hitting you. If she had hit you, she'd probably still be crying from the guilt."

ASHLYN

BOOK 5

*Ashlyn becomes the archer she always wished to be,
and Alex knows her skill better than she does.*

CHAPTER SEVENTEEN

*Ashlyn earns praise from her uncle, the great
Alex Grant, after many fought so hard against
the elusive villain MacNiven. After chastising
herself for only wounding him, her uncle viewed
her actions as something to be proud of, something
Ashlyn hadn't considered.*

ASHLYN MOVED INTO the other chamber
where her uncles, Logan and Alex, sat with
Jake and her stepsire Robbie. Jake stood and
ushered her to a chair. "Come and sit. You look
exhausted. If you've the strength, please tell us
what transpired."

She explained about the cottage they'd used for
shelter in the storm, and how they had found the
dead deer and followed the tracks to the castle.
Only two eyebrows quirked at the mention of
the two of them staying alone in the hut—her
stepsire's and Jake's. Naught was said by anyone.
She gave them the general location of the
new path, and how they had followed it to the
crumbling keep.

"Logan tells me you believe 'twas MacNiven.
Are you sure?"

"I saw him from afar with his helm on, but
Magnus recognized him. The talk we overheard
certainly sounded like him."

"Any idea what their plans are?" Uncle Alex asked, drumming his fingers on the table.

"When my arrows killed two of his men, MacNiven raced for the front of the keep. He gave instructions for one of the men to kill Magnus, then he whirled around and fled. The others followed him. I put an arrow in the belly of the man aiming for Magnus, and I tried to shoot MacNiven," she paused, trying to collect herself. "I caught him in the shoulder, but then I noticed Magnus was barely moving and another ran after him, so I shot him in his chest and climbed out of the tree."

The floodgates finally opened, and down came the tears. "I could have tried to shoot MacNiven again, but Magnus...I decided...the other man could have killed him." Her face now covered with tears, she was unable to finish her sentence.

Jake, seated next to her, wrapped his arm around her shoulder and kissed her cheek. "I'm quite pleased you chose to take care of my best friend instead of taking off after that fool. 'Twas the right thing to do."

"I could have put an end to all of this, but then I..."

"I would have done the same. I agree with Jake, you made the correct choice." Uncle Logan crossed his arms in front of his chest.

"We all agree, now you need to accept 'tis true." Uncle Alex stood and moved to the door, filling up the entire frame. "Jake, there's little more we can do. He's a strong warrior. I expect we'll talk to him by the morrow. Logan, come back to the great hall for an ale?"

Before they left, Alex stopped with his hand on the door handle. "Ashlyn, you alone wounded the man who has escaped all of us, you've made me proud to call you a Grant warrior. Hold your head high."

"My thanks, my laird." She sniffled because her tears had finally slowed. The reality of what her laird had just said settled on her. Was it the truth? Was she the only warrior to have injured MacNiven? She fought with everything she had back at that curtain wall, but she'd been ready to go home when in Edinburgh. There was no reason to be embarrassed. Suddenly, she looked at all that transpired in a different light. Uncle Alex was proud of her!

JAMIE

AND

GRACIE

BOOK 7

This is a powerful story of father and son.
Jamie loves Gracie but can't admit it to himself.
Alex will make certain he figures it out.

CHAPTER ELEVEN

*In this scene, the suitors arrive to see the most
beautiful lass in all the Highlands, Gracie, but Jamie
can't handle watching her with another man.
Baron Crichton learns not to raise a blade to a
woman in Castle Grant.*

"I WOULD LIKE SOME time to get to know you, my lady. Come along with me to this table where we may speak in private."

Gracie did not say anything, just nodded in agreement and then searched the crowd around them. She noticed Laird Chisholm was speaking with her sire, but she could not find Jamie. She needed to know that he was doing as he'd promised—that he was watching over her. There. He stood a short distance away, and while he was indeed watching them, he made no movement toward them. His arms were crossed and the rest of his body was in a warrior's stance. His facial expression was quite serious, but it couldn't have been any worse than hers. For some reason, she was paralyzed in fear.

Rather than stopping at the table, the baron managed to maneuver her toward a passageway off the hall. It led to her uncle Brodie's tower, which was well lit with torches, but the passageway itself was darker than she would have liked. Still, she was doing what was expected of her, was she not?

She smiled at the baron. "Forgive me, but you are the first baron I have met. How should I address you?"

"How refreshing that you choose to ask instead of risking a mistake. I am pleased with that quality. You may call me Baron Crichton. If we become more familiar, my given name is Gordon, but that would be premature at this point. Do you not agree?"

"Of course, Baron Crichton."

"An agreeable, beautiful woman. Just what I have been searching for." He reached up and ran a finger down her cheekbone. "You are quite elegant, a true beauty. The noble blood in you is so obvious. Regal, just as a baroness should be."

He gave her a tender kiss, short but sweet—a kiss that confused her because it was nice. As nice as Jamie's? Nay, nothing could be, but she still felt something.

"How do you feel about becoming a baroness, running my household, traveling to Edinburgh to see our king? I'll see that you have several maids to take care of you. You'll give me the finest sons and the loveliest daughters. Your every desire will be met."

Gracie did not know how to answer him, because she suddenly felt uncertain. She'd sworn never to leave Grant land, but if Jamie was not interested, then should she marry another? She did want her own bairns.

Suppose the worst thing possible happened. Suppose Jamie fell in love with someone else, married someone from afar who would move here. Would she be able to watch him with another? The prospect of becoming a baroness was more enticing than that. If Jamie changed his mind, she would reconsider, but what if he did not? No one else had interested her at all, but this man was different, mysterious.

A voice interrupted them. "Gracie, is he bothering you?" Jamie came down the passageway toward them.

The baron turned to address Jamie. "Nay, I am not bothering the lady. Take your leave."

"I asked the lady, not you. Gracie?"

"And I am giving you a direct order."

"I do not take orders from you." With each comment, Jamie took a step closer.

The baron pulled out his small sword, and the swish of the blade against its sheath brought two of his guards into the passageway. "Who are you?"

"I am her cousin, and 'tis my duty to ensure she is treated with respect. Is he treating you respectfully, Gracie?"

She gave a quick nod, not wishing to anger the baron, pleading with her gaze for Jamie to back down. Something told her this would not end well at all.

"Of course I am treating her with respect. She will be my baroness, and as such, deserves your respect as well. You will address her as Lady Grace, not Gracie." He gave an odd sound after he stated her childhood name. "Do I also detect a touch of jealousy?"

"Do not be ridiculous, but I will protect her reputation."

"I think you want more of her than her reputation, and I mean to put an end to it." His sword, which had been down at his side, was now raised, and the baron stood in a fighting stance.

Gracie's heart started beating doubly fast, as if it might jump out of her chest. Jamie drew his own sword as the baron's minions approached with their weapons raised. "You're on Grant land, so drop your sword unless you wish to start a clan war. We did not invite your suit, and now you may consider it rejected. Take yourself back to Duncrub, Baron. You're no longer welcome."

"I'll stay as long as I wish."

"Gracie, step back. I do not want you hurt."

"Jamie," she whispered, "three to one. Please do not…" She knew her words had not been heard and would not be heeded. The tension in the passageway was strong enough for all to feel. What if he was hurt? What if he was killed? She couldn't bear it.

"Nay, three to three." Her uncle Brodie and his son Braden appeared out of the tower room, swords drawn.

"Stand down, all of you." Uncle Alex's booming voice echoed down the passageway. Gracie leaned against the wall, trying to make herself as small as possible.

The baron was not about to give up so easily. "This fool is interfering, Grant. I am simply attempting to get to know your niece better. His actions are inappropriate."

Alex Grant's muscular body, still larger than any in the clan, blocked almost the entire passageway.

His sword was drawn, and he still had a reputation as the best swordsman in all the land. No one made a move to anger him. "You are inappropriate, Baron Crichton, by drawing your sword in my hall in front of a woman of my clan. Drop your weapon and leave my land. Take your guards with you. You are no longer welcome here."

The baron lowered his sword, but did not sheath it. "Laird Grant, I request the lady's hand in marriage, respectfully. I ask that her sire accompany her to my keep so we may become better acquainted without the presence of so many interfering suitors, including her cousin here."

Jamie barked, "I am not a suitor."

"I will take my men and depart on friendly terms if you agree to bring her to my land, escorted by any men you choose except this one." His sword made a quick lashing in Jamie's direction.

"That one is my son, and I'll do as I see fit. If you wish to do battle, it will be you and me in the lists, Baron."

While Alex waited for the baron's response, Gracie could hear the panting in the room, each of the men ready to fight at the slightest provocation. She could see Kyla had arrived at the end of the passageway along with Gracie's mother and father.

The baron paused, his gaze taking in all in the passageway, then nodded to his men. "We shall take our leave, but I have already petitioned the court for Lady Grace's hand in marriage, and I expect you to bring her to my land within half a sennight. If not, I shall bring an army of men to retrieve her myself." He sheathed his sword, then gave Gracie a short bow. "Until then, my lady."

Gracie must have heard him wrong. Petitioned the court? Did that mean what she thought it did? Had the baron asked the king for her hand in marriage? Her heart pounded loud enough to be heard by others, she feared. She attempted to lock her legs so the trembling brought on by the argument would stop.

If the baron had in truth made such a petition, her destiny would be sealed once the king agreed.

No one moved until the baron was out the door. In a low voice, Alex asked, "What provoked him, Jamie?"

"I did. I did not like that he brought her down a dark passageway, so I came to investigate." He gave Gracie a furtive glance. "'Twas a hunch—my intuition told me not to trust the man."

Alex turned to Gracie.

"Was the baron inappropriate with you?"

Gracie did not know what to say. If she said aye, the issue with the baron would be over. But did she want it to be over? Her world had always been small and simple since she'd joined the Grants, but now it seemed as if every decision she made would have an enormous impact.

"Papa, why are you putting her through this?" Jamie pressed. "Leave her be. She does not wish to leave our clan. Marrying the baron would require her to go."

The words were kind and caring, but he did not even look at her as he said it.

"You came here to tell us that the baron has petitioned the king for her hand," Alex said, his voice loud and sonorous. "You know that if the king orders the marriage, refusing him would be considered an act of treason. Torrian went through this."

Her hands shook as she reached up to brush a stray hair from her face. Dear Lord, she was doomed. She wished to tear down the passageway screaming loud enough for all to hear. She wanted no part of any of this. The only thought in her mind was that she wished to return to the safety and tranquility of the loch, her parents' home. It had been a mistake to want more.

"Can you not petition the king to refuse him?" Jamie asked, his cheeks turning red. "I do not think they suit each other. Grandmama said that we should all have a say in our marriages. Uncle Robbie may be Gracie's stepsire, but she is still a Grant."

Gracie held her breath, waiting to hear Uncle Alex's response.

"This seems to be more about what you want than about what Gracie wants."

Jamie threw his arms up in the air. "I do not know what you expect me to do, Papa. You taught me to protect the innocent, but now you've changed your mind."

"I do not think Gracie is an innocent. She's a woman grown."

Jamie's expression changed from one of anger to one of acquiescence. He bowed to Gracie. "Forgive me. I'll not intrude on your life again." He spun on his heel and stalked away without saying another word to his sire.

A moment later, Alex shouted after his son, "Jamie, in the stables at high sun on the morrow. Be there, or I'll come and find you." He said it without looking at him.

CHAPTER TWELVE

Jamie knows enough to watch out for that tic in his father's jaw. So here I reprint the entire chapter. Why? Because this is Alexander Grant. Enjoy!

JAMIE STRODE TOWARD the stables, tipping his head back to check the sun. He hadn't found Gracie last night, so he'd vowed to find her sometime later today. If he survived this meeting with his sire, he'd find her right away and explain his foolishness to her. He'd go with her if she had to go to the baron's land—of course he would. Staying behind was just unacceptable. What the hell had he been thinking?

His sire's voice called out to him as soon as he entered the stable. Jamie sighed. From the sound of his da's voice, he knew exactly where he was—Mac's stall.

That's what he'd called it for as long as he could remember. Mac had chosen a stall for himself. He'd had a storage closet built into it so he could keep all his tools there for when he groomed the horses. He always kept sweet treats for the wee ones and the horses in his special closet. It was a place where Jamie had spent a great deal of time as a lad.

"Why here, Papa?" He noticed all the stable lads were gone, not a good sign.

His father stood from the bale of hay where he'd been seated. "Why not? You are acting like a horse's arse, just as you did shortly after Mac passed on. Do you not recall?"

Jamie did not want to look at his sire. That time had been so painful for him, but he had not let himself cry. Instead, he'd become so furious with the world, he'd sniped at each and every person who crossed his path.

"Aye, I recall. But I was young, Papa. Every time I came here 'twas painful for me. Why mention it now? No one has died."

"Your mother and I believe the way you're acting now is exactly the same way you were acting then."

"So your plan is to fight me until I start crying? If I recall, 'twas what happened the first time. You swung your sword at me until I was so upset that I cried and cried. I was a lad then. You'll not be able to make me cry now. I tell you, the two situations have naught to do with each other."

"I think they do," his sire's voice came out in a whisper, and he stood there as he always did— calm and controlled.

Telling Jamie what he thought.

Telling Jamie what to do.

Telling Jamie how to run his life.

Jamie did not care to listen any longer.

His sire narrowed his gaze at his son and lifted his chin, spinning his sword with his hand, acting like he knew everything. "I think 'tis exactly the same."

And Jamie's temper blew. "I do not, and I'm tired of everyone telling me what to do, where to go. The bastard deserved to be thrown off our land, putting his hands all over Gracie."

His sire just leveled him with a look.

He'd never known anyone who could control his temper like his father could. Alex could be furious and one would never know it, but Jamie had learned the subtle signs that meant he was close to losing his temper. He'd see that wee tic in his sire's jaw and he'd nod to Jake, telling him to start running.

That tic hadn't started yet.

"You and Mama taught me that a Highlander should protect women. I protected Gracie against Sean and Chisholm and the baron just as you raised me to do. Why was I wrong?" He could feel his voice growing louder, but he did not care. It felt good to yell at his father. "Did you ever consider that mayhap I did not *want* to protect her, that it was our clan's code of honor that made me go after the baron?"

The tic in his sire's jaw started to wiggle. It did not matter. He could not stop now.

"The way the men all circled her, you should have assigned her a team of protectors. Mayhap had three guards follow her everywhere. The lass draws men like bees to a honeycomb—all of them flitting around her, trying to sniff her, trying to lick her, trying to…"

"Get your arse outside and draw your sword, lad."

Jamie stared at his father, at the tic of his jaw, at his narrowed gaze, another bad sign.

But he didn't stop, plowing ahead without any thought of the repercussions. The anger had grown in him over the past weeks, peaking last night. "They wished to stick their cock in her like she was a common wench, a whore…" he growled.

His sire's voice bellowed through the rafters. "Get your arse outside and draw your weapon, lad, or it'll be my fists."

Jamie hollered back, "Suits me. Kick my arse any way you want. Mayhap I'll kick yours." He stalked outside, took his shirt off, and grabbed his sword.

His sire came at him with a roar, his blade poised over his head, waiting for Jamie to ready himself. Once they were far enough from the building, Jamie charged toward his sire, forcing the confrontation. He would hold back nothing. Metal clashed against metal, and though Jamie's muscles begged for mercy, he would not stop. He could not. He swung and swung, stopping his father's advances. Out of the corner of his eye, he saw Jake and Connor, but they stayed back. This was between him and his sire.

He'd had enough. He could take no more of watching those bastards flitting around his Gracie.

His Gracie! Aye, he was supposed to protect her, but he'd failed.

He swung his sword from the side, hoping to catch his sire off-guard, but Alex was faster, and he swung with a force that knocked him on his arse.

He hadn't protected her as he ought to have. Those bastards had touched her.

He jumped up and ran straight at his father with his sword, and again his father knocked him on his arse.

Laird Chisholm had kissed her. *Kissed his Gracie.*

Jumping to his feet, he spun in a circle and brought his sword down on his father's weapon so hard that sparks flew.

Sean had kissed her…*his Gracie.*

He swung again and his father knocked his weapon out of his hands. He grabbed it quick and ran at him again, but he knocked him away.

The bastard baron had *kissed his Gracie*!

His sire stood in front of him, heaving, his sword down in front of him. "Jamie, this is no different than before. You couldn't handle losing Mac. Can you not see what's bothering you?"

"Nay. Naught is bothering me. Draw your weapon, Papa."

His father lifted his sword again, but with a different attitude. "Can you not see what you're doing? You're deliberately keeping your distance from the lass. She'll not hurt you like Mac did." His father let up a touch, though he continued a light parry while they talked.

"Aye, she could," he said, choking on the words.

"You've lost loved ones before, I know that, but have you watched them die in front of you? Da, a bolt of lightning shot down out of the sky and sucked the life right out of him, and there was nothing I could do but *watch*. I'll never put myself in such a position again."

"What happened to Mac was a terrible accident, but it wasn't a common one. We did not raise you to be afraid of life, Jamie. Stop hiding from it."

"I held him in my hands, Da. As soon as I touched him, I knew he was dead. Women die in childbirth, from the fever. What if…" He couldn't even say it. The thought of Gracie dying made him ill.

They continued to move and spar, but Jamie said naught. He told himself that the water around his eyes was only sweat, but part of him knew better. He'd never forget that night. Never forget seeing someone alive one moment and dead the next.

His sire's voice came again. "You need to knock that wall down, lad. If you do not, I'll do what I can to knock it down for you. You need Gracie in your life and you know it. You're afraid you're losing her. 'Tis why you are fighting everything and everyone around you."

Jamie spun in a circle and attempted to knock the sword out of his sire's hands, but his father did something new, twisting his sword in such a way that Jamie lost his grip. The weapon flew out of his hands, and his sire flipped him onto his back, putting his foot on his chest.

He stared up at Alex, shocked that his sire had beaten him so easily.

"Now, son, you're going to listen to me and I do not wish to hear a word from you." His voice fell to a whisper, low enough so no one else could hear them. "You lost to me because your emotions are ripping you apart, both your mind and your heart. You couldn't handle losing Mac, and you are about to lose another person you love, Gracie, and you cannot handle that either. I came out here to knock some sense into you, hopefully, and help you realize that your heart belongs to that wee lassie you loved many moons ago. Her smile might melt a thousand men's hearts, but her heart belongs to you. Now you have to be smart enough to accept that truth and offer for her. If you do not, you will lose her, and she'll be gone forever. You cannot spend your whole life being afraid to love. You must trust your own heart.

"Now, I have a letter that was written a long while ago, and it belongs to you. I set it in Mac's cupboard. When you've finished reading it, come see me at the door to the stables. We'll see if we cannot come up with a plan to end this foolishness."

His sire picked up his sword and strode into the stables, leaving him flat on his back. He stared at the sky for a long time, not moving, thinking about all his sire had said.

Was he right? Did Gracie truly love him? Jamie had to admit to having strong feelings for her, stronger every day, but he'd done his best to bury them. Fear had stopped him, fear of losing her, fear of her not reciprocating his feelings, fear of not being good enough, fear of too many things.

After he mulled it over for a while, he stood up and walked back toward the stables. Jake stood a good distance away, but Jamie waved him away. This was something he needed to do alone. He sheathed his sword and moved into Mac's stall. There in the cupboard sat a folded piece of parchment.

His hand shook at the sudden surety that this was a note from his beloved Mac. He opened it and began to read:

Jamie,
I had your mother pen this letter before I got to be too old to think clearly. I miss you, wee bean.

Jamie smiled at the term. He had no doubt that Mac had dictated this note to him. He had not called him wee bean in front of many.

I know you'll be upset when I go. You're young and well, so you do not understand death. But I will go willingly when my time comes so I can be with my Alice again.
I know you've told me about all the things you wish to do in your lifetime, but I wish to tell you something different. 'Tis not what's out there that is the most important, but what's at home. I know you dream of traveling and exploring, of being a hero like your da, all the things young lads wish to do.
Mayhap it sounds simple, but my advice is to find your lass. Naught will make you happier than the love of a sweet lass. You are too young to believe me now, but one day I hope you will believe me. I know she's out

*there for you, but your heart will tell you when it's time.
I fought loving my Alice, my sweet flower, but marrying
her was the best thing I've ever done. Our life together
made me happiest of all.*

*Find your flower. Follow your heart and do not fight
your feelings as I did. I almost missed the greatest gift
in my life.*

Be a good lad now. Someday we'll meet again.
Mac

Jamie folded the parchment and tucked it into his sporran.

He needed to find his flower, Gracie.

His father stood with his arms crossed, right where he'd said he would be. None of the stable lads had returned yet, probably at his sire's request.

"Did you read the note, Papa?"

"I did."

"What do you think?"

"It does not matter what I think. What do you think?"

"I think he has a good point." Jamie stared at the ground in front of him, unsure of what to say to his sire.

His sire, not one to overuse words, said, "I agree."

"Do you think Gracie is my flower?"

"I do." His father clasped his shoulder. His sire stared up at the sky, a strange look crossed his face—an expression of almost…delight. "Stablemasters are special."

"They are?"

"Aye. If 'twere not for Mac and my stablemaster

before him, Old Hugh, I never would have found and married your mother."

The thought shocked him. "Truly?"

"Aye. I would not have enjoyed my life without her. She means as much to me as Alice did to Mac. Listen to the old men of the world, Jamie."

"Did Jake go through this with Aline?"

His sire shook his head. "Jake sees what's right in front of him, but does not pay attention to what's around him. All he saw was Aline; he did not care about the circumstances that brought her to us. You see everything around you, but not what's right in front of you."

"Gracie's right in front of me."

"Aye."

"Does it matter that we're cousins?" he asked. "I worried 'twas wrong." He glanced at his sire, hoping he would approve of what he wished to do. Men that underestimated Alex Grant were foolish. He couldn't believe the battle he'd just had with his sire.

"Nay. She's not a blood cousin. I don't think Gracie sees you as a cousin."

Jamie thought that was a good sign. He did not want Gracie to see him as a cousin at all. He thought about each of the kisses they'd shared. She'd never pushed him away the way she'd pushed against Sean. She'd looked extremely uncomfortable with Laird Chisholm. Was it his imagination or had she fit him just perfectly? She'd never pushed away from him but instead found the perfect way to melt into him, her softness something he suddenly craved. "I need to find her, talk to her. Do you think Uncle Robbie would accept my request for her hand?"

"Aye. But I would suggest courting her. You need to talk to Gracie first."

His father's tone had changed to one of encouragement, the rough edge he'd had before their swordplay now gone. He'd been crude about Gracie, said horrible things, all signs of his jealousy. For some unknown reason, it all started to make sense to him. His attitude had been all about her, though he wouldn't admit it to many.

"You and Mama will support me?"

"Aye." His sire smiled, sheathing his sword.

"I need to find Gracie, then talk to Uncle Robbie and Aunt Caralyn."

His father nodded before he glanced up at the sky. "That could be a problem."

"Why?"

"Because Gracie decided she wished to go to the baron's this morn. They left at dawn."

CHAPTER TWENTY

Alex in battle, defending his clan…

KYLA TOOK HER hand and said, "We have no time to waste, just come." She tugged her down the passageway and up the long staircase to the parapets. Once outside, they ran around the curtain wall until they reached the front, where they had a good view of the gates. Some of the guards who waited in the crenellations with their bows pushed them out of the way.

The sight sent a wave of panic through Gracie. "There are so many." A sea of warriors sat on their horses in the meadow, the Baron of Duncrub's flag waving above them in the breeze. Uncle Alex took his time getting out there, making their enemy wait as he often did. Her sire, Uncle Brodie, Jake, and Jamie already sat on their horses in front of the gates, and a score of Grant guards waited behind them and off to the side of the field.

"Will we be able to hear? What do you think he wants?" Kyla whispered.

Gracie said, with as much conviction as she could muster, "He cannot want me unless he wishes to tie me to a whipping post and give me forty lashes in' front of his clan." She chewed on her thumbnail as she stared out over the land. The sight of the baron, even from a distance, sickened her. "We might be able to hear. There's no wind."

Alex moved to the front of the Grants, and the guards all moved aside for their laird.

"Da looks bigger than everyone," Kyla said. "Still…it frightens me when he goes to battle. What would I do if I ever lost him? The baron thinks he's weak."

Gracie reached down to clasp Kyla's hand in hers, giving it a squeeze. "He's the strongest laird in all the land. Everyone knows that but the baron."

Uncle Alex roared loud enough for all to hear.

"State your business. You're not welcome on my land."

"I'll be quick, Grant," the baron bellowed back, his voice sickeningly familiar. "I want your niece, Grace. We arranged for our betrothal before the mighty storm hit us. She became frightened and ran away. I want her back."

"You gave my niece bruises on her face and neck. She'll go nowhere with you."

"I'll not leave until I get her."

Gracie could almost see the fire in the baron's eyes. She saw Jamie's horse prance a bit, and fear clutched her heart, but Jake grabbed the mare's reins and shot his brother a quieting look.

"You did not hear me, Crichton. You'll not get her. And you will have to get past my sword to get to her."

"You have twenty-four hours to send her out. If she's not here by then, we will attack and kill as many of your clan as we can, including your women and children. I have a priest who will marry us as soon as she leaves your gate. Think on it, Grant. You may have many men, but I have two hundred more warriors coming."

"You have no right to the lass, so leave now."

"Och," the baron chuckled. "You are wrong about that. I took her maidenhead. She belongs to me. The king will grant my request as soon as my expert examines her. Twenty-four hours."

Gracie turned around and ran all the way back to the doorway, down the staircase, and into her room. Now what was she to do? The vile man had lied about her. Jamie was the one who'd taken her maidenhead, but if she were examined, the doctor would say it was gone.

She would lose no matter what.

CHAPTER TWENTY-ONE

Alex goes down in battle…

JAMIE RODE HIS horse to the left of his sire, and slightly behind him. The laird was always in the center, flanked by Uncle Robbie on one side, and Uncle Brodie on the other. Uncle Logan had been placed in charge of the warriors in the periphery so was not with them. Alex's sons rode behind him—Jake on one end, Jamie on the other, and Connor in the center—but their cousins Roddy and Braden rode between them. This was done to ensure that two of the laird's heirs could not be taken out in one swing. Magnus was behind Jake, and Finlay sat behind Jamie, their primary job to protect the laird's heirs.

A sea of warriors in the Grant plaid fanned out behind them including Tormod.

Jamie had seen the archers in the curtain wall. He'd bet his cousins Molly and Ashlyn were among them, sickness and all for Ashlyn, because they were both so powerful and true. Wee Kenzie was perched on the wall with his slinger.

The baron came forward as far as the Grant warriors allowed him, riding side by side with another man, probably Simon de La Porte. He guided his horse to a stop in front of Jamie's sire. "Where is Gracie?"

"Gracie, who is married to my son, Jamie, is inside where I told her to stay. She'll not be going anywhere with you."

"That's either a lie or they were just married," the man said, his eyes practically glowing with fury. "I told you I took her maidenhead. You'd allow your pup to marry a wench? She gave it freely to me."

Anger burned Jamie from the inside out, but he soothed himself with the thought that the baron would pay. It was only a matter of when.

"You have the tongue of a viper, and you disrespect my daughter-in-law," Alex bellowed. "Take your men from my land or prepare to do battle, Crichton."

He knew his sire's tactics. The baron would never make it off their land in one piece. Alex was only acting reticent about the attack because he wanted the baron to believe he'd been right to think the Grants weak.

By the time he realized how wrong he was, it would be too late.

No one moved for several moments. Jamie took the time to size up their opponents. He noted that some looked young, though that meant little enough on a battlefield. He knew wee Kenzie could be deadly with his sling, and he was just a laddie. A moment later, the baron let out his war whoop. He swung his sword arm over his head as he rode straight for Jamie's sire.

Alex fought him off, giving his own war whoop to signal to the Grant warriors that the battle had begun.

The field erupted into chaos and death.

Jamie moved in next to Uncle Brodie, keeping an eye on his sire as he blocked blows and made them, but Alex did not need anyone's help—he sent the baron back easily, though two other warriors rode in to take his place. Jake forged ahead as he usually did, mounting his attack from in front of his sire but off to his right.

The sound of swords clashing echoed across the Highlands. The reverberation was so deafening that Jamie could not hear aught else. His knees controlled his steed as his weapon caught one rider in the belly, then another in the arm. Men's screams rent the air as arrows flew overhead. He fought and fought, fueled by thoughts of the baron and Gracie—he wanted to be the one to kill the man who'd attacked his wife—yet trying to keep his emotions in check.

The baron had backed up after the initial onslaught, showing his true spirit. Jamie decided to make his way in that direction. He would knock that smirk off the baron's face.

As the battle raged on, he noticed the number of red plaids now outnumbered the number of green plaids. He attempted to search the injured for Grants, but it was almost impossible because warriors were still coming at them from many directions. Bodies were strewn all over the ground, and horses fell and rolled in the skirmish, some getting up and wandering off.

Jamie's sword arm, aching and tired, continued to strike and defend, but something caught him from the corner of his eye—his sire tumbling off his horse.

The man who'd dealt Alex a blow was preparing to strike him again, but Jamie rode hard toward them and took the man out. His war whoop came next, followed by the words they'd always dreaded to hear, "Protect your laird!"

Immediately men on horseback surrounded his sire, who still lay on the ground, blood darkening his plaid. His eyes were open, but he appeared dazed. He'd never thought to see the time his sire would be beaten on the battlefield, the man had appeared invincible to all. Yet here he was flat on the ground, unable to protect himself. He prayed his eyes deceived him and his sire would get up soon.

There was no sign of Jake either. Magnus, Connor, Braden, and Roddy had all joined him in the circle around his sire, but where the hell was Jake? When he finally set eyes on his brother, he saw he was far ahead of them, still fighting like a fierce warrior. He had no idea their sire was down.

Jamie yelled again, "Protect your laird!" Two more rode in hard to join them, and the weight on Jamie's shoulders eased a slight bit. He could protect his sire from further damage until the conflict ended. The number of green plaids were dwindling, so the battle would end sooner rather than later. Then he saw something that took his breath away and stole what was left of his composure.

Gracie on horseback. Gracie was riding hard off into the forest, far away from the battle. But why? What had possessed her to leave the safety of the keep?

Jamie's composure left him. Did he chase after Gracie and leave his sire undefended? There was no one around to take his place in the circle. He swung his sword again and took two more bastards down. From his position, he could see a sea of red plaids streaming toward the baron's men from behind—Uncle Logan's warriors.

They would help end this.

"Gracie! What are you doing?" Frantic, he called out to Finlay, "Finlay, cover my sire. I must go after Gracie."

Finlay answered his call immediately.

The worst of all happened. The baron had also seen Gracie leave and charged after her. Jamie tried again to get his brother back, but he was too far away to see or hear what was happening. Two Grant warriors came up from the back of the field, so he bellowed. "Here. Protect your laird." Three had filled the spaces, so he galloped after Gracie as fast as he could.

Gracie was still ahead of both of them, but the melee slowed her. She stopped once to cover her head with her arms, screaming for them to end the battle. Jamie knew the precise moment when the baron realized he would catch her because an evil grin crossed the man's face. He moved toward Gracie at about the same pace Jamie was moving—slow but persistent. There were too many warriors between him and Gracie and the baron.

Jamie yelled again. "Kill him. Take the baron out." No one could hear him over all the screams. He glanced back at his sire again. The blood stain at his midsection continued to grow and his eyes were now squeezed shut. "Da, fight, do you hear me? Fight, stay alert."

What the hell was he to do? All of a sudden, all the faces around him seemed to blend together. Dirt and sweat and spit and blood flew everywhere. He was losing the ability to distinguish between the enemy and his brethren. A shock of bright hair popped out against the others, and he saw the baron was now only a short distance from his bride.

Jamie lost all control. He kneed his horse and headed straight for the baron, swinging his sword arm over his head. The strike did not land, which threw Jamie's balance off and gave the baron a chance to flee toward Gracie. Horror overtook Jamie as he watched the baron ride hard in her direction.

His sire's words rang out in his mind. *Take your emotions out of it, Jamie. You'll not best your enemy if you allow your emotions to overtake your reason.*

Then, a miracle happened. A horse appeared out of the dust, cutting the baron off from behind, forcing him to slow enough for Jamie to catch him. Tormod. His friend had given him the chance he needed.

Forcing Gracie out of his mind, Jamie slashed

his sword at the baron again. The bastard locked gazes with him, smiling that hideous grin.

Jamie swung at him, but the baron easily blocked his blow. They parried a few more times before the baron struck at his lowest point with words.

"She's a whore, Grant. You married a whore, and I liked her."

Jamie ignored him, knowing the feint for what it was. He would not be distracted. He faked a swing at the man, who immediately raised his sword to block it, then changed his direction at the last instant and buried his sword in the baron's belly, a death blow for sure. Tormod struck him with another blow from behind.

The baron dropped his sword and grabbed his belly, and Jamie pulled his sword out, wiping his blade across the man's legs just before he fell to the ground. Jamie took a moment to gather his strength, searching his immediate area for any more warriors in green. Mayhap they'd leave now that their baron was dead.

But it wasn't to be. The man who'd rode in with the baron, probably Simon de La Porte, barked orders at the remaining guards. Four warriors came toward Jamie and Tormod, but they managed to fight them off together. Tormod did battle from one side while Jamie attacked from the other, slicing bellies and flesh everywhere they could. Men fell to their right and to their left.

A voice came from atop of one of the towers. "Kill them all, Tormod! That's my brother."

Lyall. His brother was standing watch on the parapets, and he'd seen Tormod fighting like a man set on fire.

Uncle Logan and four more Grant warriors joined them, and together they fought off the last few green-clad warriors around them. When Jamie glanced at his brother in the front lines, he saw that Jake was still holding strong, fighting two of the green-clad men at once.

Moments later, the few remaining enemy warriors fled the scene, Simon de La Porte with them.

Jamie immediately searched the area for any sign of Gracie. There was none. He'd lost sight of her when he'd met with the baron, but she could not have gone far. Perhaps she was hiding in the trees.

His breathing still ragged, Jamie rode back to the circle of protectors surrounding his sire.

"Where's Gracie?" he asked.

No one answered.

"She was just here on horseback." He searched the grounds for light hair, but there was no sign of her.

Jake came up behind him. "Nice battle with the baron. Great way to put an end to this ruckus. Why is everyone in a circle?" He pointed toward the spot where their sire lay, clearly still unaware of what had happened.

"Da took a sword to his belly," Jamie said bluntly, wiping his sleeve across his face to get the blood off.

Jake stunned, asked, "What? Da? But he's…

where is he?" He jumped off his horse and raced to the circle, pushing everyone aside as Jamie shouted to him.

Jamie followed. "He was bleeding heavily when I last saw him. He couldn't get up, but I saw his eyes open and close."

He dismounted and pushed his way into the circle. Uncle Brodie was already kneeling beside Alex, whose eyes remained closed.

"Papa?" Jamie leaned closer to him, searching for any signs of life. His heart was beating hard in his chest, yet his limbs felt almost numb, and he could not find any beats of life in his arm or his wrist. His face was so pale, that alone frightened him. Jamie's mind clouded again as he tried to reason through all that had transpired.

This could not be happening. Could not. He should be going after Gracie, but she'd probably run off to hide. The threat had lessened now that the baron was dead and his men were gone. Loki rode up from the outside, staring down at Alex with a strange look on his face. "Loki, see if you can find Gracie. She was on horseback headed west."

Loki simply nodded and rode off.

Jamie grabbed his sire's arm and shook it, attempting to get a reaction. Alex's eyes fluttered open and then shut again. "Papa!" Jamie lifted his head and shouted, "Someone bring Aunt Caralyn."

"Robbie's already gone for her," Uncle Brodie said. "He's barely alive."

Connor moved next to Jake. "Papa?"

Jamie put his hand up on his sire's neck, searching for a sign that he still lived. "I feel it. He's still alive. Papa!"

Alex's eyes opened and he glanced at Jamie. "My thanks," he said in a weak voice, "your actions saved me. Take me inside…Maddie."

"He's alive. I heard him, Jamie. He'll come back." Connor's voice was full of hope.

Jamie wished he had the same hope inside him right now.

Caralyn arrived moments later on foot, Maddie by her side. Jamie bolted up before they reached the circle, hoping to lessen the pain of what his mother was about to see. He grasped her shoulder. "Mama, remember how strong Da is."

"Is he dead? He looks dead… Nay, Alex, please, nay…our time is not done yet." Maddie's fist went into her mouth and tears streamed down her cheeks. "Help me, Jamie, Jake. My knees. Help me get down, I must be close to him, please, please." Jake came over to help console his mother.

Jamie did as she asked as more and more people gathered around. Magnus had stepped away from their group to give instructions on cleaning the area up, gathering the dead, and looking for wounded men. There was a dampened mood, and many of the warriors surrounded their fallen laird at a distance. Some had even dropped to their knees to pray.

"Alex?" Maddie brushed his long locks away from his face and kissed his forehead. "Alex, come back to me, please." Her voice had broken into sobs. Jamie watched as his sire reached for her hand and squeezed it, though it was obvious he had no strength.

"Fine…, Maddie. I'll be fine. Do not…worry." His eyes closed again.

Jake asked, "Aunt Caralyn?"

She looked at Uncle Robbie and Uncle Brodie and shook her head. "I…'tis naught I can… Healing a belly wound is beyond my abilities. I'm sorry."

Maddie screamed and rested her head on her husband's chest.

Jamie whispered, "How long before he's dead?"

"Not long," Caralyn said. "Mayhap a day."

∼∼∼

They finally get Alex to Jennie…

A
S SOON AS Jamie arrived inside the Cameron gates, Aunt Jennie flew out to Alex's side, oblivious to everyone but Alex and Maddie in the cart. Alex and Jennie held a special relationship, and they were all witnesses to it.

"Alex. Please, Alex. Wake up, open your eyes for me." She jiggled his shoulder but he did not move. "Alex!"

"Maddie, how long has he been like this? When was the last time he opened his eyes?"

"It has been a couple of hours. I tried to keep him awake, Jennie, but he kept falling asleep."

"Alex," she shouted in his face. "You listen to me. You shall not give up. Do you hear me?" She poked her finger into his chest, tears beginning to clog her voice. "'Tis too early for you, you need to stay here. You have not even met your first grandson yet. How could you think about leaving all of us? Your lads still need you and so do your lassies. Do you not want to meet your grandson, the future laird of your clan?"

She gave a few curt instructions to those around her to get him into the keep. Jamie helped his mother out of the cart.

"Alex, I'm warning you. *Wake up*."

He stirred and opened his eyes. "Mayhap I'd prefer a grandlassie first."

Jennie laughed and kissed his cheek. "I love you, Alex. Do not go, please? Aye, you may have a granddaughter if the heavens abide your wishes."

They used another large blanket to get Alex inside, though he was too pale to Jamie's liking. At least they had made it. He'd had been petrified he would die on the journey here.

Aunt Jennie could save him, he had faith in her.

An hour later, he was pacing the Cameron great hall when the door flew open with a bang. He rushed over to the door, blurting out the only thing he could think of at the moment. "Did you find her?"

He knew the answer by the look in Aunt Caralyn's face, wet with tears. Uncle Robbie said, "Nay. We had a possible trail with one other horse, but with all the horses in the area for the war, it was impossible to trail her. She has not come here? We'd hoped she might have ridden in this direction."

Jamie said, "Nay." His belly churned so hard he thought he might be ill. Images of the worst possible scenarios flashed through his mind—wild boars, reivers, Simon de La Porte. Nay, he could not let that happen. He had to find his wife.

"I'll go search outside for her," Kenzie said. "I'll not give up until I find her."

He started to say, "Kenzie, I doubt she's…" but Loki clasped his shoulder.

"Let him go. 'Twill give the lad something to do."

Kenzie dashed out of the hall. As soon as he left, Uncle Robbie asked, "My brother? How is he?"

"Aunt Jennie's checking him now," Jamie said, running a hand through his hair. "It does not look good. He's pale and weak. He only awakened when Aunt Jennie yelled at him. Tell me which trail you followed. I'm going back out after Gracie."

"I'll go with you," Finlay got up from the trestle table and said, "She has to show up somewhere."

They headed to the chamber when the door flew open a second time. Aunt Brenna flew past him with a short, "Greetings, all. I must go to my sister's healing chamber." Uncle Quade, Uncle Logan, and Aunt Gwyneth followed. The Ramsays had arrived. The churning in his belly slowed at their presence. Aunt Brenna was still renowned as one of the best healers in all the land, and she had taught Aunt Jennie. The aunts working together gave him new hope, gave them all hope.

Uncle Robbie said, "Nice work, Logan. That was fast."

Uncle Logan wiped the grime from his face

with his plaid. Logan's gaze searched everyone in the hall, catching the slow but unenthusiastic nods. "He's still that bad?"

Slow nods followed.

Uncle Robbie said, "Glad to see you came along with my sister, Quade. How are your joints?"

"Riding horseback is easy. I know how she loves her brother, and after we heard how bad he is, I had to come. Fill me in while they work on him."

Jamie said, "Finlay, I'm going to check with my mother, then we'll head out."

His pacing slowed as he approached the room they'd been referring to as the sick chamber. Aedan Cameron stepped out of the chamber as he approached it. "Jamie, go on inside. I must go greet Quade and Logan. Have faith in your aunts. I do."

Jamie stepped inside the chamber, the smell making him wish to run the other way. He had no idea how healers could do what they did. His mother rushed up to him and grasped his hand.

He whispered, "Any change?"

"Hush, listen to Aunt Brenna for a moment."

Aunt Brenna and Aunt Jennie peered at the wound on the right side of Alex's belly.

"Based on the book that Aedan gave me, I think this is his liver," Jennie said, "and that looks to be where most of the damage is. 'Twas a clean stab. It did not go through the entire organ to his back."

Aunt Brenna nodded. "I wonder if he would have enough left to serve him if we were to cut out the small portion that is shredded. 'Tis a verra large organ, and he would still have most of it. Quade never suffered any lasting effects from the organ I once removed from him. Granted, it was small in comparison, but based on what I've learned, the liver does not have an inner cavity the way the heart or the stomach does. Mayhap he can survive with most of it left intact. The rest of it appears to be healthy."

"I think 'tis our only chance," Aunt Jennie said softly. "Otherwise, he will continue to bleed from all those tears. I think we cut here—" she made a motion across the organ, "—and sew him up to stem the bleeding. His outside wound is clean, so we'll stitch him up. Hopefully, he'll awaken before the fever sets in. We must try to get enough fluids in him."

"I think we must do this as quickly as possible. I do not like how slow his vessels are beating."

"Aye, 'tis Mama's most basic healing rule. Keep fluids in the body and keep it clean."

Jamie had heard many of the elders talk of his grandmama and her sire. They'd been amazing healers. All had admired her sire, but when his mother had grown of age, they'd worked together and done some wonderful things for the clan. It had been his grandmama that had pushed them to be clean about their wounds. Though he had no idea why, he had to agree that the cleaner a wound was, the less chance of fever.

"This is good timing. I just cleaned all of my surgical tools, so we do not have to take the time to do that. This time the water had come to a boil before I dropped the tools in. Surprised me how much easier they cleaned in the hot water. I hardly had to touch them. I'll wash my hands and get my tools."

Aunt Brenna looked up at them as Aunt Jennie went for her instruments. "I'm hopeful, Maddie. The bowel was not pierced, so that is the good news. I think we can repair his liver. Jamie, 'tis a good thing you brought him here. Caralyn does not do much surgery. Why not take your mother down to the hall? This may take a while, and if Alex wakes up, which I doubt, we will put him to sleep again."

EPILOGUE

Alex steps down from the lairdship…

JAMIE GLANCED AT his brother Jake, the two of them standing at the entrance to the great hall, waiting to see why they'd been summoned to the keep from the lists. Jamie fidgeted every once in a while, unable to stop himself.

"Can you not hold still? You never could when you were wee either."

"Why?" Jamie whispered. "Does it bother you? Because if it does, I'll make sure to do it more often."

Jake gave him a wide grin. "I have two fists behind my back that might change your mind."

The hall was empty except for the elders seated at the dais. It was a special meeting that had been called, but neither Jake nor Jamie knew the reason for it.

At the table were three of the elders who had been part of the group, the *dearbh fine*, since Alex had been chosen laird. In their clan, the laird did the disciplining with his second, but Alex had always had two seconds—his brothers—so Uncle Robbie and Uncle Brodie were both elders. Nicol; Edwin, Nicol's sire; Taran, the eldest male in the clan and also Edwin's sire; and Solas.

Jamie glanced over at them: Taran, Solas, Edwin—the eldest three, and the newer members—Nicol, Robbie, and Brodie. After the laird, the *dearbh fine* held most of the power in the clan.

"I'm thinking this is about Da." Jake leaned toward Jamie, doing his best to keep his voice down.

"Why do you think 'tis about Da?" Jamie asked.

"Because he has not healed as fast as everyone thought he would."

"There's naught wrong with his mind," Jamie insisted. "He can lead from a horse, he just cannot do battle."

Jake sighed. "I agree with you, but I'm not sure Taran and Solas agree with us."

The door opened at the end of the great hall, the new area built especially for Alex and Maddie. Their mother held it as their father made his way through it with slow, deliberate steps. He used a whittled oak branch to keep him upright, something Kenzie and Loki had whittled until it was smooth as a stone plucked out of the bottom of a rushing riverbed.

Alex Grant nodded to the men at the dais and his two sons who'd been instructed to remain by the entrance to the great hall until they were called forward.

Jake whispered, "I still can't believe he survived. Damn good thing you were there to argue with me. I was sure our sire was a dead man. They say he may never get back to full strength."

"He does not need to," Jamie whispered. "He's the great Laird Alexander Grant. His days as the best swordsman in the Highlands might be over, but I think he'll swing one again."

Jake glanced at his twin. "I hope you're right."

"Mama and Papa love their new chamber. You did a nice job with that. They'll never go back upstairs," Jamie said.

Their sire would not be able to handle the keep's stairways for a while, so Jake had overseen the addition of a chamber near Uncle Brodie's tower, but at the end of the hall instead of in the corner. He'd added a hearth and a sitting area for their mother.

Once their parents had settled, Taran, the chief of the elders, asked, "For what purpose did you call this meeting, Laird?"

Jamie couldn't believe what he'd heard...his sire had called this meeting?

"I've called this meeting because I believe it's time for me to step down as laird of Clan Grant."

A huge uproar followed. So many comments

were made that Jamie could not keep them straight.

"You cannot step down."

"Why is your wife here? She's a woman."

"Women are not allowed at our meetings."

"You'll be fine in no time."

"Who could possibly replace you?"

"Give yourself time to recuperate."

Alex finally brought his fist down on the table to gain everyone's silence.

They all stared at him wide-eyed, though Jamie was not sure whether it was due to his father's statement or his fist.

"You cannot mean that, brother," Uncle Robbie said.

"If I may, I'd like to continue."

Taran banged his hand down on the table in agreement. "I'd like to hear what he has to say. If he wants to step down, then we should vote on his eldest son, Jake, taking over."

Jamie glanced at his brother, who'd paled at that statement. He elbowed him, but said nothing. Jake's moment was finally here.

It was Jake's right as the laird's eldest son, and Jamie did not want to see it go to anyone but his brother. This was their clan, and they needed a sound leader.

"Allow him the opportunity to speak his mind, he's our laird," Solas said with an emphatic nod.

They quieted and gave his sire the chance to speak.

"First of all, I brought my wife along because

she will have an important contribution to this meeting." Alex cleared his throat. "Understand, *dearbh fine*, that 'tis an honor for me to serve my clan, but I also firmly believe that I should be in this role only as long as I am fit for it. I would like to suggest that the lairdship be passed down to my sons."

"Sons?" Taran asked.

"Sons?" Edwin echoed.

"Aye, my sons. I suggest that the lairdship be shared equally between our firstborn sons, Jake and Jamie."

Jamie's knees nearly buckled, though he somehow managed to stay upright. This possibility had never occurred to him.

"But Jake is your firstborn son, Laird," Edwin said. "And our custom is to pass the lairdship over to the laird's firstborn son unless he is unfit. Jake is perfectly fit for the job, though the matter would need to be voted on."

"Is he our firstborn? Who on the dais can answer that question for me?" Alex leaned back in his chair and crossed his arms.

Taran glanced at the others at the table. "Robbie? Brodie? What say you?"

Uncle Robbie shrugged his shoulders. "I was not there. I cannot say for certain."

Uncle Brodie said the same. "I was with Robbie in the hall."

Taran turned to look at Jamie and Jake standing near the doorway. Jake said, "We were there, but I do not think either of us recall." Their comment gained a ripple of laughter from everyone in the council but Taran, who had a more of a scowl than usual.

Jamie and Jake exchanged a glance, grinning at each other.

"Who was there?" Taran asked. "Alex, you were there, were you not? Your poor wife was attacked in the middle of the long event. Did you not stay in the chamber after the birth? 'Tis the tale the minstrels tell."

"Aye, I was there. Besides the two of us, Maddie's dear maid, Alice, who has since passed on, was also present. So was my sister Brenna, who now lives with the Ramsays."

"Enough of this foolishness, Laird," said Solas, who was red in the face. "When the first bairn was born, what did you name him? Jake, was it not? Then it's Jake."

Alex looked at Maddie. "We did not name them until much later. I do not recall myself which one came out first."

Taran stood up, banging his hand on the table. "Here, here, Laird." His frustration was evident in the way the words spewed from his mouth, spittle flying everywhere. Taran had sat as the head of the *dearbh fine* for some time now. He was as old as dirt, according to the lads of the clan, and his long beard was a testament to his age. "We need not hear the details about women's work. Just tell us who was first."

Jamie could not believe the spectacle in front of him. All these years, he'd been told he was the second born. His sire had planned this perfectly. Of course, everyone knew the lads looked nothing alike—Jamie was fair, and Jake was dark-haired—but no one could openly accuse the laird of lying.

His father said, "I'll ask their mother. Maddie, what say you?"

"I was verra busy trying to deliver the second one to pay attention to the first. I cannot answer that. And we could not decide on names. We never even thought about it 'til after the bairns had been brought downstairs into the hall and then back up to me. Then we decided to name the dark-haired lad after Alex's sire, John, because he had the same coloring, and the light-haired lad after my sire, James, for the same reason. It had naught to do with who came out first. John became Jake, James became Jamie, and there you have it."

Taran bellowed. "Again, must I hear about issues that took place inside a woman's chamber? I care not to think on it. Just tell us who was first. The clan's *dearbh fine* commands you to reveal the truth." He sat down and stroked his grizzled beard as he awaited the laird's response, his beady eyes aimed directly at him.

Alex said, "Please calm down, Taran. With all due respect, I tell you this because in my eyes, it does not matter. Maddie feels the same way. We did not pay close attention because she'd had a dagger at her throat minutes before the bairns were born. But here is what I'd like to present to you. Our sons are two verra different men, and this past year has illustrated as much. Jake is the type of warrior who focuses on the big issues, while Jamie is more likely to concern himself with details. Jake is an expert on knowing how to do what's needed immediately, while Jamie recognizes what is needed in the long-term. They are two verra different leaders, and I believe we are best served by having them both lead our clan. Just as my two brothers, who have both been invaluable to me, are verra different, so are Jake and Jamie. Together, they will be more powerful."

Jamie looked into Jake's eyes as he thought about what his sire had said. He could see the truth of it. Was his brother appraising him the same way?

"He makes a valid point," Uncle Brodie said. "They worked well together both at our fight with MacNiven and Hew Gordon at Castle Dubh and in the battle with Baron Crichton."

"But it was Jake who led the battle against the baron," Solas argued. "I saw him do it. He was at the forefront of the battle all the way."

"True," Nicol said, "but it was Jamie who saw our laird go down and who called for our warriors to protect him. He was farther back. Jake had no idea our laird was injured."

Uncle Robbie said, "And if it had been up to Jake and me, my brother would not be here. He would have died within a day's time. Jake and I wished to allow you to die in peace. 'Twas Jamie and Brodie who said to take you to Jennie's, and your sisters are the reason you are still here."

Taran waved to Jake and Jamie, summoning them over to the dais. Jamie's head was spinning. What would come next?

Taran stood when they came to a stop in front of the dais. "Lads, would you accept our decision if we ask both of you to step into your sire's position as laird of Clan Grant?"

Jamie glanced at his brother, unsure how he would take this. They'd both believed their entire life that when the time came, Jake would become laird. He'd wait to see what his brother said first. It would be his choice.

Jake thought for a moment, then said, "Aye. I trust my brother's judgment. We often have different ways of approaching a problem, but we always seem to come to terms. I think the clan would benefit from having two lairds."

Jamie was shocked. He was about to be named chief of Clan Grant alongside his brother? Many times over the years, he'd thought of becoming the laird instead of his brother, but alongside him? The possibility had never occurred to him. He thought it was a sound plan.

"Jamie? Your brother accepts. We must hear from you."

Jamie nodded. "I am honored to be included. I would accept on one condition."

The elders looked aghast that he would consider making a demand of the elders.

"I'll hear that condition, Jamie," his sire said.

"On the condition that when you are strong enough to take the lairdship back, we will relinquish it until we are again needed."

His mother pulled a linen square out of the folds of her dress and dabbed her eyes.

"Accepted," Alex said.

Taran banged the table and said, "How many are in favor of this, say aye."

A chorus of ayes greeted him.

"Nays?"

Silence.

Taran said, "James Alexander Grant, John Alexander Grant, you are now the new lairds of Clan Grant, based on the *dearbh fine's* recommendation."

The entire table erupted into cheers and smiles.

Jamie looked at his brother and asked, "What have we done?"

Alex and Maddie…

AT THE END of the table, Alex Grant looked at his wife of more years than he could count and said, "Does this please you, wife?" He kept his voice low so the others would not hear him.

"Aye, Alex, but I'm still surprised you decided to do this. You still have an able mind to lead."

"Maddie, I must tell you something." Alex had dreaded telling her this, but he knew it was time.

"What is it?"

"Did you know that all your hairs have turned white? I fear I must have put you through too much with this last injury."

"What? But I have had a few white hairs for some time now."

Alex tipped his head, his gaze traveling to the bound hair hanging down her back. "A few?"

Maddie grabbed the bottom of her plaited hair, tugging it over her shoulder and as far into the air as much as she could. She stared at her long tresses for a moment and then whispered, "Why, so it has. Why has no one told me?"

"Because you're still as beautiful as the day I met you. 'Tis time for me to spend all my time with you." He tugged her onto his lap and kissed her.

Taran barked, "Och, for the love of God. Look at the two of them." He tossed his hands into the air and scurried out the door.

SORCHA

BOOK 8

Sorcha and Cailean, always a favorite.

CHAPTER SEVENTEEN

*A group of Ramsays make the trek to
visit Alex to make sure he's healing.
Fortunately, Alex continues to improve…*

"NAY." SORCHA WAS so wrapped up in her own troubles, she hardly noticed the people who had entered the hall until the newcomers were almost upon them.

She jumped to her feet as Uncle Alex made his way over to a cushioned chair by the hearth, assisted by Connor. "Uncle Alex! 'Tis so good to see you." She waited until he was seated before rushing over to kiss his cheek.

"Good eve to you, lass. Maddie sends her apologies as she's in her night rail. In truth, Connor is better at supporting me. From time to time, I still falter." He motioned for his youngest son to take a seat next to him.

"How do you feel?" Sorcha asked.

"Much better. I'll not be swinging my sword yet, but I'm improving every day."

She couldn't help but smile. His condition was so much better than the stories had inclined her to believe. His voice was as booming and authoritative as ever, and his body was clearly well on its way to recovery. "We have not stopped worrying since we heard the news. I feared the worst, Uncle Alex. I thought…Pay me no mind. Connor, you're almost as tall as your sire."

Uncle Alex chuckled. "He's trying to beat his brothers. Neither has surpassed my height, but Connor insists he will. He's convinced he has some growing time left. We shall see." Connor grinned and nodded his head in agreement. "I hear you had a difficult journey and there's a lad in the healing chamber who is in rough shape."

"Aye, a mudslide caught my horse, but Cailean went over the side with me."

Her uncle arched his brow at her.

"He was on a different horse, but his mount was right next to mine. He tried to stop me from going over the embankment—instead, we both toppled over it. He protected me." She wrung her hands, caught up in the entire event again. She'd never been so frightened in her life.

"Any good Ramsay warrior would do as he did. Your sire was not close enough?"

"Nay, he was in the front, leading us through the section."

"He was lucky Cailean was close by."

She leaned in closer and whispered, "Uncle Alex, would you mention that to him, please?"

Her uncle gave her a wide grin. "Your sire does not wish to admit you're a woman grown? 'Tis tough for us old fathers." He tipped his head toward Kyla. "I suppose I'll be forced to go through the same myself soon."

Kyla said, "Oh, Papa, you know I'll pick someone you'll like."

Connor chuckled, looking at his father. "But

will he be good enough for you? I imagine you'll want to test his sword skills."

Sorcha rolled her eyes. "Papa already tested Cailean's skills."

"And did he pass?" Alex asked.

"Aye, or he wouldn't have been allowed to come along." She scowled, thinking again about the trials the poor man had been forced to endure just to travel along with the other Ramsay guards.

Just then, Sorcha's sire stepped out of the solar, closing the door behind him. A wide grin spread across his face as he moved to join them at the hearth. "Alex, you're looking much better." He stood by the big man's side, clapping a hand on Alex's shoulder.

"Aye, I'm improving. My thanks for getting my sister to my side so quickly, Ramsay."

"I doubt 'twill be long before you've got your hands on that sword again. Your son here can help you the first time. He's growing into a fine lad, I see."

"Do not worry. I'll be back." He shot a wry look at Kyla. "If for no other reason than to test the skills of my daughter's suitors, just as you did, Ramsay."

Her father smirked at her, but then turned back to Alex. "He passed. The poor lad took a rough tumble after that, but he's a Ramsay warrior. He'll survive. You're welcome to join us, laird. I need to confer with your sons and your brothers to see what's been transpiring in the Highlands."

Alex shook his head before nodding to Connor. "Nay, I'll leave all to the new lairds. Connor will help me back to my chamber. I'll sit with Maddie for a while."

With one last nod and grin, Sorcha's sire left for the solar. Kyla bolted out of her chair as soon as Alex started to lift himself up. "I'll help you, Papa."

"Nay, daughter. Stay and enjoy your cousin. Connor will come back to the solar in a few moments."

They watched the two cross the hall to Alex and Maddie's new chamber before they continued their conversation.

KYLA

BOOK 9

*Alex with his eldest daughter,
some of the best scenes ever…*

CHAPTER FIVE

*Kyla decided to sneak away to make sure
Davina was fine. But the truth is she is just
beginning to deal with nearly losing her father.
Have the tissues ready!*

KYLA'S RECKONING FINALLY came that
evening. Her mother had sent word that
she was to meet her parents in the solar in ten
minutes. After delaying as long as she dared, she
trudged down the staircase and knocked on the
door.

"Enter," her sire's voice boomed.

She peeked around the door, pleased to see only
her parents inside, her father seated at his desk
and her mother in a chair off to his side. Much
better to face them alone than with a board of
witnesses. "Greetings, Papa. You sound so much
better. Is he better, Mama?"

Her sire narrowed his gaze at her. "Sit. You'll
not distract us from our purpose, daughter."

She sat down in the chair in front of the desk,
fussing with the folds of her skirt. "Mama, forgive
me for my transgression. I…"

"How could you?" Tears fell down her mother's
face, exactly what she did *not* want to see. "After
everything your sire and I have been through,
how could you put us through this worry?"

Her father clasped her mother's hand and said, "I'd like to hear Kyla's reasons, Maddie. Let's allow her to explain herself. She has rarely been defiant, so she must believe she had a good reason."

Her mother took out her linen square, dabbed at her tears, and folded her hands in her lap. "Aye, I wish to hear your reasons, Kyla."

She took a deep breath and began, hoping she could convince her parents she'd done the right thing. "After listening to Jamie and Uncle Logan talk about the mercenaries and their ill intent toward us, I could not just sit by idly and watch. We've been through too much, and so much of it is because of our quarrel with the Buchan and MacNiven. I could not watch my family be torn apart again.

"Papa, it was so hard when you fell in battle. We did not know whether you would see the next day." Tears began to fall down her cheeks, but she managed to control them for the most part. She would explain her intentions and gain their support. "After our celebrations for Jamie and Gracie and Sorcha and Cailean, we got back some semblance of what we'd been before. You were home, and we were happy again. Our clan was functioning again. I was proud of how we all pulled together, of the fine job Jake and Jamie were doing as lairds, and I...I was willing to do aught I could to keep it that way.

"We must persevere." Her tone changed and the anger she had about what her loved ones had been forced to endure seeped out. "Mama, I could not allow it. And why can I never go along on any missions? Connor is always left behind as well. 'Tis not fair to him."

Her father said, "We're discussing your situation, not Connor's. Your brothers have all been training for years in the lists to be able to protect themselves. You know how talented the Ramsay women are as archers, but you've never been interested in learning to fight. How did you plan to protect yourself?"

"There were plenty of guards with us. Finlay was assigned as my protector. I had a plan," she insisted, looking back and forth between her parents. "I wanted to speak to Davina. I believed that we could come to an agreement, woman to woman. My hope was that she would divulge what her sire was planning, and that I could convince her to help establish peace between our clans."

"And were you successful?" her sire asked.

"In a way, aye. Davina told me something no one else from our group uncovered. And we have to help her, Papa. Please tell me you'll help her."

"What did she tell you?"

She gave her attention to her mother, who had been grossly abused before Alex had rescued her from her stepbrother's keep. Her mama would want to help Davina; she was sure of it. "Mama, her sire gives her to whatever man he wants. She has no say in the matter. He wishes to give her to Simon de La Porte who will be arriving soon."

Her mother gasped, just as she'd expected.

"And she has a bairn now, MacNiven's daughter, and she only wishes to raise the wee lassie in peace. Her sire wanted me to convince her to do his bidding, I believe, but I would not do it. How could her own father treat her so poorly?"

"Is that the reason you were ordered off their land?" her sire asked.

"Aye, he was angry because I did not agree with him. He swung his sword over his head and struck a stone bench. Finlay pulled out his sword and protected me."

"So instead of helping, you hindered the attempt to make peace." Her father's voice had turned into that quiet tone they all dreaded, that tone of judgment that could make her cry at just the sound.

"But Papa." She sat on the edge of her chair, gripping the arms tight. "We must help her. Can you not see that? We must send an army back to get her away, take her and her bairn to a safe place. I promised her we would help her."

"Did you see de La Porte?"

"Nay, but I would not know him if I saw him. Uncle Logan never saw him. We must save her before he is forced on her. Even if she has a babe, 'tis still rape, is it not? Mama?" She had to make them understand.

Her sire got up from his chair behind the desk and moved around to the front. He sat on the edge and tugged her out of the chair, wrapping his arms around her and setting his chin on the top of her head.

The tears came and she could not stop them.

"Papa, am I not hurting you?" She sobbed into his chest, taking in her father's familiar scent and the warmth of his embrace as she melted into her favorite place in the entire world.

"Nay, you're not hurting me. The only way you can hurt me is if something happens to you."

"Don't you see I was afraid you'd never be able to hug me again?" She sobbed harder, her breath hitching as she swallowed her tears. "I must do something to prevent that from happening again. I just got you back, Papa. I cannot bear to lose you."

"You are too soft-hearted." He gave a large sigh as he rubbed her back. "Just like your mother."

<hr>

CHAPTER ELEVEN

★Simon de la Porte and
Glenn of Buchan have Kyla…

ALEX GRANT SAT in his solar, mulling over all he'd just heard. His eldest sons and acting lairds were there, along with Quade and Logan Ramsay, and the group that had returned with the news—his youngest son, Connor, and Roddy and Braden.

Logan had just returned from a journey intended to uncover new information about the mercenaries and Buchan's plot—a mission that had proved unsuccessful. The man had started pacing the room the moment he'd entered it, and he now turned to the younger men and barked, "What the hell were you thinking, taking Kyla straight to the enemy? I could order lashings for all five of you. And Finlay? I'll kill him with my bare hands. You've given the enemy just what they wanted, something to use against us."

"Admonishments will get us nowhere at this point," Alex said. "They used the innocence and inexperience of our young people against us. Now, we must do what's necessary to right the situation. The bastard has my daughter, and we need to settle on a strategy to get her back. Jake, make a call to arms. Three hundred men will march with me on the morrow. Get them ready. Get their mounts ready. Jamie, find messengers and send them to Menzie land and Drummond land. I would ask for one hundred guards from each of them. Micheil has likely brought Gavin and Gregor back to Drummond land with him, but we can send another messenger to Edinburgh to be sure. And someone should be sent to Cameron land telling them we're coming and bringing our women for safety. Aedan's to keep his guards at home to protect his land and the abbey. Dusk outside Buchan land on the morrow."

"Send a messenger to Torrian," Quade added. "Tell him to ready two hundred."

Jake and Jamie left the room to carry out their instructions.

Logan continued to pace. He stopped for a moment and said, "Alex, are you sure you're ready to sit on a mount for that long? It will take nearly a day to get there."

"Aye, 'tis perfect. We'll attack at night while half of them are in their cups," Alex said.

Connor said, "I doubt they'll be in their cups. We saw no evidence of such."

Logan sat down and said, "Connor, Roddy, Braden. Tell us every detail of what you know."

The door opened and the Grant's brothers came in quietly and sat.

"De La Porte and his mercenaries had just arrived," Connor said. "We saw no more than two hundred men."

A knock sounded at the door. Brodie said, "I'll go."

Alex nodded. His brother opened the door to find Maddie standing there.

"A messenger," Maddie motioned to the door.

Brodie returned a few moments later, holding a scroll. "A messenger handed me this and hustled away." Maddie followed him in.

All conversation stopped as they waited to hear what Brodie had to say. Alex motioned for Maddie to come to him behind the desk.

Brodie read the message on the scroll. "This is from Glenn of Buchan," he said, looking up. "He has Kyla and promises no harm to her in exchange for…" he paused, reading it again as if to convince himself of what it said.

Alex pulled Maddie down onto his lap, afraid she would collapse onto the floor. He could feel her fine tremors. This was too much for his wee wife.

Robbie stared at him. Alex said, "Go ahead, Brodie."

"He'll return Kyla to us safely when we

relinquish Grant Castle to him. We have two days
to decide."

Maddie gasped and fell against Alex, but after a
moment, she stood up and squared her shoulders.

She folded her hands in front of her and said,
"Husband, you need to put a dagger in that man's
black heart."

CHAPTER SIXTEEN

Alex learns how many allies he has.

ALEX GRANT RODE with a heavy heart.
Not at his peak, he worried he'd fail his
daughter and his wife, yet he pushed himself
onward. His side ached after being on horseback
for so long, but it was nothing he couldn't
handle. But how long could he swing his sword?
He'd been practicing privately so as not to worry
Maddie, but his strength had been slow to return.
He was no longer the best swordsman in the
Highlands, and mayhap that title would never
be his again. Still, Alex had chosen his usual war
garb, his leine and his red and black Grant plaid.
While some warriors fought in muted plaids, he
wished for his enemy to remember him well.

Despite his lingering ailments, he was
confident in their plan. Logan had his archers all
ready, and he knew his old friend would do his
job well. Numbers were in their favor as well.
Aedan had offered to send men with them, but
Alex had advised him to keep all his warriors at

home to protect Lochluin Abbey and his land. It comforted him to know that Maddie and his sisters were safe.

Then something miraculous happened. Alex led his warriors over the last hill on their way off Cameron land, only to see a sea of warriors waiting below him—there were blue Ramsay plaids, Menzie plaids, and he was quite sure he could see a slew of Drummond plaids, too. There were horses everywhere and banners waving in the wind. This stood for everything his clan had built over the years, all the friendships they had nurtured. He glanced at his brothers to his right, both clearly feeling the same pride that swelled in his chest.

Together, they would get Kyla back and end Clan Buchan's reign of terror.

Once in the valley, he held his hand up to halt his guards behind him so he could move forward to speak with the group of leaders who awaited him—Torrian, whose sire had already joined his side; Micheil; and Drew Menzie. "Any news of Kyla or Finlay?"

Micheil shook his head. "We'll get them back, Alex. 'Tis time for us to put an end to this treachery."

Alex was about to speak when a noise interrupted him. He turned his head to see two of his warriors, one of them Finlay's brother, escorting a young lad he didn't recognize toward him. Though he looked small on his horse, he held his head high.

Fergus held onto the reins of the lad's horse.

"My laird, our pardon, but the lad says he can take you to Kyla."

"Fergus, 'tis probably a trap," Alex rumbled. "Let him go." He'd had enough of Simon de La Porte's games.

"Your pardon, my laird," Fergus said. "I think you should hear what the lad has to say."

Alex glanced to his brothers and his sons. He knew Fergus was upset about Finlay's situation. Could he really be objective? Connor, Loki, and Brodie all nodded at him, so he decided to listen. Besides, there was something about the boy that called to him. "Speak up, lad. Your name first."

"My name is Gillie, and Finlay sent me here because I was assigned as Kyla's protector."

His words came out in a rush so fast that Alex could hardly understand him.

"My real name is Gilleasp, but everyone calls me Gillie, Finlay promised me that if I helped him he would bring me to Grant land to live because I don't want to live with the Buchan anymore but I helped Finlay with the horses and we got Kyla out and he has her behind the waterfall and I'm to bring you to them and then he offered to take me with him to Grant land." He let his breath out and stared up at Alex. "Are you truly Alexander Grant, the one who fought at the Battle of Largs?"

"I am, lad. Now tell me why I should believe you. How do I know Buchan did not send you to lead me into a trap?"

Gillie whispered, "Och, I almost forgot. Finlay said to tell you Inga and Uncle Geordie both helped him," the lad paused. "And he said to give you this. Kyla said you would know them."

Fergus took something out of the lad's hand and handed it over to him. Alex opened his palm and stared at the necklace of pearls, the same ones he'd placed around his wife's neck before they married. Maddie had told him she had given them to Kyla.

CHAPTER SEVENTEEN

One of my all-time favorites.
The one chapter that makes me cry.
Every. Single. Time…

"ARE THOSE PEARLS not the ones you gave Maddie?" Brodie asked.

Alex nodded.

"You're certain?"

"Aye." He held the clasp up for Brodie to see. "I had the jeweler engrave it with FMG for Father MacGregor, who gave me the idea. Maddie adored him."

He placed the pearls in his sporran and said, "Brodie, Jamie, you'll come with me. Jamie, choose ten other guards to join us." He saw Nicol out of the corner of his eye—the man had ridden up to speak with his son. "You, too, Nicol." He then turned to the lad and said, "Gillie, take me to my daughter."

Gillie took the reins of his horse and was about to turn around when he stopped. "Oh, Finlay

said I'm to warn you that Kyla was beaten bad.
She does not look too good…my laird. That is, I
hope you'll be my laird."

Alex motioned for him to continue, and they
headed into the forest, leaving the lines of warriors
behind. She was alive. That was all that mattered
at present. He needed to see her for himself.

"She's a strong lass like her mother and sire,
Alex," Brodie said. "Remember that."

He nodded, unable to speak due to the huge
lump that had found its way into his throat. They
hit a meadow and Alex waved to Gillie to speed
his horse into a gallop.

It felt like they rode for an eternity, though it
had to be less than an hour, before Gillie led them
to a burn. They followed it as it widened, and a
short time later he heard the musical sounds of
the waterfall nearby. Alex said a quick prayer that
this was indeed Kyla and Finley and not a trap.
If his daughter was indeed safe, Gillie would be
joining Clan Grant soon.

Gillie tipped his head back and whistled a bird
call. Within seconds, Finlay stepped out from
behind the waterfall, carrying Kyla in his arms.
He could see the tears rolling down the lad's
face and his gut clenched. Had they come too
late? Was she gone? Her eyes were closed, but
her color, what he could see past the bruises and
swelling, was not the worst he'd ever seen.

Dismounting, he pulled on his inner strength
not to fall to his knees, instead moving over to
stand in front of Finlay, who'd stepped into the
grass, still clutching Kyla to his chest.

"Is she alive, Finlay?"

Finlay nodded. "Aye, she still breathes."

"Are you alone?"

"We have not been followed."

Alex reached for his daughter, but Finlay stepped away from him. "I would like to, my laird, but movement pains her terribly."

Alex stood back and nodded, his eyes traveling across his daughter's beautiful face. It was covered with purple and blue marks, one eye was badly swollen, and her lips were cut and scabbed. As his gaze traveled the length of her body, fury built inside him like a raging fire.

He'd experienced a fury like this once before, when he'd watched a depraved bastard take a lash to his wife's back, but this was different. Now, he was older and more capable of controlling his fury, channeling it into vengeance. This was fury that would turn him into a predator, a cat that would pace around his enemy until he had the bastard just where he wanted him.

They had done this to his daughter, the one who had been strapped to his chest as a bairn, her giggles and blue eyes ensuring she had a special place in his heart all her own.

This. Was. His. *Baby*.

He leaned down and kissed her forehead, letting the tears fall onto his cheeks unabashedly. He wished to cuddle her as he had when she was a bairn, keep everyone away from her.

Finlay nodded to Alex and the others. His sire, Nicol, took a step toward him. The warrior finally spoke, "I have something I'd like to say."

Alex nodded. "Go ahead. You have a few moments before I send her to Cameron land. My sisters can help her heal."

Finlay kissed Kyla's cheek and said, "My apologies to all of you for my hand in this travesty. My laird, I need you to know that I love your daughter. Naught would please me more than to ask for her hand in marriage, but I understand that first I must prove my worth. I foolishly thought I should leave Clan Grant after my mother's passing, but now I realize that there is no place I'd rather be than by this woman's side. I set out to prove my worthiness to you as a suitor for your daughter, but I bungled everything terribly. I will accept your decision, whatever 'tis, but I do love her with all my heart."

He waited, his gaze on him. Alex had been struck speechless. It was the last thing he'd expected Finlay to say at this moment. "Lad, I think 'tis something I need to think on…"

Kyla opened her eyes and did her best to smile. "Papa? 'Tis you truly? And Finlay…would you mind repeating what you just said?"

Gillie hurried up to her and shouted, "He says he loves you and wishes to marry you."

Finlay chuckled and kissed her gently. "Aye, I do love you. But I know I must prove myself."

"Finlay, set her down please," Alex said.

"Nay, it pains her to stand, my laird. Either her ankle is twisted or her foot broken, so with all due respect, I cannot set her down in good conscience."

"Is there a boulder I could sit on behind that waterfall?" Alex pointed in that direction.

Gillie said, "Aye, there are two large ones."

"I'd like a few moments alone with my daughter. Please hand her to me." Alex reached for his daughter and scooped her into his arms as carefully as he could.

She winced but was able to grab his shoulders, and he carried her behind the cascading water, feeling a few cool splashes on his face. It helped ground him in the moment as he settled on the boulder with Kyla on his lap. "You are comfortable enough to talk?"

"Aye, Papa. I'm so sorry for all the trouble I've caused. Finlay only came along because I swore I'd go alone without him. The message was a ruse, but I believed it. I was terrified for Davina."

He rested his chin on his daughter's head as she continued to babble, explaining her actions, but all he could do was take in the familiar scent and softness of his wee daughter. Kyla had become such a strong woman, just as her mother was. How could he fault her for doing what was right and fighting against the abuse of women? Nay, he was proud of her, and Maddie would be, too. "Daughter, I do not fault you for your good heart, nor do I fault Finlay for protecting you. The fault lies at Buchan's feet. Forgive me, but I must ask. Were you raped?"

Kyla pulled her head back and cupped her sire's cheek. "Nay, Papa. Finlay and Davina and Gillie protected me. I may not walk for a while, but I'll survive. Oh, Davina is fine and so is her daughter."

She brushed away the wetness she found on his cheeks. "Papa, I'm sorry. What will happen now?"

"Do you love Finlay?"

"Aye, I do love him. After watching my brothers and my cousins find such happiness in marriage, I was afraid I'd never find the same, but my love has been in front of me all along. And the best part is that he's part of our clan. I'll not be leaving you and Mama. I couldn't bear it."

"You've been through much, so we'll not decide now. Uncle Brodie and Finlay's sire will escort you to Cameron land. Your mother is there with your aunts, who will tend to your wounds. I need to finish this so the Buchans and de La Porte will not disrupt my clan again." He stood, lifting her with him, then stooped to kiss her cheek. "I love you, lassie. My heart was nearly broken from worrying about you, but I am proud of you."

He stepped out from behind the waterfall and said, "Brodie, Nicol, please deliver Kyla to her mother on Cameron land. Take seven guards with you."

After Brodie mounted, Alex carefully lifted Kyla up to him. "Papa, be careful," Kyla said. "I love you and Finlay."

"What about me?" Gillie asked. "Where do I go?"

Alex beckoned to the lad and gestured for him to stand in front of him. When Gillie did as instructed and lifted his gaze to him, Alex set his hand on the lad's shoulder and asked, "Are you not my daughter's protector?"

He grinned and said "Aye, my laird." His eyes grew wide, waiting to see what would come next.

"Welcome to Clan Grant. You may ride with Nicol. Take care of my daughter until Finlay and I return for her."

"Aye, my laird." He raced to Nicol's horse and jumped so high he almost flew over the back of the horse, but Nicol caught him. It was good to see the man grinning—the loss of his wife had weighed on him.

After taking a final look at his daughter, ensuring himself she was all right, Alex moved over to speak with Nicol. "Your son made me proud today. I do not fault him for what transpired. He brought my daughter back to me safely."

After the group bound for the Camerons left, Alex motioned for Jamie and the other two guards to patrol the area. "Jamie, I'll speak to Finlay alone, then we shall head back. Give us a few minutes."

Alex strode up to stand in front of Finlay. Hell, but when had the lad grown so large? He remembered him as a little sprite of a laddie, just as he remembered all of these young ones. He could see the lad bore his own share of bruises, telling him how hard he'd fought to free Kyla from her imprisonment.

"Finlay, my thanks for returning my daughter to me and for joining her in her endeavor to ensure she did not go off alone. I know how headstrong she can be, so I do not need the particular details. I lay all the blame on Buchan and de La Porte.

You are still a valued member of our clan, should you choose to stay."

"I do, my laird."

"That pleases me." He glanced up at the sky, pausing before he dropped his gaze back to Finlay's. "Then I only have one other question for you. Which one would you like—Glenn of Buchan or Simon de La Porte? I'll give you first choice."

Finlay smiled. "I choose de La Porte. I've dreamed of killing that bastard."

"He's all yours. I will gladly take on Glenn of Buchan." He moved over to his stallion and mounted.

"Time to end this."

CHAPTER EIGHTEEN

*Alex rides into battle with a
need for vengeance unlike any
he's ever felt before…*

ALEX GRANT NODDED to Jake and Jamie to give their final instructions to their men. He needed a quiet moment of clarity, something he often found helpful before battle.

He rode Black Lightning down the lines of horses covering the landscape. He found a small knoll and led his horse up to the top so he could look over the leagues of men here to fight for his *clann*.

Dusk was descending fast and he closed his eyes to feel the light breeze coming in from the mountains, the sweet Scottish air feeding his soul, exhilarating him like nothing else could. His nephews, David, Roddy, Braden, and his youngest son, Connor, all wore expressions of anticipation. They were eager to be involved in the action for the first time.

His eldest sons, Jake and Jamie, carried the hardness of experience across their cheekbones, their gazes discerning, always searching for something unusual, anything to help in their preparation for battle. He and Maddie had done a fine job raising their bairns.

Hellfire, he was a proud man. Proud of his wife and all she'd endured over the years, of his sons and daughters, of how deeply they'd connected with the Ramsay clan, of how both clans dared to bring women warriors along with them. He thought of his sire and mother and how proud they would be of all they had become.

The breeze lifted the Grant banner and the Ramsay banner not far away, the snapping and billowing of the flags the only other sound to be heard outside his sons' voices and the occasional shifting of horses' hooves. His sons finished giving the instructions necessary to guarantee they would fight strong and dominate the battle.

Good must triumph over evil today.

The last thing he did was to bow his head in prayer that the Lord would see them all through this battle and that he would fare better than he had in the last one, the one that had nearly cost him his life. All was quiet as his men followed him, honoring his moment of silence.

Black Lightning was so in tune with his rider that when Alex finished his prayer, the great beast lifted his front legs and stood on his hind legs, his dark head raised up as he whinnied, giving the warriors the signal that his master was ready for battle.

The Grant war whoop, uttered by hundreds, rang out over the valley.

CHAPTER NINETEEN

*Finlay battles de la Porte inside
Buchan Castle and saves Alex.*

OUT OF THE corner of his eye, he (Finlay) saw de La Porte leaving through the tower door. Cailean, who'd already knocked his second attacker down, shouted, "I've got this. Go after him."

Finlay didn't need to be told twice. He followed the bastard out the door and searched the area at the back of the keep. De La Porte was heading for the wall behind the kitchens, so Finlay pursued him without hesitation. The bastard was almost at the wall when Finlay shouted, "You'll never get up there without my sword in your back. Fight me like a true warrior, or are you all talk? I never did see you use your sword in the lists."

Simon spun around with his sword in his hands and lunged at Finlay, first from the left, then from the right. They parried for a short time while de La Porte did his best to taunt him. "That lass of yours sure had nice breasts. Did she tell you I tasted her everywhere while she was my captive? She offered me her maidenhead, too." His grin hatched from the devil itself.

Finlay blocked out his comments, fighting for all he was worth. Off to the side, he noticed two of Buchan's men about to join in the melee, but one was taken out with an arrow to his chest and the second took a dagger right between his eyes.

Logan shouted, "Say the word and I'll have one of my archers take him out, MacNicol."

"Stay out. He's mine." Finlay growled, then brought his sword against de La Porte's so hard that sparks flew overhead. Their duel continued, Finlay doing his best to drive his sword home. He needed to finish this for Kyla and for himself.

"You have no skills, wee laddie. You'll never beat me. I'm going to steal Kyla again as soon as I get out of here. All the Grants are here, so my path will be obstacle free. My guess is you took her to Cameron land, right near the wealthy coffers of Lochluin Abbey, which is exactly where I'm headed."

Finlay swung again, but was blocked. "See? You savages think being a Highlander makes you stronger than other warriors? See the truth in front of you. You're nothing. You don't deserve the lass. I'll take her with me. She'll gladly trade you for a true man."

That comment sunk in, so he tried a move he'd

only done a few times. He brought his sword across without completing his swing, faking his opponent into blocking his blow. At the last moment, he changed the path of his weapon and brought it down on de La Porte's arm as hard as he could.

He connected with flesh, rendering the man's sword arm useless. Simon de La Porte stared at him in shock as blood poured out of his body.

"How are my skills now?" Finlay drawled.

Simon hadn't moved so Finlay brought his sword down again, severing the fiend's arm from his body. His blood shot out in a pulsating fountain, his other arm reaching for a way to stanch the bleeding. Moments later, he collapsed to the ground.

Shouts of support came from the archers above, but he couldn't take time to appreciate them. He wiped his sword across the now lifeless body of de La Porte and rushed back to the keep, hoping the others had taken care of Glenn of Buchan.

When he stepped into the great hall, he saw about a dozen of the enemy fighting five Grants. Jamie, Connor, Loki, Cailean, and Alex Grant stood near the back with Glenn of Buchan huddling in the opposite corner. There was no sign of Davina.

Connor, Jamie, Loki, and Cailean fought like beasts, downing every man who dared to swing a sword their way, but Alex was losing strength. He fought hard, taking a couple out, but he didn't have the power of the other three.

Then the worst thing possible happened. Glenn of Buchan came running from the opposite side of the hall, his sword arm raised and heading directly toward Alex Grant's back.

CHAPTER TWENTY

Alex Grant, the might warrior and swordsman, is back!

"MY LAIRD, YOUR back!" Finlay bellowed. He buried a sword in the back of the man Alex had been parrying with in front of him, freeing the Grant to face his foe.

Alex Grant spun around, and in a beautifully choreographed move, knocked the sword out of Buchan's hands and plunged his sword into the swine's heart. Buchan fell to the floor, cursing the Grants and the Ramsays as he clutched his chest.

Connor and Jamie finished the last two and they all paused, staring around at the carnage, gasping for breath. "Anyone injured?" Jamie asked. "Papa?"

"I'm fine." He glanced at Finlay. "Good timing, lad. I never saw him coming."

"My laird, you finished him. 'Tis what counts and what all the Scots need to know," Finlay said as he cleaned his sword and sheathed it.

"De La Porte?" Jamie asked.

Logan came in through the back, chuckling. "MacNicol made sure he'll never be taking a sword to anyone again." Then he frowned for a moment. "And damn if somebody isn't deadly with a dagger. I still don't know who threw the one that hit that bastard between the eyes before Molly could send off another arrow."

Finlay had a vague recollection of that happening out in back. At the time, his mind had been fixed on de La Porte.

Connor took his sire by the elbow and led him to one of the few upright chairs. "Papa, sit. You did what you set out to do—you ended this man's tyranny. But your color isn't good. Mama will have my hide if I don't watch over you."

Alex sat, heaving to catch his breath. "Jamie, Finlay," he gasped. "Check the progress outside." Connor hurried off to find him something to drink.

Finlay peered over Jamie's shoulder as he opened the door, but they both broke into huge smiles when they saw nothing but red plaids and blue plaids filling the courtyard, either standing or on horseback.

"'Tis done, brother?" Jake yelled out. "Father is hale?"

Jamie nodded. "Aye, 'tis done. Alex Grant took Glenn of Buchan out, and Finlay MacNicol finished Simon de La Porte."

Jamie and Jake nodded to each other. Then they lifted their swords in celebration as they led a chant of Grant and Ramsay war whoops that spread like fire down the valley and across the surrounding moors.

A few moments later, Alex came out the front door, Loki directly behind him, and raised his sword to cheers from his comrades, but his arm fell to his side quickly. His color had improved, but his face was drawn. He'd apparently seen enough battle. Finlay caught the looks exchanged between the acting lairds and knew they'd be taking the former laird home soon.

Torrian raced across the courtyard and up the steps.

"What is it?" Jamie asked.

"I need to see for myself."

The fierce expression on the Ramsay laird's face left Finlay with no doubt that the Grants would let him in.

Everyone in the Highlands had heard the story of the beginning of the Buchan's tyranny. Glenn had tried to force Torrian Ramsay to marry Davina. Together with Ranulf MacNiven, he had conspired to use trickery to convince their king that Torrian had taken the lass's maidenhead. The Ramsays had been able to prove the truth with the assistance of Torrian's wee sister, Jennet. But the Buchan's plan had almost worked. Moreover, the Buchan's sons had tormented both Torrian's wife and his sister.

Jamie led Torrian into the great hall, and Finlay and the others followed them inside. While Alex took to a chair again, Torrian strode to the back to see Glenn of Buchan.

Logan, still in the hall, moved over and placed his hand on the Ramsay laird's shoulder as a show of support.

"Stand back, Uncle Logan." Torrian whispered. "I need a moment."

Logan did as his nephew asked, glancing at Finlay, Loki, and Cailean.

Torrian stared at the man, spat on him, then pulled his sword out, before going down on one knee before Alex Grant and bowing his head. "My thanks to you, Uncle Alex."

Alex grasped his shoulder and said, "My stroke was for Kyla, Finlay, and all the Ramsays." He nodded to Finlay. "There were many hands guiding my arm. His evil spirit did great harm, but it's done."

Torrian stood and turned to Jamie. "Any instructions, laird?"

Jamie nodded to his sire, giving him that honor.

"We're heading home," Alex announced. "We shall take one hundred guards with us. Have the rest bury the dead. Ten guards should stay to take Buchan and de La Porte to Edinburgh for the king to see."

Torrian said, "Kyle Maule and I respectfully request that duty."

Alex nodded to him. "See it done. Then we hope the two of you will join our celebrations on Cameron land."

"With pleasure." Torrian nodded and left.

CHAPTER TWENTY-TWO

The wedding of his eldest daughter…

HER MOTHER LEANED down and kissed her youngest daughters before sending them over to Aunt Jennie. "Go along with your aunties. I'll follow soon. This moment is for your sister and her father. Her brothers will lead them."

After much rustling and arranging, the others left. Her mother kissed her on the cheek and said, "You are a stunning bride, daughter."

"Even with all my bruises, Mama?"

She kissed her forehead. "Even with your bruises. I hardly noticed them. You've chosen a fine man, and I wish you nothing but happiness."

Jake kissed Kyla on the cheek before he left to escort their mother to the abbey.

Jamie and Connor stood on either side of their father. Kyla stared at Connor. "Oh my, Papa."

Her sire lifted his brow in question.

"Connor looks exactly like you, and he's the same height."

Connor gave them all a mischievous grin, and her sire rolled his eyes.

Her father glanced at his sons and pointed to the door. "Go check if Gillie and Kenzie have the horses ready."

For the first time since the battle, she was alone with her sire. She pushed on the crutch Aunt Jennie had fixed for her, but her father took it and tossed it off to the side. "I'll support my daughter."

Tears began to flow as soon as her gaze lifted to his.

"Why do you cry on your wedding day, lassie?" His thumb wiped her tears from her face.

"Oh, Papa." He'd just called her lassie, sending

her heart into her belly. "I was so worried about you, and I know I was the cause of much of this trouble. I had hoped to help, and I did the very opposite. I just wanted our *clann* to stay the same forever. I tried to take over for both of you because you were wounded and Mama was so worried. I want you and Mama hale and hearty, and for everything to stay the same forever."

He kissed her cheek. "Life is forever changing. You must accept that. Look at the fine young man you've found. He's been there all along—you just needed to find him for yourself."

"Aye. I do love him so. I cry out of guilt *and* gratefulness."

"Buchan would have caused trouble one way or another. You just helped bring it to a conclusion a wee bit faster. Please do not think on it any longer. I slept much better last eve knowing that blight on our land was gone. And now, since I can no longer carry you on my chest, it pleases me to give you to a man I know will protect you. But if you ever sneak off again like that, I'll be chasing you next time." He grinned as he said it.

She giggled. "I promise, never again. You stay at home with Mama." Her hand reached up to brush a piece of lint from his leine. "You look so handsome in your finery, though I know you don't have your best plaid."

"This day is for you. You've chosen a fine man." He held his arm out to her. "Shall we go, my wee princess?"

She smiled and took his arm, happy they'd had this moment together. Jamie and Connor held the doors as they exited the Cameron keep. Kenzie and Gillie fussed over the horses, their eyes on her father, both clearly eager to please. Connor settled her on her horse and fixed her skirts the best he could, which sent Jamie and the two lads into gales of laughter.

"You're just like a lass, Connor," Kenzie said in delight.

Loki had been leaning against a tree keeping an eye on Kenzie and Gillie. He came over and said, "I'll do it, Connor. Hell, know you naught about women?" When he finished, he kissed Kyla's cheek and said, "And that's how you do it, lads."

Kenzie and Gillie laughed so hard everyone else started chuckling with them. Then Alex cleared his throat, and the two lads jumped to attention.

"Aye, my laird."

"Aye, my laird."

Kenzie and Gillie were getting along together even better than she and Finlay had expected.

Loki gave them direction. "Take the reins of the horses. Connor and Jamie will lead with their steeds."

Her father sat atop Black Lightning, looking as regal as any king. Her horse was a beautiful white mare. Her cousins Lily, Sorcha, and Bethia had braided the horse's mane and tail with silver ribbons and had even woven in a small bouquet of bluebells above her forelock. They'd attempted to do the same to Black Lightning, but her sire had balked.

They rode toward the abbey, a much longer

ride than it was to the Grant chapel from the castle.

The sun sat high in the blue sky and shone down on the abbey, but an even more impressive sight was the rows and rows of warriors arranged before the abbey. As they got closer, two lines of warriors created a path for them to follow. The guards were all on horseback with their swords held high in the air as a tribute to their lairds. They did not lower their weapons until all had passed them by. Her father held her hand and nodded to his warriors.

At this point, Kyla had eyes only for Finlay, who was also mounted and had ridden out to greet them. He awaited them with his father and brother, all on horseback, at the end of the warrior lines, and he and his family escorted them the rest of the way to the abbey.

Lines of nuns stood along the walkway in front of the church. Several priests were present, too, their cassocks billowing in the wind. This was the abbey's way of showing respect and appreciation to the Grants, Ramsays, Drummonds, Menzies, and Camerons, who had saved them from de La Porte's planned attack.

The Cameron guards had spread out around the two buildings of the abbey, demonstrating their dedication to always protecting the church.

At the end of their procession, Connor helped Kyla down and her sire leaned over to kiss her. "You've chosen well," he whispered in her ear. Then he stepped back to be with her mother.

Kyla could hear her mother's sobs, a bit stronger

than she expected, but when she took Finlay's arm and moved to the front of the abbey to stand in front of the priest, she discovered why.

A gray-haired man pushed himself out of a chair to stand in front of them. Though he struggled a little to get to his feet, a young lad in vestments assisted him.

The man straightened his robe and nodded to them. "Good evening, Kyla and Finlay. My name is Father MacGregor, and since I performed the ceremony at the marriage of your parents, Kyla, nothing could please me more in my old age than to preside over your wedding." He took a moment to greet her parents with a nod. Kyla glanced over her shoulder to smile at them.

Finlay squeezed her hand, bringing her attention back to him, the tall, handsome Highlander who'd stolen her heart in such a short time. He was such a rugged warrior, yet so gentle with her. His bright smile and twinkling eyes lit up her heart, reminding her of his quick wit, and how easily he could send her into gales of laughter.

Soon after he held her hand, his thumb reached around to caress the inside of her wrist, their small intimacy she'd never, ever forget.

Father MacGregor wrapped the Grant plaid over their hands as he continued in Gaelic, and all she could do was say many, many prayers of thanks as she stood in front of Lochluin Abbey, all her *clann* behind her.

When Father told Finlay to kiss the bride, she had to keep herself from leaping into his arms with joy. She and Finlay were husband and wife.

LOKI'S
CHRISTMAS
STORY

BOOK 11

Alex and Loki's purpose.

CHAPTER TEN

Loki talks with Uncle Alex
about his life's purpose…

LOKI LEANED DOWN to kiss Bella on the cheek. "I'll be right back." He needed a moment alone after all that had happened. His mother and Aunt Maddie were tending to Bella and Ami, so he thought it a good time to leave. Stepping into the courtyard, he huddled into his clothing as he lifted his face toward the sky, surprised to see a few glittering snowflakes dusting the air. Winter was here.

A tear caught in his eye as he thought about the daughter he and Bella had lost. Abi was a most beautiful name. What would she have been like? Would she have looked like him or Bella? He strode across his land, still unable to understand the workings of the world—why one child had been given to him and another taken away. Would aught have happened differently if he had not left for Ayr? Bella seemed truly happy to accept wee Ami into their family, but had he agreed to do something that would prove to be too much for him and his clan? For his wife?

Uncle Alex came up behind him, clasping his shoulder. "My sympathies on the loss of your bairn, Loki."

He peered up at his uncle and nodded. "The

loss is painful, Uncle, and I know we will always grieve her." His uncle was known for his wisdom, so he decided to ask for his opinion. "My laird, I was asked to assist someone…" He struggled for the right words, but he knew his uncle would allow him the time to form his thoughts. All he could think of was a small hut near Edinburgh full of wee ones without parents. "I met a man who provides care for orphans. He's dying and asked me if I would take over his life's mission, to seek out and care for the orphans in our land. Bring them home to Castle Curanta."

Uncle Alex thought for a moment and said, "I can't think of a better person to take over that task. What say you?"

"I agreed, but I said I would need your support and Bella's."

"Is this the man from your dreams? The one with the furs?"

"Aye. I'm having trouble believing all that transpired. If I hadn't been there, seen how closely the man matched my vision…"

"May I give a word of advice?"

"I would value it." More than anything, he needed someone to convince him he was not losing his mind.

"I don't ever say 'why me' anymore. Fate can be a wondrous facet of life if you look at it as an opportunity instead of always questioning everything. You were chosen for this calling for a reason." He clasped Loki's shoulder again. "We will support you completely when the time comes. Just tell me whatever you need."

DEAR READER,
  You've completed the first half of Alexander Grant's life, twenty books in all. I hope you're enjoying this walk through Alex's life—his formation of the clan, his loves, battles, and wisdom.

  Book two will take you through the Band of Cousins, Highland Healers, Highland Swords, Highland Hunters, and finally, Clans of Mull.

  Elizabeth's story, the last book in The Highland Clan, by timeline, will come after the Band of Cousins.

  Please tell me what you think!
  And thanks for reading!

Keira Montclair
www.keiramontclair.com

HIGHLAND HIGHLIGHTS
THE BEST OF...

Alexander Grant, Part 1 and 2
Madeline Grant
Brenna Grant
Logan Ramsay, Part 1 and 2
Gwyneth Ramsay
Loki Grant
Torrian Ramsay
Connor Grant
Maitland Menzie
Dyna Grant
The Bairns, Part 1 and 2
The Pets, The Ghosts, and Spirits
My Favorite Scenes

ABOUT THE AUTHOR

KEIRA MONTCLAIR IS the pen name of an author who lives in South Carolina with her husband. She loves to write fast-paced, emotional romance, especially with children as secondary characters.

When she's not writing, she loves to spend time with her grandchildren. She's worked as a high school math teacher, a registered nurse, and an office manager. She loves ballet, mathematics, puzzles, learning anything new, and creating new characters for her readers to fall in love with.

She writes historical romantic suspense. Her best-selling series is a family saga that follows two medieval Scottish clans through four generations and now numbers over thirty books.

Contact her through her website:
www.keiramontclair.com